Best Tennis
Players
I Know
God Bless
& Keep you

Sharn
2/24/19
"In Joy"

Artist Wife

Artist Wife

A Suspense Story of Love, Intrigue, and Triumph

SHARRON BEDFORD-VINES

ARCHWAY
PUBLISHING

Interior Image Credit: Roederick Vines

Scripture quotations are taken from the King James Version of the Bible.

Archway Publishing books may be ordered through booksellers or by contacting:

Archway Publishing
1663 Liberty Drive
Bloomington, IN 47403
www.archwaypublishing.com
1 (888) 242-5904

ISBN: 978-1-4808-7377-3 (sc)
ISBN: 978-1-4808-7376-6 (hc)
ISBN: 978-1-4808-7378-0 (e)

Library of Congress Control Number: 2019932003

Print information available on the last page.

Archway Publishing rev. date: 01/25/2019

Live purposefully, accurately, and worthy.
—Ephesians 5:15

For Alice Roby-Bedford (1929–2003), my dear
mother and an angel in disguise, and Deidra Louise
Burton-Vines (1986–2010), our daughter

Acknowledgments

All praises to my Lord and Savior, Jesus Christ, who made this publication possible by His love, grace, and mercy. My gifted husband, Roederick, for helping birth the concept of the book. Thank you for your continuous love, patience, and robust enthusiasm. Thanks to the Archway Publishing team. My editor, W. Calvin Anderson, for perceptive comments that shaped the book. My mentors: Donnie Rose Smith, Precious Colclough and Dottie Toney Ransom, for your guidance and spiritual counsel. My loving family and special friends who supported me with diligent prayers. It is well!

The Celebration

*G*race approached Dr. Monica Wolf lovingly, knowing that she only recently had just about forgiven her for so intimately saving Wellington's life years ago. Grace no longer needed to brace her heart for any hard feelings. As Monica approached her on the stage, a quick thought passed through Grace's mind about Monica's deceased husband. Daniel had been an exceptionally talented California artist she'd faithfully supported until his untimely death two years earlier. The mystery surrounding his unsolved death left the entire art community baffled. After the accident, Monica moved to Dern, Switzerland, to embark on a medical research project for the Centers for Disease Control and Prevention in molecular biology for unspecified animals.

Startled by the loud applause, as though a hypnotist had snapped her out of a daze, Grace quickly came back to reality. A dream was unfolding right before her brown eyes. Grace's eyes teared as she approached the stage, and the crowd clapped loudly. She called Monica to the podium and presented her an award. The occasion was a fund-raiser for the Artists' Wives of Green Village.

"I would like to thank God for his grace, his mercy, and his love for me. Finally, thanks to all Grace's colleagues, the Artist Wife Association, and our dear friends for supporting me," Monica said, sheepishly accepting the award from Grace.

Grace's mind drifted again to happy thoughts of the past. *For years, the artists' wives in our group have supported their husbands. In many instances, this has included the preproduction loading and unpacking, smiling and sweating at exhibits, and of course, the postproduction repacking and inventory accounting. Our husbands have taken care of photo opportunities, business arrangements, and new leads. Some wives felt they were not appreciated for their labors of love and dedication, and some wives really felt insignificant in their mates' lives too. Our group has helped all the wives understand the traveling, managing, and continuous encouragement of their spouses. Wives have earned their renowned positions, and then some, assisting in their husbands' successes. We've shared business leads and information resources, as well as venting about our trials along the undefined road of being the infamous wives of sterling fine artists. The organization has been vital for us to continue our support of our "better halves" just based on the nature of who we are and what they must do to be a name and brand in the national and international art world. Tonight, at the New York Plaza Hotel, we honored Dr. Monica Wolf.*

"A special shout-out and love to all. I love you madly, and you can't do anything about it," Monica concluded as she took a final bow and blew a kiss to the crowd. A roar went up as we exited the stage and the house lights came on. All of New York's finest gallery owners, politicians, athletes, and movie celebrities were present in their display of vibrant colors. Many men wore casual slacks and shirts, and women paraded in their sexy, flowing gowns, minidresses, and flashy jewelry. They chattered loudly in the ballroom.

Moving across the ballroom floor, Grace hugged and greeted several friends and picked up a glass of sparkling champagne. She tugged at her Zee Wear's designer peach chiffon gown that hugged her round figure, which was beginning to show her small baby bump. The upsweep hairstyle added an inch to her five-foot-six-inch, 120-pound frame, making her feel like an elite model. Assessing the room, Grace's eyes met Monica's big, sparkling brown eyes. They nodded and smiled as Grace continued in her direction. Monica looked dazzling in a maroon gown with matching spike heels. Her short-bobbed haircut flipped perfectly at the ends, making her look younger than thirty. Monica was pretty, and her new black glass rims made her look studious. But what a callous tongue she had, begetting many enemies early, including Grace. Grace got wind of a rumor of an affair between Monica and Grace's husband, Wellington Holmes, when he was commissioned to paint her portrait. It made Grace feel insecure and jealous. Wellington assured Grace nothing happened, but she felt it hard to believe in the presence of an attractive and seductive woman. Those uneasy feelings were trying to rise right now and overtake Grace's emotions, but she rejected them. Grace knew and understood those were feelings of insecurity, which she overcame.

Grace felt Wellington's reassuring soft touch on her shoulder. His sleek six-foot-four-inch frame, wavy black hair, and smooth bronze skin looked extremely sexy in the black designer tuxedo. Grace was so proud to be next to him.

"Grace, are you okay?" he asked.

Grace quickly thought past circumstances and their renewed relationship. "I'm great. Just overwhelmed."

Wellington hugged her and wiped the tears from her cheeks.

Releasing from his embrace, Grace stepped in Monica's direction. "This is going to be a night we will remember forever," Grace whispered in Monica's ear as they embraced.

"I thank God for you and Wellington for returning life and love back in my life. It feels good to be back home." Monica smiled.

CHAPTER

2

Developing Passion

Growing up Samuel and Ruth Green's only child in Santa Barbara, California, had its advantages. Grace was given a lot of love, nurturing, and a strong foundation. Recognizing their child's artistic talents at an early age, they enrolled her in private art classes at the age of seven. Grace's dad bought her first paint set. Little did he know that was the beginning of her love for art. Grace spent a lot of time alone in her room drawing. By the time she was ten, Grace knew she wanted to be an artist. Her dad, a successful lawyer, kept his own dream alive that she would one day follow in his footsteps, but that didn't happen. Mr. Smith, Grace's eleventh grade art teacher, dashed her dad's dream of her becoming a lawyer by encouraging and fine-tuning her growing artistic talent. That gave Grace an informed passion for art.

Grace's family established many personal standards and values for her to follow. Her dad enrolled her in the best private schools and instilled an importance in critical thinking. She loved his responsible ways, and it seemed to inform her sense of determination from an early age. Grace wanted to be successful in everything she did. He enrolled her in a martial arts class to teach her discipline and learn how to protect herself. It gave Grace an opportunity to interact with other races outside her community and opportunities to learn cultural differences.

Grace's mom was an educator. She was a motivator, very persuasive, responsible, and always had a positive attitude about everything. She never discouraged her and believed Grace could do anything she tried. Many of Grace's characteristics reflected her mom. She was known for her simple style. She nurtured, guided, and mentored Grace with love and kindness. She had lost a child before Grace, but through that challenge, she and Grace's dad never gave up hope God would grant them another child one day. She said his grace got them through that difficult period, and if he so kindly blessed her with a, girl, she would name her Grace. She used to always say, "Rhythm of grace," when they went through a challenge or a storm, and they always got through it. Grace didn't understand it then, but after growing up, she grew to. The most important gift her mom revealed about herself was her gentleness.

Mr. Smith recommended Hope Art College in Connecticut, one of the finest art schools in the Northeast. Sadly, Grace's dad did not have an opportunity to see that day. He was an avid smoker, and at age forty, he was diagnosed with lung cancer. He died during her senior year of high school. It was tragic for their small family. Grace never forgot the strength her mom possessed during that ill-timed period in their lives. As a woman of faith, she didn't show any signs of weakness.

When Grace was a young child, she remembered her mom whispering prayers in her ear. Prayers of endearment, love, and reinforcing strength. Even today, when she wasn't around, Grace still heard gentle whispers reminding her that she must look for joy in her brokenness and find it during adversity. She reminded Grace of the significance of her name and how God would see them through that difficult time. She encouraged Grace to attend Hope College and prophesied, "Your life is but a shadow of the good things that the good Lord has in store for your future." Grace believed her and held onto her encouraging words.

CHAPTER

3

Hope College

Hope College was founded in 1940 in Hartford, Connecticut. The East Coast was completely different from California. It was flat but full of history and culture, and it was thriving with preppy and energetic young people. The small campus had only 2,500 students. The buildings were old and surrounded by trees, cobblestone streets, and hills. Modern eateries and quaint mom-and-pop stores populated the two-square-mile radius, all contained within fenced walls. Life on the East Coast, Grace could foresee, was going to be a transformation for a California beach, girl.

Jana Smith turned the knob to the dorm room at the same time Grace turned the key, causing Grace to stumble and trip into the room. At first glance, Jana was around five feet five, with hazel eyes and a natural, short hairstyle.

8

"I'm so sorry," she chuckled, extending a hand to help Grace up. "I'm Jana Smith, your roommate."

Grace stood and shook her hand. "I'm Grace. And as you see, that name doesn't quite go along with my movements." Grace chuckled and picked up her purse. Somehow Jana's warmth did not allow room for Grace to feel embarrassed. They talked very easily and discovered their backgrounds were very different. Jana grew up in Chicago in a lower-class family with three brothers and two sisters. She was a sophomore, forthright, spunky, talkative, and had an infectious laugh.

Grace had grown up in a middle-class family and attended a private school. She was a top student and leader in many school organizations, which made her popular among groups as well as at church. When it came to social events, Grace did not participate a lot; she preferred private time alone to paint. But the one thing Grace and Jana had in common was an eye for design and color.

4

The Dream

In the line registering for classes, Grace could feel eyes on her from across the room. Turning slightly to the right to get a glimpse of the individual, she knocked the books out of the hands of the person behind her. By the time she helped pick up the books, the mysterious guy had disappeared. Grace recalled his piercing eyes though that evening when she mentioned it, but Jana shrugged it off—as she did most of their conversations. The thought preoccupied Grace and lingered in her memory when she fell asleep that evening.

"Is this your ticket?" someone asked in a rich baritone voice.

Grace turned around, absorbed by a manly voice and was face-to-face with the person posing the question. She didn't realize she had dropped her ticket to the theater. Grace was rattled when she encountered the same intriguing brown twinkling eyes from school staring straight into hers. He was amazingly striking six foot two, dressed in a cool brown shirt that matched his brown eyes, muscular frame, smooth complexion, and curly black hair.

Hmmm, Grace thought, scanning him up and down, *not bad.* Stunned by his appearance, she didn't realize her mouth was wide open.

"Is this yours?" he repeated.

"Thanks," Grace replied, reaching for the ticket. "It must have slipped out of my hand." She felt self-conscious and embarrassed that she was looking so plain in a simple blue jean skirt, funky top, and hat to match—and no hint of makeup.

"Are you waiting for someone?" he asked.

"No, I'm not," Grace responded softly.

He introduced himself, but she didn't catch his name as he held out his hand to shake hers. "What's yours?"

"Grace" she replied, shaking his soft, strong hand.

His feet shifted closer to hers, and she could feel the cool of his breath and smell the sweet scent of cologne.

"That name fits you," he whispered.

Feeling nervous, Grace took a step back. "What do you mean by that?" she responded.

"Well, the way you walk and talk is so graceful one could almost—"

"Almost what?" Grace said. "How would you know anything about me?"

"Don't be alarmed. I'm harmless. I have been watching you," he said shyly. "And with much delight," he added with a wink and smile.

"Thank you … and nice meeting you," Grace replied quickly and abruptly hurried to her seat. She touched her flushed face and held her trembling hands. She dared not look back to see if he had followed her or where he sat. She tried to focus on the show, but the encounter left her in such deep thought that she couldn't recall what movie was about.

Preparing for the First Day

The shrieking alarm clock startled Grace. She jumped straight out of bed, tripping over the white fluffy down bed covers. It took a few moments to regain her footing and stand straight up. Her pajamas were soaked with sweat.

Realizing she was recovering from a dream, Grace wiped her eyes and brushed back her tousled hair. *Hmmm … another puzzling dream*, Grace thought. She had many, and they always bore intrigue and flavored significance.

She pulled the lacy curtains aside to view the blue sky and clicked on the TV to channel 5 just in time to hear the weather forecast. It was sixty-five degrees, and there were pictures of seasonal foliage with brown, yellow, and red leaves.

Grace dragged herself into the bathroom. After showering, she dried off and walked over to the closet. She pulled a blue cashmere sweater from the top shelf and stepped into her stretch jeans. Pulling her shoulder-length hair into a ponytail, she grabbed a big hat and a jacket and headed for the door.

Jana had left a note on the table for her to pick up food for dinner.

Somehow, Grace stepped into the younger sister role and did all the errands. It was okay though because Grace felt like she finally had a sister.

6

Classroom Shock

The activity at Hope College was high-pitched for the first day of class. Grace pushed her way through the bustling students to make one last-minute schedule change for an early-afternoon class.

Malcolm Jenkins, a friend from one of her high school art classes, approached her as she finished signing up. Grace was shocked. They were both members of the National Honor Society and had some interaction in high school, but he never really said much to her.

"Hey, Grace. I didn't know you chose Hope College. I guess Mr. Smith made an impression on both of us." He smiled.

"Yes, he was one of my best teachers and a mentor to me," Grace said.

"Nice school, huh?"

"Yes, I'm loving it so far. What art classes did you take?"

"I have Art Appreciation this semester."

"Yes, that's one of the classes I have too. It's the last class of the day."

"Well, I'll see you there," he said as he turned to leave.

That was a welcome surprise and a little strange too, Grace thought.

Malcolm, who was a scholar and voted "most likely to succeed" could be anything he wanted, but like her, he had a love for the arts.

When Grace arrived at her last class of the day, the teacher's back was turned to the bulletin board as he talked to another student. She chose a seat near the back of the room, noticed Malcolm, and gave him a nod.

When the teacher turned and faced the class, Grace's mouth dropped to the floor. She couldn't believe it. It was the emerging artist of the era: Wellington Holmes. She had followed his work since her junior year of high school. She could barely catch her breath. He was better-looking than his photos had suggested.

"Welcome, class," he said in an electrifying baritone voice. "I'm Dr. Wellington Holmes, your teacher."

Grace's hearing slowly began to leave her. She was a self-conscious mess, and she knew she was infatuated by him too.

He briefed the class on the syllabus for the semester and asked a few students to give a little background on themselves.

Grace lost all equilibrium when his eyes connected with hers, and he pointed to her. Grace silently prayed that the "God of mercy," at least that was what her mother called him, would help her regain her composure. Grace held her breath, touched her rumbling stomach with both hands, and listened to her thumping heart. She managed to stand and opened her mouth to speak. Before any words came out, her legs gave out. As she collapsed, Grace heard faint screams and felt movement around her.

"Move out of the way and make room," someone shouted.

Grace caught a glimpse of someone standing over her and felt someone touching her arm. She coughed and tried to sit up. "What's going on?"

"You passed out," Professor Holmes said, slowly moving away from her.

"Passed out?" she mumbled.

Professor Holmes helped Grace up and to a chair.

Regaining her breath, she stroked her hair and wondered if she looked as disarrayed as she felt.

Malcolm looked concerned.

Someone produced a glass of water, and Grace took a few sips, trying to recall what had happened. Gazing into Professor Holmes's gleaming eyes, it slowly came back to her. *Talk about embarrassment!*

Professor Holmes dismissed the class and reminded everyone to read chapters 1 and 2 and to be ready to discuss the material next week.

The other students filed out of the room.

"I guess that's one way to have class dismissed early on the first day," Grace said, trying to make light of the issue.

"Not if your life depends on it," Professor Holmes replied.

Grace attempted to get up but fell back into the chair.

"Are you sure you are okay?" Professor Holmes gently helped her up from the chair. "Perhaps you should wait a few more moments."

Grace could not handle looking into his disarming brown eyes. "My dorm is just across campus. I think I can manage." She shrugged as he extended his hand. "Thank you, Professor Holmes. Sorry I interrupted your class." She gathered her books and left hastily. Her heart was racing from his touch as she left the classroom.

Grace was embarrassed, but she was also mesmerized by his eyes, his voice, and his touch. She felt less attractive and a little foolish. After all, he was her first professor, and it was her first day in class.

7

Unlikely Date

The answering machine light was flashing when Grace entered her dorm room. She tapped the replay button.

"I'm checking to see if you got home okay. Call me, this is Professor Holmes."

This is weird! She anxiously hit the redial button.

"Hey there," Professor Holmes said. "I thought I'd call to make sure you were okay.

"How did you get my number?" Grace asked in a nervous voice.

"I have my contacts," he replied. "No, seriously, you looked a little wobbly, and I wanted to make sure you got home. The administrators gave me your number after I told them about the incident. In case of emergencies, we are able to call the student."

Surprised by his concern, she adjusted her tone. "Thanks for checking. I skipped lunch today, which probably had a negative effect on me," she lied. "But I'm feeling better now."

"Did you get something to eat—or are you going to starve yourself some more?" He chuckled.

"I really haven't given it much thought," she responded.

"Well, would you like to go get something to eat this evening?"

Grace paused before answering, surprised by the request. "Well ..."

"A girl's gotta eat, right?" Professor Wellington said.

"Yes, okay. I guess I owe you that much for coming to my rescue," Grace replied.

"Consider it done then. I'll be there by five—or I'm not coming," he said before hanging up.

Grace smiled and began humming one of her favorite songs, "Not There by Five."

"I thought Christmas wasn't until December," Jana said as she closed the door. "What brings on this joy?" She placed her books on the table.

Grace immediately stopped singing. Jana was her only friend at school, and she couldn't wait to share the news with her. "You won't believe this. I ran into one of my high school classmates, and then I found out my art professor is Dr. Wellington Holmes."

"Am I supposed to know him?" she asked.

"Well, if you don't follow art, I guess you wouldn't," Grace said.

Jana answered, "Never heard of him."

"Anyway, I'm going to get a sandwich with him this evening." Grace giggled.

"Are you serious?"

"Is that bad?"

"Yes. You don't even know him," she said.

"Well, let me tell you what happened first and what led up to this before you start judging me," Grace said. "I walked into class, and when I saw him, my stomach started doing flips. When I stood up, I passed out. I was so embarrassed. It felt like I was hit by lightning."

"Hold it, woman. You're moving too fast," Jana said. "Let me get this straight. You fainted? Are you for real?" She laughed heartily.

"Yes, my heart was beating so fast I thought it was going to explode," Grace said.

"Here we go again. You never cease to amaze me, child." Jana walked away.

"No. This is real … I promise you." Grace grabbed Jana and looked into her eyes. "He was the first one to my side. When I got home, he called and invited me to dinner."

"Sounds like a chapter out of Cinderella to me," Jana snorted, bending over to contain her laughter. "You know the whole glass slipper incident. First, you meet Prince Charming, then you faint, and he comes to your rescue. And now you're having dinner with him? All of this is accomplished by you in just a few hours? Did I get that right?"

"No silly," Grace said. "I mean yes, sorta."

"So how did it progress into dinner?" Jana folded her arms.

"He called and left a message, and I called him back. He wanted to make sure I had something to eat because that was the excuse for fainting. That's when he asked me to dinner,"

"Come on, girl! You accepted a date with your professor on the first day of school? You can't be serious. That's crazy. You barely know him. He could be a stalker or even a rapist. You know the stuff that is happening on campuses these days. You sound sorta smitten too. Besides, I thought you were stopping at the store and making dinner for us tonight. You, and I were supposed to spend the evening together. I guess that's a dead matter now?" Jana looked into the small and empty refrigerator.

"Sorry. I completely forgot about dinner," Grace said. "This is not like me to immediately go out with strangers, but somehow it seems different."

"Different how?" Jana responded.

"I can't help if something feels different this time," Grace said. "Unlike you, I didn't date a lot in my teens, and I never had a serious relationship. I'm excited about someone paying attention to me—even if it is my professor. I'll take it slow and will also make dinner for you tomorrow. I promise."

"Are you meeting him in a safe place?" Jana asked.

"He's picking me up at five, and I'm not sure where we're going for dinner. I feel like he's trustworthy," Grace said.

"Well, just be careful," she replied.

"My problem is what I'm going to wear." Grace threw her hands in the air. "Do you have something I can borrow?" Grace headed for Jana's closet.

"Settle down, child!" Jana said, pulling Grace by the arm. "You look fine just as you are. Why do you always doubt your looks? You are so adorable. You've got to believe in yourself. Otherwise, you'll compromise your soul."

"You have a good point," Grace said. "Then again, you don't have the problem of getting dates. You are so pretty the guys are lined up for you." Grace pouted. "You have Jeff, that cute guy who walks you down the hall. Robert is always winking at you, and although it's only been a few days of school, you are already popular."

"Grace, you are a beautiful, girl, inside and out. Just be yourself." Jana patted Grace's head.

They both laughed.

Grace reached onto the top shelf and pulled down her stretch jeans and a sassy blouse. She stepped into the bathroom, applied a little makeup, and grabbed her jacket. She took one last look around the room and yelled goodbye to Jana before heading to the lobby to wait for Professor Holmes. She didn't want to be late. Grace paced nervously for what seemed liked hours, hoping it was not a dream.

8

Dinner with Professor Holmes

At five o'clock, Professor Holmes pulled up in a dark blue BMW 325i. He ran over to open the door as Grace approached the car. "Hi there. You are looking much better."

"Hello," Grace responded softly as she slipped into the low seat. "I feel better too."

The sun gleamed magically through the windshield as they rode to a quaint Italian café.

"Isn't it strange to dine with one of your students on the first day?" Grace asked.

"Well, this is a little unusual on the first day. I think I'm good to have a bite to eat with one of my students. No harm, no foul!" he said with a wide smile.

"Did you invite me because you thought I was a starving artist?" Grace grinned as he pulled into the parking lot.

"Absolutely not! You look pretty healthy to me. He sized up her frame. You just don't know when to eat." Professor Holmes grinned, and she smiled back. "I saw your face beaming when you started to speak in class, and unless my eyes played tricks, I thought I saw a halo too." He laughed. "I was confused about why you fainted before you even got a chance to speak. All I asked was one question." He smiled.

"I can see that you have a good sense of humor," Grace said.

The waitress approached the table and took their order.

Professor Holmes cleared his throat and said, "You passing out was a little concerning, and that's why I called. I couldn't help myself. There was something so radiant about you that I couldn't resist."

The sound of his voice sent chills up Grace's spine.

They ordered pizza and chatted about life and their families.

Professor Holmes was twenty-eight and had a younger sister and an older brother who lived in New York. His parents were deceased. He had begun painting at an early age, had never married, and had been an art teacher at Hope for three years. On many weekends, he exhibited his artwork at museums and in diverse shows. He was very humble.

At nineteen, Grace had never had close male relationships. The electricity between them concerned her because of the age difference. His commanding presence had a lasting effect on her. Besides his good looks, he had a contagious personality.

They laughed and talked about art and Grace's future in the arts.

Professor Holmes dropped her off at the dorm at seven thirty.

Grace was glad that Jana was not home to tell her it was all just a silly crush. Grace could savor the moment alone and not be judged. She knew her dreams were going to be sweet that night.

9

The Letdown

Grace anticipated special attention from Professor Holmes the following day, but he never looked in her direction. Several students asked about her health, including Malcolm.

Grace thanked her classmates and played it off concerning professor. When the bell rang, she left the classroom in a big hurry. On the way home, she felt a tap on her shoulder. She turned and saw Jana behind her. "What are you doing sneaking up on me?" Grace said. "Don't scare me like that."

"Scare you like what? I barely touched you," Jana said. "Where are you racing off to in such a hurry?"

"I'm going to the library to do some research," Grace responded without looking up.

Jana grabbed Grace's arm and stopped her. "Well, how did it go last night?"

"We had an okay time." She shrugged. "We ate at Tony's, enjoyed small talk, and I got home pretty early. It was cool."

Jana said, "So, why don't you sound like you had fun?"

"Well, he barely looked my way in class today. It was as if nothing—"

"Nothing what? You didn't on the first night, did you, girl?" Jana asked with a wink.

"Don't be ridiculous," Grace said with her hands on her hips. "It wasn't that kind of date. We didn't even kiss. He was very respectful. I thought I felt a little connection between us. Maybe I'm just tripping over nothing."

"You just met him. Besides he's way older than you."

"It's not like that at all. You just don't understand," Grace said. "I never had anyone approach me in the manner he did and make me feel so different, so special."

"Just stop worrying, girl," Jana said. "When it's right, you'll know."

"Yeah, I guess."

"Maybe he's just another boring guy like the rest of them," Jana said with a chuckle.

"See you at home." Grace pushed past her and headed home.

The Pursuit

Studying for hours on a late evening in November caused Grace's eyes to dry out and become bloodshot. She removed her glasses and reached for a tissue.

"Need one?" Professor Holmes asked.

"Thanks," she said, blushing harder than she wanted to as she picked a few tissues from the box.

"Looks like you could use a cup of coffee. I'm heading to the coffee shop. Would you like to join me?"

Grace nodded, slowly stood, and gathered her books.

Professor Holmes helped her put on her coat and gently wrapped the black and white scarf across her neck. His closeness gave her chills and was almost too much to bear. They walked across the campus toward the coffee shop in the first snow of the season. He playfully stepped back and threw a snowball her way.

She ducked just in time, and it hit a tree. She laughed and responded with a left-handed snowball that curved straight into his chest. She took off running toward the coffee shop and slipped.

He slipped too and landed on top of her.

Grace gazed into his eyes. *This dream is live and in spectacular color.*

Laughing and brushing off the snow, they entered the coffee shop, ordered Frappuccinos, and sat near the fireplace.

"How's a California girl like you adjusting to this weather?" he asked.

"It's not such a big difference. I ski every winter in California, so I'm somewhat used to the cold."

"I didn't hear much from you in class today," he said as he blew on his hands.

"Yes, I'm staying low-key, seeing that I made such a stir in class," Grace said.

"I don't think the students hold that against you," he added with raised eyebrows.

The waitress approached our table with their coffees.

"You seem a little distant," he said. "What's on your mind?"

"I'm just adjusting to the classes and missing my mom, I guess," Grace replied.

"The snow is so romantic, and it offers everyone a time to slow down and reflect on some life changes."

"Yes, I'm reflecting all right—about how a certain person always seems to show up when I least expect it."

"Are you talking about me?" Professor Holmes said.

"Yes, I'm talking about you. I don't understand why you are constantly bumping into me."

"Am I?" he asked.

"It's okay, but it makes me a little nervous. You always show up unexpectedly—or am I dreaming?" Grace said.

"Okay, you want a direct answer again?" Without warning, he grabbed Grace's hand, pulled her chair closer and whispered, "It's crazy that I barely know you, but there is something about you. I'm trying to keep my distance. That way, I won't get into trouble. But you are making it impossible." He released Grace's hand, finished his coffee, and stood up to leave.

Grace rolled her eyes in disbelief as she watched him disappear. He almost had her, and she was still responding to the lingering cologne on her hands. *He is such a man. He is energetic, breathtaking, and unpredictable—all at the same time. I really need to sort out my feelings.*

She left the coffee shop by herself.

11

An Encounter with Malcolm

Grace saw Malcolm a few times in the cafeteria and found out just how talented he was in creating abstracts. Whenever she saw him in the hallway, which was quite often, he would stop chat with her. They decided to study together in the library a few times.

Grace discovered two things: new abstract techniques and a hint that he had a crush on her. Grace wondered if he was the mysterious guy who was looking at her from a distance on the first day of school or even the man in her dream. She thought he liked her, but he never made any advances.

While they were studying, their shoulders bumped.

Grace saw a twinkle in his eye, which gave her an indication of how he felt about her. Grace sensed his embarrassment and played it off. Nothing else developed between them.

Saturday was Grace's only day to paint without distractions. In class, the focus was on drawing the human figure, which was a problem area for her. She preferred to study techniques in the use of color and the opportunity to manipulate and determine juxtaposition in free form. She never wanted to be concerned with the "politics" of drawing the human figure. Drawing the human figure made her feel vulnerable and revealed more about her inhibitions than she wanted to share.

Grace was too insecure to express herself via the human form. She didn't want to be held accountable for drawing or painting human figures. She liked capturing the frenzy and various techniques and patterns on a canvas. Color, form, and texture are tools that provide a real foundation for abstract expressions.

Grace couldn't wait to start a new abstract. It had become a deep passion for her.

Professor Holmes stressed the need for artists to find their niche. "The foundation of good art, painting, or illustration is good draftsmanship. Everything hinges on that. If you don't get the fundamentals of drawing, you are not going to be as good an artist as you could be. Some artists want quick results, but they don't want to put in the time. You need to put in time for that which you love, and that will help you discover your niche."

Grace splashed a mixture of colors on the canvas and stepped back to check out her new creation. She would rather have spent the day with him, but she rarely saw him outside of the classroom.

He traveled to his exhibitions on the weekends, and Grace was lonely. He always seemed to pop up in her life. She wanted to approach him about it, but she didn't want to appear too pushy since he was building a body of work, a brand, and a career. Being too forward wasn't her style, and she hadn't let go of the thought that he was her elder, her superior, and her professor.

Grace thought the fantasy love life she had dreamed about had come to an end. As time went on, her lack of focus in his class and struggles with painting the human figure led her to make new decisions. She wanted to drop out of his class at the end of the semester. She wanted to take control of what she wanted and decided to enroll in an interior design class to strengthen her decorating skills and enjoy creating her abstract designs. Now, she only needed to get her mind completely off of him.

Wavering Thoughts of Love

An irresistible urge made Grace pass by his classroom, which wasn't even in the direction she was going at the time. She couldn't help peeking into Professor Holmes's class to get a glimpse of him—and she got the surprise of her life. Sitting on the edge of his desk was none other than Jana: legs crossed, short skirt, and giggling hysterically. He seemed engrossed in whatever she was saying. He was smiling, giving her high fives, and looking at her passionately.

Grace scurried around the corner, hoping Jana did not see her. Grace's heart was racing. He had not looked her way in weeks. Could that be the reason why he hadn't paid any attention to her and why

Jana got her to change classes? *How could Jana do this and not tell me?* Grace wanted to approach them, but she didn't have the guts. What a nerve to move in on her dream man! Grace was fuming with anger. Even though she had not spoken of him lately, Jana knew how she felt about him.

Grace would need the right moment, the right words, and the courage to approach Jana about her betrayal. She decided to wait and talk to her that evening. Grace arrived at the dorm around five. After what seemed like hours, she gave up and decided to work on her abstract. That didn't work. Her creativity was not flowing.

Around nine, Grace heard the door close and peeked through her bedroom door. Jana was all smiles. Her heart sank, and her anxieties rose. *Why am I such a chicken?* She slapped her leg. She needed to approach Jana, but she also knew that she needed more evidence before cornering her. Grace quietly shut the door without Jana noticing her and decided to wait and confront her the next day.

The next morning, Jana did not go to their interior decorating class. After class, Grace called Jana and said, "Where are you?"

"I had some business to take care of and couldn't make it to class," she replied.

"Yeah? What kind of business?"

"Oh, girl, please. I don't think my mamma came to school with me, so you don't need to check up on me."

"Sorry," Grace replied. "You sound busy, so I'll let you go. I was just making sure you were okay since you weren't in class."

"I'm fine, just busy. I'll talk to you later," Jana said, clicking the receiver.

Grace stepped back and rubbed her ear. A million thoughts shot through her mind. Something wasn't quite right. *She's very defensive.*

From that day on, Grace decided to keep an eye on her.

Jana began spending less time at home, but Grace wasn't sure what to make of it. Grace expected her to tell the truth about the professor—and she dared not ask him. *Of all the students, why would he choose Jana? He's using her to either make me jealous or break my heart.*

Grace needed to talk to her mom and dialed her number.

"Hey, Mom," she said. "Just called to say hi."

"I can tell by your voice there's more to this call," Ruth said. "Is everything okay at school? Are you feeling okay?"

"I'm feeling fine, Ma. I just need a shoulder to lean on. I really thought Jana was a friend until she slipped behind my back to see someone I was interested in."

"Oh my," Ruth replied softly. "I didn't know you were dating anyone, honey."

"Well, yes and no, Mom. We saw each other a few times. I really felt we had a connection, but he just stopped talking to me."

"Oh! What dummy would do that?" Ruth asked.

"Mom, you may not agree with me, so when I tell you this, please don't criticize me."

"It can't be that bad, child. You said you called to talk, so I'm here to listen."

"Mom, the guy I'm talking about is my professor," Grace said, moving the telephone away from her ear and waiting for a reply.

There was silence on the other end.

"Okay. Sweetie, are you sure?"

"Sure about what, Mom?"

"Sure he felt the same way about you as you did about him. After all, you know professors get approached by many of their students."

"Mom, I didn't approach him," Grace replied. "We saw each other a few times, and just when I thought things were getting started, he stopped paying attention to me. What did I do wrong, Mom? I'm feeling very low right now. He's very nice, and ... I think I've fallen for him." Grace sighed.

"Dear, it sounds like you are experiencing your first love. That's all." Ruth laughed.

"Mom, the real reason I called is because I suspect Jana might be pursuing him. What am I going to do?"

"Darling you are very emotional right now. Love is inclined to do that to you. All I can say is do not move too fast or do something you'll regret. Be patient. If it's meant for you, it'll come to pass."

Grace let out a sigh. "Thanks, Mom. You always have the right words to encourage me. I love you so much."

"I love you too—and so does God. Keep him in your thoughts. Talk with him, and he will direct you through every chapter of your life." Ruth sounded like she was smiling as she said goodbye.

13

The Scuffle

Jana nearly knocked Grace over when she opened the door to their interior decorating class.

Grace said, "Where are you going in such a rush?"

"I have to catch someone before he leaves for the day. I'll talk with you later," she said.

Jana ran past Grace, approached Professor Holmes's office, and walked up to him.

Professor Holmes was seated at his desk, and Jana sat on the edge, revealing long, shapely legs under a short, tight black skirt.

How dare that bitch move into my territory? Grace thought wondering how those words flowed from her lips. Steaming with jealousy, Grace wanted to burst through the door, but she lacked the courage. Unable to hold back her tears, Grace headed to the bathroom. She looked in the mirror and wipe the smeared makeup from under her eyes.

Jana entered the bathroom and said, "Grace, are you okay?" She softly touched Grace's shoulder.

"No," Grace shouted between sobs. "I'm not. Don't act like you are a friend. I saw you in his office—all up in his face. You know how I feel about him. How could you do this to me?"

"Wait one damn minute," Jana shouted with her hands on her round hips. "Since when do you have a claim on him? You haven't mentioned him in weeks."

"But you know how I feel about him!" Grace replied.

Jana stepped forward and pointed her long fingers at Grace. "I know how to use what I have to get what I need. That's more than I can say for you. You're always dreaming, but you don't have enough guts to speak up or go after anything you want."

Grace charged at Jana, shoved her into the sink, and caused her to slip and fall. "You snake!"

Two girls entered the bathroom and moved to the side of the room.

Jana got up slowly and ran toward Grace with balled fists.

Grace held out her hand to deflect the punch, catching Jana in the stomach with her knee.

Jana crumbled to the floor, and her nose was bleeding.

Grace bent down, grabbed Jana's hair, and dragged her to the garbage can. "There you go, slut. That's where you belong—in the garbage with all the other trash." Grace released Jana's hair and cleaned her hands in disgust.

Jana fell back to the floor.

"I don't need friends like you." Grace grabbed her books and walked out of the bathroom.

It was the first time Grace had stood up to Jana, and it felt good.

Halfway across campus, Grace's cell phone rang. It was Jana. "Didn't you get enough?" Grace asked. "What do you want?"

"Girl, this isn't the way this should end," Jana said between sobs. "I didn't know you were holding those strong feelings for Professor Holmes because you never talked to me about him. You acted like a wild woman back there. What's really going on with you?"

"I saw you with him on two occasions, and I saw how you looked at him. Legs crossed on his desk, showing all your stuff."

"You were spying on me?"

"Sort of. I was curious because of your strange actions lately. I stopped by his class, and I saw you two together. I thought maybe you were his new interest."

"I'm sorry," Jana said. "I didn't know you felt that way. I thought if you weren't paying him attention, then someone should … 'cause he's a good catch."

"I should have told you how I felt," Grace said. "I guess I really didn't know until now. It's a buildup of frustration over him, and I took it out on you. Are you all right? I hope I didn't hurt you badly."

"Yes. My stomach is aching, but I'll live. Didn't know you had fight in you, girlfriend."

"I took martial arts in high school, and I still remember a few moves. Jana, I'm so confused. Maybe the best thing is for us to just keep some distance until I can sort out these feelings. I think I am far too emotional right now, and I also think I have fallen in love with him. Whatever this feeling is, it's different—and I can't control it."

"Yeah. With the way you attacked me, I would have to agree." Jana laughed.

"Yeah, I know it's uncharacteristic of me. I didn't know I felt so strongly about him."

"You have to learn to speak what's inside of you and release how you are feeling. Otherwise, you can end good relationships."

Grace sighed. She knew Jana had a good point. "I'm sorry. I need more time to sort out some thoughts. Maybe it is best if I move to another dorm. I'm also dropping out of his class at the end of the semester. It'll help clear my head completely."

"I'm sorry you feel that way. It's not the only way to handle this, Grace. You can't run from your feelings forever. I hope we can still be friends. When you are ready to talk, please reach out to me. If it makes you feel any better, he never looked my way—not even once."

Right. As pretty as you are? Grace thought. *She makes an indelible impact on most men, but it would be nice if she is right about this one.*

14

Reinforcement

Ruth's telephone rang several times. "Please be home, Mom. I need you now," Grace cried.

"Hello?"

"Hey, Mom," Grace said dryly.

"What's wrong now?"

"Jana and I had a fight. I decided I'm going to move to another dorm," Grace replied.

"Just like that honey? What happened?"

"Our friendship has been compromised," Grace said.

"Would you like me to come visit for the weekend and make you feel better?"

"No thanks, Mom. I'll be okay. This is something I'll work through, and I know I'll get over it. I just need to hear your reassuring voice. That's why I called. I never mentioned this, but at times like these, I wish I had a sister to talk to. Then I wouldn't have to call you so much."

"I wish you had one too. After the trouble I went through delivering you, your dad didn't want me to go through that pain again. We worried about you being an only child, and we hoped it wouldn't have a negative impact on you. But you know what I always say?"

"Mom, which saying? You have so many great ones." Grace laughed.

"I always say, 'Talk to the Man above. He's your friend, and he knows all about you already.' Have you given any further thought to our conversation about finding a campus Christian fellowship? It's a really practical way to meet people and make friends."

"Not yet, Mom. It'll happen. Right now, I just need time alone."

"Okay, dear, but you are always alone! Just remember that you can't function by yourself forever. I know you remember all those faith-based teachings you had throughout your youth. I pray that you will consider them, when appropriate. That's all I ask, dear. If you want victory in your life, you must go through him."

"Yes, Mom. I hear you. Listen, I'll call you next week," Grace said. "I love you."

The Adjustment

Grace did follow through with the ideas to change her entire direction and her lifestyle at Hope College. Within the month, she moved to another dorm, and she dropped Professor Holmes's class at the end of the semester. She rarely saw Jana other than in their interior decorating class. They only spoke as a matter of courtesy. She really had hurt Grace, and while Grace thought she had forgiven her, every time she saw Jana, the pain in her heart would suddenly return. From time to time, she did think of her anyway. She was the only close girlfriend Grace had ever had. Grace wasn't sure if they would still be friends today if she had been a little more mature. At any rate, her life was moving in a positive direction.

Grace became engrossed in developing her own painting style and began learning even more abstract shortcuts from Malcolm. It helped give birth to her brand, and Grace's talents took her to the top of her class. She painted a unique abstract design on a window treatment that won top honors. The work was selected among fifty pieces to be exhibited at Hope College's spring art show. Grace was beginning to find the niche artists discover for themselves.

Spring came early that year, and love oddly blossomed. Grace noticed someone reading a newspaper after a Sunday morning bike ride. He leaped toward her bike and almost made her crash. Professor Holmes had a bouquet of the prettiest roses she'd ever seen.

"On a beautiful day like this, a certain angel deserves something that smells as sweet as her, don't you think?" He planted a light kiss on Grace's cheek and held the flowers up to her nose.

Grace stepped off her bike, and her heart started thumping. "Thank you, Professor Holmes. These are gorgeous. What's the occasion?"

"Just because," he said.

"I don't get it. Just because what?" Grace grinned.

"Just because I can." He smiled.

Her face lit up when she saw his brilliant smile. "Okay," Grace said.

"And, by the way, can you stop calling me Professor Holmes? Just call me Wellington."

"Okay, but it sounds weird calling a professor by his first name," Grace replied.

"But I'm not your professor, right?" He smiled.

"I guess you have a point there. How did you get my address?"

"You know me. I have ways to find out things," he replied. "I heard about the little scrape in the girl's room between you and Jana, and I thought it was time I put an end to your agitation with me." He looked at Grace like he was studying her, and she tried to smile. "I admit that I have avoided you. It wasn't appropriate for me to pursue you while you were my student, and that's why I backed off. I knew you didn't feel comfortable either, but I was enchanted with you—and my heart never let me rest. I have been busy pursuing my career and traveling to art exhibitions almost every weekend. That's what kept my mind busy, but I have thought of you often. Anyway, now that you are no longer in my class, will you give me the pleasure of your company today?"

"I don't know what to say." Grace looked down at the flowers.

"Come on, girl." He grabbed her hand and pulled her across the grass. "You are finally going with me," he said playfully.

Grace couldn't help but laugh and relax around him. She enjoyed the wind in her hair, the smell of fresh flowers, and sound of chirping birds. She felt spring and love flowing inside of her. "What about the bike?"

"No worries. It'll be here when we return," he replied.

Grace knew why she was attracted to him. It was his jovial spirit, his self-confidence, and his passion for the arts. He put all his energy into whatever he was involved in. And now he was intimately involved with her!

16

Love Flourishes

In the next month, Grace watched their love blossom. She came to know and understand true love for the first time in her life.

Wellington stayed busy teaching and traveling on the weekends, and she prepared for the art fair. Surprisingly, she won first place—and an award of five thousand dollars. Her entry was an abstract design on a window treatment.

Wellington was taken aback by her new skills and the recognition. He encouraged her to continue painting in her fine arts medium of choice and assured her that she was on to something very promising.

When school ended, Wellington's travel schedule increased.

Grace applied for a summer job at a local interior design shop.

Wellington's career was developing, and it didn't look like he would return to teaching at Hope College in the fall. She wondered how it would affect their relationship. *Would he meet some other fine lady and lose his attraction for her? Would he never return?* Grace was feeling uncomfortable.

Daniel—a gifted sculptor and friend of Wellington—lived in New York. Ricardo Azul, an international agent in his thirties, had established Daniel's brand in Europe. There were rumors that Azul had been involved in a scandal with art smugglers, but his name was cleared. Wellington went to meet Azul for lunch in Los Angeles and sent Grace a plane ticket.

Grace was thrilled that he was including her, and it helped restore her confidence in their relationship. She immediately phoned her mother in hopes that she could drive from Santa Barbara and meet them during the weekend. Grace was delighted that her mom would finally meet Wellington.

Everything was coming together. The Beverly Hills Hotel was very upscale. Azul was dressed all in white and seated near a large window with a wonderful view of the garden. He had a reputation for handling big deals and powerful clients.

"Good afternoon," Azul said.

"Hey, Azul, good to meet you," Wellington said as they shook hands. "This is my beautiful friend Grace."

"Beautiful indeed. Nice meeting you," he said, kissing Grace's hand.

"You're looking spiffy today. Plan on playing golf today?" Wellington asked.

"No, man. I can't stand still long enough to learn that game." Azul laughed.

A waiter approached and said, "Would you care for some coffee?"

"I'll have some peppermint tea," Grace said.

"Black coffee please," Azul and Wellington said almost in unison.

"Okay, shall we get right down to business?" Azul asked. "I have so many awesome opportunities I can line up for you. With your talent, we are going to rock the world! I brought a contract that you

can read over and sign when you are ready, but don't take too long."
He laughed.

Wellington said, "You put Daniel's name on the map, and I'm looking forward to you advancing my career in the same manner."

"Well, you've come to the right place, my man. I specialize in what I call the Next-level performance, and I guarantee you won't be disappointed."

A man in dark sunglasses and a fedora passed by the table and exchanged glances with Azul. Grace couldn't put her finger on it, but there was something sly about the interaction.

Wellington didn't notice, but Grace's intuition wouldn't let it slide. It was recorded in her mind.

17

Reconciliation

Wellington's absence during the summer provided an opportunity for Grace to renew her relationship with Jana. After Wellington convinced Grace that he was never interested in Jana, Grace admitted that she missed Jana getting on her case and talking about her.

Jana made Grace look at herself and helped her grow up. They began shopping together and going to the movies on a regular basis. Grace began to understand the need for a sustainable friend and a sister she could talk to. She learned to trust Jana again, and they never spoke about the bathroom incident again.

A dozen roses were delivered to Grace's job on Monday morning with a note: "You are invited to attend a special exhibition on Friday, July 20, at the Museum of Modern Art in New York featuring artist Wellington Holmes. Airline arrangements have been made, and a car will pick you up on Friday morning at eight o'clock. Love Wellington."

Grace screamed with delight and almost dropped the vase she was painting. She was so engaged with the note that she forgot a customer was waiting for her to finish a business transaction. Hurriedly, she completed wrapping and bagging the vase.

Kyra, her boss, came into the room. When she saw the flowers and the note, she hugged Grace. "So, I know what's next. You need the weekend off, right?"

Grace laughed. "I'm hoping you say yes—so I don't disappoint the artist."

It would be her first time going to New York, and she didn't want to miss the opportunity so see one of his exhibits.

Grace said, "I will be mixing with the crème de la crème of the art world."

"Take the entire week off if you want," Kyra said.

They hugged and laughed.

Grace grinned and said, "Thank you, boss lady!"

18

New York City

At JFK, a man in a black suit held up a large sign: "Looking for an angel."

"I'm Grace Green, the angel you are looking for," Grace said as she approached him.

"Welcome to New York, ma'am." Grace followed him to baggage claim and picked up her bags. A long black limo was waiting at the curb.

In the car, the driver handed her a note: "Sweetie, welcome to New York. Get ready to have some fun. Here's your schedule for the day: Your first appointment is at 11:00 at Jazzy's Spa on Fifth Avenue, where you will receive the Master Works Treatment. At 2:00, the driver will take you to Eric's Hair Salon for your hair appointment and makeup. At 5:00, the driver will pick you up and take you to the hotel. I still have several preparations for the exhibition and may not see you before the limo picks you up again at 7:00 for the event. Nevertheless, my love for you is intense, and I can't wait to see your lovely face. Love, Wellington."

After Grace's appointments, the driver drove her to the Plaza Hotel. A beautiful bouquet of yellow roses greeted Grace at the door. She was filled with delight. Another surprise was waiting in the bedroom. On the bed was a mid-length red gown with silver tiny beads around the low neckline and flared at the bottom. A silver handbag and matching shoes were next to the outfit. Grace had never owned such an exquisite ensemble. She picked up the gown and danced in front of the mirror. The dress and shoes she had brought with her certainly could not top this.

The professor has plans, honey. She laughed out loud. Realizing all the fuss Wellington had gone through caused her to tear up. She quickly dotted her eyes with a Kleenex to avoid ruining her makeup.

The sharp ring of the telephone startled her.

"Hello?" Grace said.

"Hi, sweetheart. Did you have a great day?"

"Darling, did I? You are the sweetest and most generous man I know." Grace smiled. "You didn't have to go to all this trouble. You must have spent hundreds to make this day special. The spa, the plane ride, just everything is unbelievable. You're really not going to be able to stand me when you see me in this dress."

"Never too much for a princess. I'm sorry I couldn't meet you at the airport. I have a lot of last-minute changes and am still running behind. I'm sending a car to pick you up around seven. Will you be ready?"

"Sure, I understand, and yes, I'll be ready."

He chuckled and said, "Remember—seven o'clock!"

Wellington had excellent taste in clothes and was a genius with an appreciation for colors. He didn't spare any expense to make her look elegant. The red dress accented Grace's tanned skin and the streaks of honey blonde in her dark brown hair. The heart-shaped diamond earrings and a matching necklace were almost too delicate to handle.

The phone rang again, and Grace tried not to wrinkle her clothes.

"Hi, dear, are you settled in?"

"Mom, I'm in heaven. Wellington has made everything so lovely. It's a dream come true."

"I know, dear. It is everything God ordered for my little angel. Wellington told me his plans for you."

"Mom, thanks for praying and supporting me. I know that you love me, and I'm grateful to have your support. You told me everything would work out. Mom, you are always telling me to pray and trust God—that kind of stuff—and I'm trying to do more of that."

"I'm happy to hear that, sweetie. Have a wonderful time tonight. I'll see you soon. I know you will be among some bigwigs tonight but remember to just be you. That's the person he fell in love with. Like the proverb says: 'As water reflects a face, a man's heart reflects the man.'"

"Thanks, Mom. I won't forget. I love you. I will see you tomorrow."

Grace looked in the mirror once more, looking at her few freckles, and was happy her makeup did not cover them. She had learned to like them and felt that they were a unique part of her. Grace could hear her mom's voice with another of her prized sayings: "You're one of God's special children. He's got treasures waiting for you. You haven't come to the full knowledge of it yet, but you will. It's inevitable."

Her mom always had a way of lifting her spirits. She was kind and full of confidence in the Lord and in her daughter. Grace hoped to follow in her footsteps. The phone rang, and she thought it might be her driver.

"Hello, can I speak to Wellington Holmes?" a man said.

"He's not available. Can I take a message?"

"No, ma'am. It's a private matter. I'll see him later. Thank you." The man hung up the telephone.

What a strange call, Grace thought.

By the time the limo arrived, Grace understood Cinderella's transformation. *Glamour, sophistication,* and *sexy* were not words usually with her, but she totally fit the bill. The thought that her man would finally see her blossom in front of his eyes—just for him—tickled her inside.

19

The Museum of Modern Art

The door to the limo opened, and the camera flashes blinded Grace. When she cleared her eyes, she saw Wellington. He looked handsome and chic in a black suit and red tie that matched her dress. She hugged him tightly. She was proud and happy to be with him.

He remained humble despite his numerous accomplishments in the art world. In the classroom, he appeared to be just an ordinary teacher. He never let his students know what a well-known artist he was.

That night, Grace recognized his worth as a fine artist—and not just as her former teacher. Walking up the stairs and through the barrage of cameras, Grace begged Wellington not to release her hand. She feared that everyone would see her hands shaking.

He squeezed her hand tightly, kissed her cheek, and whispered words of assurance.

Grace managed to smile at the cameras and walk along the long red carpet without tripping. Entering the ballroom, she was in awe when she saw Wellington's massive display of paintings on the walls and on easels. Each painting revealed a unique passion and told a story. She was overwhelmed by the beauty and the extraordinary array of colors.

"You surprised me," Grace whispered.

"How's that?" he asked, tenderly stroking her bare back.

"You never revealed your talents to the class. We only saw sketches. I knew you exhibited in San Francisco, Los Angeles, Washington, and internationally, but I had no idea it was on this scale. Why did you hold that back?"

"I was waiting for a special moment like this." He smiled, rubbing his smooth face against hers. "I had a few big collectors and some companies that purchased my work, but my vision is a much larger platform."

"I see. You camouflage well. Should I call you Master Wellington Holmes now? And what other secrets are you hiding that I need to know about?"

"That's for me to know—and for you to find out," he answered.

"Oh, by the way, before I left the hotel, you got a strange call from a guy, and he didn't want to leave a message. He said he would see you later."

The waiter approached with drinks as they mingled with the crowd. Somehow, they got separated, but Grace could see him speaking to numerous people.

"Ladies and Gentlemen, can I have your attention? Please help me welcome Wellington Holmes to the podium."

Everyone clapped as Wellington approached the stage. He gave an overview of his work. The next thing that happened came as a surprise to the entire room. Without warning, he stepped down from the podium and began walking toward Grace.

Her heart beat rapidly as she recalled begging him not to introduce her and hoped he would keep her wish. The feeling from art class on the first day was gradually returning. She tried not to panic or faint.

He planted a kiss on her cheek, dropped a red rose at her feet, bent down to pick it up with his teeth, and handed it to her. He took Grace's hand and said, "Will you marry me?"

Grace had never been so embarrassed or delighted. She managed to whisper, "Yes," and the whole room exploded with excitement. It was a dream coming true and the most endearing moment of her life.

Suddenly the speakers began playing "The First Time Ever I Saw Your Face" by Roberta Flack.

Wellington grabbed her hand and pulled her into an open area.

Grace couldn't hold back her tears of joy. Although she had never seen Wellington cry, she saw tears forming in his eyes.

As they danced, he squeezed her and stared into her eyes. *I'm going to be the artist's wife,* Grace thought. *This is like heaven on earth. Just like Mom said.*

Everyone clapped as they made their way back to their seats. Several people came over to congratulate them.

A short, burly man introduced himself as Detective Carlos Ramos. "Congratulations on your engagement and your show. I admire your work." He smiled, handed Wellington a business card, and asked him to call him.

"Thank you. What is this concerning?" Wellington asked.

"Nothing you should worry about for the moment. Just call me— and I'll explain."

Wellington placed the card in his jacket as the man walked away. That must be the person who called earlier," Grace said.

Wellington said, "That was an interesting time for him to approach me. It must be something of grave importance."

"It's not important as this special moment we are enjoying together right now," Grace added, kissing him softly on the lips.

20

Detective Carlos Ramos

Two months passed before Wellington spoke with Detective Carlos Ramos. Wellington called on a Saturday morning from his studio.

"Hi, this is Detective Ramos. I never heard back from you."

"I apologize. I've been so busy working. It totally slipped my mind," Wellington said.

"How's everything going?" Detective Ramos asked.

"It's all good. I'm home for a week and finishing up an important project in my studio."

"You got a moment?" he asked.

"Sure, I'll make one," Wellington replied.

"I want to talk to you about Ricardo Azul. I figured this was a good time to catch you, and I hope I didn't startle you and cause any concern."

"I did think it was a little odd for you to approach me at the show, but it's okay. What's your question about Azul?"

"The CIA has been investigating him for years. He was involved in criminal activity about five years ago in Europe, and we have him on the radar for recent activity. Several artists he represented have mysteriously died in the past five years. Did you know anything about this investigation?"

"No, nothing at all," Wellington said.

"One of the artists Azul represented—I can't mention his name—lived in California. Azul was part of a huge art scheme, but we never could directly tie anything to him. He got a call from a studio that leased ten paintings for a movie shoot. They used Azul's name as the contact person. The negotiations appeared to be set. It all happened so fast. It was the opportunity of a lifetime for the artist. He moved on it quickly, but he failed to check out the small print and some important details.

"The studio asked that he provide the images so they could decide on the ones they wanted. They asked him to send them an invoice for ten thousand dollars to cover the initial rental fee for a week. Because the production was in process, they needed the paintings right away. The production coordinator set up a time that the shipping truck could pick up the paintings.

"Everything was very professional in terms of communication with the production coordinator, so it seemed legit. The workers came within four hours with a car that was too small, but they called for a backup truck, which took another hour. The artist didn't think it was odd and was not suspicious. The workers remained at the house, talking and entertaining the artist, and he was elated that his work was getting national attention.

"When the truck arrived, they packed the paintings neatly, loaded them on the truck, said their goodbyes—and that was the last he heard of it. When he followed up the next day for the check, the telephone numbers were disconnected. It had all been a setup. That particular production company and movie set never existed. Azul denied any connection to the scheme. He appeared as shocked as the artist."

"Really? This is shocking."

"That's just a small example of the illegal operations in the art world. To be safe, I suggest that you keep an eye on Azul—and on your paintings. Azul moves very fast, and he is very illusive. You are truly gifted and have a great future ahead. I wouldn't want you to get mixed up with a potential criminal."

"That's the last thing I need right now," Wellington replied.

"If you suspect anything out of the norm, I would appreciate you giving me a call," Detective Ramos said.

"I will, sir. Thank you for calling."

After hanging up, Wellington thought, *Art smuggling? Grace always said there was something suspicious about Azul, but she couldn't put her finger on it.* The conversation with Detective Ramos sparked a thought. He walked over to his desk and pulled out a letter from Daniel's widow after his death. It was still sealed. Up to that point, it had been too painful to open.

Daniel and Wellington had exhibited together for three years at many galleries and art exhibitions. They were close friends and collaborated on a few pieces.

Dr. Monica Wolf was a microscopy researcher at the Center for Disease Control.

Before reading the letter, Wellington reflected on the last time he and Daniel were together. On a Saturday afternoon, they headed to Michael's Art Supplies in Wellington's Nissan. As they walked toward the store, a dark blue Chevy pickup sped up and hit Daniel, throwing him across the parking lot. The car sped off quickly. Wellington was stunned because the car looked like it was intended for Wellington. He looked at Daniel's mangled body and yelled out for someone to call 911. Daniel died before reaching the hospital. In addition, the toxicology report revealed poison in his blood.

Monica was so traumatized over his death that she moved to Dern, Switzerland, for a work assignment to escape the sorrow and pain. It was a hard time for all of them.

Wellington opened the letter and began reading:

> I know you have seen how depressed I've been lately. I just need someone to talk to. I am so disenchanted with Azul and wanted to let you know the reason why. I know I introduced you to him, but I'm not so sure that was the right thing to do. A deal he was working on for me went sour, and tensions rose between us. I gave him fifteen paintings to sell, and they all came up missing. They were valued at fifty thousand dollars. He said they were stolen from his warehouse, but I don't believe him. Maybe I'm making more of it than I should, but my mind won't let it go. All I know is that from that point, my relationship with him and my career took a hit and nosedived. I can't seem to recover. Azul blames everything on me and said he lost millions because of me. He turned the tables on me. I'm just asking that you watch your back. He's devious and highly connected.

Wellington paused. *What if Azul arranged his death? Naw. That is too farfetched. He doesn't seem to be a murderer.*

Wellington placed the letter back in his desk and went into his studio. His instincts were flaring. *Too many coincidences.* After reading Daniel's letter, he decided he would hold onto the detective's card and follow up with him.

Wedding Bells

The following September, Grace and Wellington were married in a small ceremony at Wellington's home on Sixth Avenue in Manhattan.

Jana was the maid of honor, and Wellington's brother, Peter, was the best man. The guest list consisted of fifty people.

Grace's dress was simply beautiful, a strapless ivory chiffon A-line fitted bodice, slightly flared at the waist, with embroidery on the bodice and on the train. Her bouquet had ranunculus, tulips, and hyacinths in various shades of pink. Jana wore a pink-shaded halter dress that draped the floor. Wellington wore a black tux with a baby pink tie to match Grace's flowers.

They spent their honeymoon week in the British Virgin Islands, walking the white beaches, sailing, and relaxing. Grace moved in with Wellington right after the honeymoon. It was a lovely two-story townhouse with stained glass windows, beautiful hand-painted french doors, hardwood floors, and a tall winding staircase leading to two bedrooms. The studio was on the first floor. Wellington created an area within his studio that Grace could call her own and separated it with a rattan divider.

Although Wellington's schedule forced him to stop teaching at the college, Grace continued her studies at Hope College and graduated with honors. After graduation, she landed a job at Dee's, an elite wearable arts boutique in Manhattan. Many of her abstract designs painted on clothing began appearing on models in designer magazines and were wanted by international buyers. Grace's flourishing career left little time to travel with Wellington or paint for relaxation.

A series of events changed Wellington's career forever. Azul invited Niklas Johansson, a prominent gallery owner from Europe, to attend a show for Wellington at the High-Strung Gallery on Seventh Avenue. This exquisite gallery was known for its high ceilings and was considered the East Coast's leading art museum. It featured paintings of famous artists.

On opening night, people filled the room and chatted as Wellington greeted the guests.

Grace moved from room to room, smiling and greeting guests.

Wellington wore a dark blue sports jacket with dark blue pants, and Grace wore a light blue floor-length flowing dress with spaghetti straps. Her hair was pulled back in a french braid. Out of the corner of her eye, Grace noticed an unusual couple roaming from one of Wellington's paintings to the next. Grace moved closer to hear their conversation.

"How stunning," the lady said as they moved to one of the smaller rooms.

Grace pretended to straighten up the room.

"Absolutely fabulous," the man said, pointing to a large painting of a man and woman in the park with the New York city skyline in the background. He was short and plump with a distinguished salt-and-pepper mustache and a strong British accent.

The female was also short, and a large hat covered her face.

Grace saw Wellington motion for her to join him in the larger showroom. As she turned to leave the room, she heard footsteps behind her and felt a tap on her shoulder.

"Hello, madam. Would you be so kind as to point out the artist?" the man asked.

"Yes, sir," Grace responded. "He's the gentleman in the dark blue suit jacket. I'm his wife, Grace." She extended her hand.

"Oh, goodness, my dear lady," he said, extending his hand. "I'm Niklas Johansson. Congratulations! You must be extremely proud of your husband."

Grace continued to shake his hand and said, "Sweetie, I'd like to introduce you to Niklas Johansson, and I believe his wife. I didn't catch your name, ma'am."

"Glad to meet you," Wellington said, extending his hand and a smile.

"This is my lovely wife, Laine. It is nice to finally meet you. Ricardo Azul spoke so highly of you and invited us to this event. We are gallery owners in Switzerland, and he invited us to see your work. We have admired your work from afar, but we've never had the pleasure of seeing the work up close. It is remarkable! You have a wonderful eye for detail and color. These are the signs of greatness!"

"Thank you." Wellington blushed. "We are happy you could come."

Niklas said, "We would love to feature and showcase some of your art in our gallery in Switzerland. Perhaps we can have dinner before we leave and talk more about it. Are you busy tomorrow evening? We'd love the pleasure of your company before we return home."

"The pleasure would truly be ours," Wellington said. "I will make reservations at the 900 Club and get the directions for you—or we could have a car pick you up."

"You don't have to go out of your way. We will find it," Niklas replied.

"I'll make it for seven o'clock and meet you there," Wellington replied.

"Sounds like a date then," Niklas concluded. "Congratulations on your show, and we look forward to talking more tomorrow evening."

After they left, Azul rushed over with sparkles in his brown eyes. "You have no idea who you just met, do you?"

"They are a very nice couple and are interested in my work. That's all I know," Wellington replied.

"My God, Mr. and Mrs. Johansson are the top exclusive gallery owners in Europe. This could be the break we're looking for, Wellington," Azul said with raised eyebrows.

"He did say they wanted to have dinner tomorrow to talk about my work."

"Well, what did you tell him?" Azul started scratching his head.

"We agreed to meet him at the 900 Club," Wellington replied coolly.

"That's great. I'll clear my calendar," Azul said, turning to walk away.

Wellington grabbed him by the arm and said, "The dinner is with me, Grace, and the Johanssons. It will be more informal that way."

Azul lowered his head and shrugged.

"Don't worry. I can handle this," Wellington said. "When it's time to do business, you know I'll include you."

Grace held back a smirk, thanking God that Wellington stood his ground and did not allow Azul to impose his will.

"Well, call me as soon as you finish dinner and tell me what happened," Azul said.

"Don't worry. I'll call you." Wellington smiled as they turned to rejoin the growing crowd.

"You've got a real problem here," Grace whispered.

"What are you talking about?" Wellington asked.

"You know … the control issues he has."

"Leave that to me, honey. I can handle him," he said.

"Okay, have it your way."

"But don't let it be said that I told you so."

The Search

The footsteps moved beyond the doors, and Detective Ramos peeked through the window shade. He saw nothing. The detectives stood still while the footsteps moved on. Detective Ramos fumbled with the key to the wooden warehouse door and dropped it.

After several attempts, the door squeaked open. Brushing away the cobwebs, he slowly walked forward to find a light switch. "Strike a match, can you?" he called to his assistant who was walking behind him.

Detective Fernando Mendez reached in his pocket to locate his lighter. "Looks like I found something." He pulled a string hanging from the ceiling, and the lights came on. Everything in the room was covered with dusty white sheets that had tiny moth holes in them. "We didn't obtain a search warrant. What if we get caught?"

Detective Mendez whispered, "Why in the world did I bring you along? My goodness, I thought you liked investigating. You know how this works. Now hold this flashlight and follow me." Detective Ramos uncovered a package on the table and brushed off the dust. The initials on top were AZ. "Looks like some important notes," Detective Ramos said, flipping through the pages.

Detective Mendez slid over to look and knocked a lamp to the ground.

"Stand still and don't touch anything!" Detective Ramos placed the book in his pocket. "This may be the thing that can help us uncover more information. He's a slick fellow who covers his tracks well. Remember Big Stoney who was in the pen for ten years for drug dealing?"

"Yes. African American, slick talker, nice dresser, bald," Mendez said.

"From the day of his release, he's been with Azul. They are up to something, but I can't tie anything together yet."

The detectives looked around a little longer, but they did not find anything else of interest.

"Let's get out of here," Detective Ramos whispered.

Moving toward the door, they heard voices and footsteps.

"Turn that light off!" Detective Ramos opened the door and peeked outside. He saw no one.

When the voices faded, they ducked around the corner, jumped into Detective Ramos's blue Fiat, and sped away.

"Whew, that was really a close call." Mendez wiped the sweat from his brow.

Detective Ramos laughed and slapped him hard on the back. "Boy, you ain't seen nothing. I'm going to make a good detective out of you yet. Just stick with me. The fun is just beginning."

"Man, I may be wrong, but it seems you have a huge vendetta against Azul. Do you just want to catch a bad guy in this art scheme? What's up with that?"

"You are right, man. He has been my nemesis, appearing to win at every turn. Twice in the past, I had him in the palm of my hand for crimes he committed. He's always been smooth enough to cleanly get out of the situation and escape punishment. This time, it isn't going to happen. Justice will prevail!"

23

The Agreement

Wellington lingered in his studio, taking one last look at his latest painting.

"Wellington, it is six o'clock," Grace yelled from upstairs. "We have to meet the Johanssons at seven. You still need to shave and shower. Help me out please!"

"One more stroke, and I'll be there, dear," Wellington shouted.

Dang, he's so slow I could scream. Grace pressed out a crease in her dress.

Wellington ran up the stairs and caught her in his arms.

"Stop!" Grace said. "You are wrinkling my clothes!"

"You don't have to be so mean," he replied.

"This is not a time to play. We have someplace to be," she said, smoothing her dress and her hair.

Wellington slammed the bathroom door and jumped into the shower. "Nag, nag, nag. God, please help me with this woman. What's wrong with her? All I want to do is paint and make some money. Is that too much to ask?"

They arrived at the 900 Club at five minutes after seven, and the Johanssons were waiting in the lobby.

"Sorry we are late. Have you been waiting long?" Wellington flashed his big smile.

"No, we actually just walked in moments before you," Niklas said.

"Good." Wellington winked at Grace, and she grinned.

Dinner was delightful, and the Johanssons loved the restaurant. They lingered over the meal and exchanged small talk until Niklas abruptly cleared his throat and said, "We have been following your work and are very pleased with what we see. We are convinced you are the artist for our special project."

"What project is that?" Wellington asked.

"We want to commission you to create a masterpiece for our collector's annual spring event. A lot of well-known art dealers and consumers will be in attendance. Would this be of interest to you?"

Wellington gulped. "I must admit you've caught me off guard. Yes, I would be honored to create something special for your event."

"Let me assure you this project involves some prestigious buyers across Europe. The theme for the event is 'Angel in Disguise,' but we leave the creative process to you. The art community is wondering who will step up and be the next great master, and we think it just might be you. Here's another business card. Give me a call so I can explain more about the project—and we can discuss how you can fit this project into your busy schedule. We are anxious to have something in hand by early winter. Do you think that is possible?"

"I'll rearrange my schedule to ensure that I'll have something for you no later than November 30."

"We have a deal then, fellow," Niklas said, shaking Wellington's hand.

Edgy Azul

The telephone was ringing when they entered the house.

Wellington grabbed it.

"How did it go?" Azul said.

"Man, either you have good timing—or you were watching us in the restaurant and knew exactly what time we arrived home."

"Aw, you are being cynical. What happened at dinner?"

"He asked me to create a masterpiece for their collector's fundraiser. He will speak with me in a few days to discuss the terms of the agreement."

"Cool. I've been waiting for a break such as this," Azul said.

"What do you mean?" Wellington asked.

"Oh sorry, man. My bad. I meant a break for *us*—as a team. Both of us have been working so hard, right?" Azul laughed.

"Yes, I guess we have," Wellington said.

"Man, let me hang up this phone so you can start sketching," Azul said.

"Me, sketch right now?" Wellington laughed. "It's ten o'clock. I stay up late painting most nights. Tonight, the only sketch and creative design I'm doing is with my wife—and it won't be on a canvas!" Wellington hung up the receiver.

Pregnancy

A contract was drawn up by the end of the week for Wellington to receive fifty thousand dollars with ten thousand up front. Wellington agreed to provide sketches within a month, and Niklas would send them to his clients to drum up interest in the work.

Wellington provided sketches, and calls from the overseas galleries streamed in. The extra income gave Wellington some wiggle room and the ability to slow his travel schedule.

Grace was extremely tired and had no energy for anything except sleep and visiting the spa, which she did regularly.

She parked next to Spa 52 and dropped her purse when she got out of the car. Bending down to pick it up, she got lightheaded, her knees buckled, and she felt faint. Luckily, she was in front of Café

Bonnet, and they had an outdoor sitting area. Grace gathered her purse and walked over to sit down.

A waiter ran outside to help her. "Are you all right, ma'am? Can I get you some water?"

"Yes, please. I could use some water. Thank you very much." Grace held her head down between her knees. "Whatever you are cooking inside is making me nauseous." Grace tried to remember what she ate that morning. *Two eggs, a piece of toast, and orange juice. Nothing out of the norm.*

The waiter ran inside and came right back.

Grace had regained her strength and was feeling stronger. "Thank you so much." She drank the water and stood up.

"Can I help you to your destination?" he asked, grabbing her arm.

"No, I think I can manage. I still feel a little lightheaded. Thanks for everything," Grace said as she left the café. Grace was ten minutes early for her appointment, and she was still not feeling well.

Ellona, her masseuse and new friend, had not arrived.

Grace was in dire need of the full treatment—facial, manicure, and massage—and sat down to wait.

"Hey, girl. Sorry I'm late." Ellona said as the door slammed.

"That's okay," Grace said. "I just arrived."

"You don't look so good today. What's up, girl?" Ellona asked.

"I'm okay. I guess I need all the treatment my body can stand today. Just give me the premier spa package."

"Okay, let's get started."

They walked to a room in the back.

"Here's your sheet. You know what to do. I'll give you a few minutes to change, and I'll be back in a few." Ellona closed the door behind her.

The smell of the incense and scented candles made the nausea reappear. Grace decided to lie down on the cot. She closed her eyes, hoping the feeling would leave.

Ellona came back into the room and said, "Are you okay?"

"I'm not sure. This feeling came over me this morning," Grace said between hiccups.

"Are you pregnant? Did you miss your monthly?" Ellona asked. "You're trying to have children, right?"

"No, we aren't actually trying, but we aren't preventing it either." Grace wiped the sweat from her face with a wet cloth.

Ellona touched her forehead. "You are pretty clammy. The flu is going around."

"I absolutely don't have the flu," Grace said. "I was feeling fine until today. Now that I think about it, I don't remember having my period this month."

"It would be a good idea to see a doctor to make sure," Ellona said. "You look like you saw a ghost. You scared me to death."

"You are so dramatic, Ellona." Grace managed a smile. "I'm sorry about that."

"Come on, girl," Ellona said. "Let's see if we can make you feel better. Just lie down. I'll make it all go away."

"I'll do so on one condition," Grace said.

"What's that?"

"If you promise to remove those stinky candles and incense."

They both laughed.

Confirmation

Upon leaving the spa, Grace called Dr. Harding. Two days after her tests, the results came back as a shock—and a tremendous surprise. She was two months pregnant, and the baby was due in June.

Grace's mom was ecstatic to hear that she would finally have a grandchild. She convinced Grace to shorten her work hours. It would allow more time for Grace to work on Wellington's birthday painting. She planned to surprise him with what she felt was her first masterpiece.

Wellington was extremely happy when she told him he was going to be a father. Grace was unsure if he would be happy with the timing of growing a family because his concentration was on completing artwork for an upcoming show in Japan and Niklas's project. Wellington confirmed his delight by celebrating that evening with a candlelight dinner, champagne, and more.

On Friday morning, Grace woke up to a bittersweet fragrance: the smell of paint. The baby's room was nearly complete, but the paint made her nauseous.

When the doctor confirmed she was having a, girl, Grace went overboard on girly stuff. She selected pink with purple and white wallpaper displaying baby dolls for the baby's room. The crib was handcrafted by one of their artist friends. The curtains were white lace with pink and purple bows. Toys and teddy bears lined the bed, awaiting their sweet princess.

Grace wobbled down the staircase and paused on the bottom step to rest. Rafa, their golden retriever, faithfully greeted her with wet licks. Grace rubbed him gently and continued toward the kitchen.

A light shining from Wellington's studio indicated that he had risen earlier. Sweet melodies streamed from his guitar.

"Good morning, sweet," Grace said. She heard a faint "hey" and continued down the long hall to prepare breakfast. He had just a few hours before boarding his plane to Japan. Grace made her way through the rubbish in the hallway. The remodel had added to Grace's daily nagging. She made tea, dreading the thought of the workers knocking on the door.

Wellington entered the kitchen and said, "Honey, have you seen my art portfolio?"

How do you get along without me?" she teased. "You can't seem to find anything yourself!"

"You seem to move everything out of reach!" Wellington slammed down a book. "It's not that I don't appreciate your cleanliness, but just for once, please leave my stuff where it is!"

They looked at each other and burst out laughing, realizing how silly they sounded.

"A good-morning hug would be a better way to greet your almost-famous husband." Wellington held his arms open to embrace her.

Grace reluctantly moved into his arms.

"All right. Doesn't that feel better?" he asked rubbing her stomach. "Do you have a little playtime for me before I leave. I didn't want to wake you last night. You looked like you were sleeping so well." He kissed her neckline.

"Time for what?" she asked, trying to pull away. "Your plane leaves in a couple of hours, and I have yet to fix your breakfast."

"I know, but a little pleasure would be nice." Wellington grabbed her robe and pulled her closer.

"Wellington, please!"

He picked her up, took her to the studio, and gently laid her on the sofa.

"All right, Mr. Magic. I give up." She smiled as her robe slid to the floor.

Airport Scare

Awakened by the sound of the doorbell, Grace grabbed the side of the couch and pulled herself up. Wellington had left a note on the table: "Sweetheart, thanks for your tender love. I'll call you from the airport." Grace smiled and headed to open the door. She was surprised it was already ten, and the workers were there. She pulled back the curtains, motioned for them to go to the back entrance, and opened the door for them. She sat at the kitchen table for a moment to catch her breath and grabbed the TV remote.

"We interrupt this show to bring you breaking news. A bomb reported on United Airlines Flight #775 to Tokyo was detonated this morning at 9:00 a.m. The plane never left the ground. A Serbian man in his thirties was arrested. Please stay tuned for further coverage."

"What?" She grabbed her stomach. "That's Wellington's plane."

The telephone rang, and Grace picked it up immediately.

"Hello?"

"Sweetie, you'll never guess what just happened?" Wellington said.

"I know. I just heard." Grace slowed her breathing. "Are you okay? What's happened?"

"Calm down, honey. Everything is okay. Nobody got hurt. We were waiting to take off when we saw several policemen and the bomb squad rushing onto the plane. The stewardesses asked everyone to quickly exit the plane without an explanation. We knew something was wrong. Man, people started to panic and push. The authorities received a tip that a bomb was on our plane. They detonated it in a matter of minutes. I don't know what this world is coming to."

"Well, I'm just thankful you're okay—and that nobody got hurt," Grace said. "Are they putting you on another plane?"

"Yes, but I'll have to wait another hour to catch a connecting flight. No problem."

"When I heard the news, the baby jumped," Grace said, holding her growing stomach.

"Sweetie, I want you to relax. Call Ellona and see if she can fit you in today for a spa treatment. I'll be back next Thursday, and we'll go out to dinner, okay?"

"Okay, I'll do that. I want you to have a great trip and not worry about us. Okay?"

"I love you," he said.

Grace smiled, sending a kiss through the telephone. By noon, she had had enough of the banging and knocking from the workers. Her appointment wasn't until one o'clock, but it was a good time to take a break from painting Wellington's birthday present, which was almost finished. The only thing left to do was to add finishing spray.

As she reached for her sweater and the car keys, the telephone rang. "God, I hope this isn't Wellington telling me he missed his plane. I am counting on a few days of rest."

"Hello, is this Grace?" Niklas said.

"Yes, this is Grace."

"Hi, Grace. Laine and I are in town for a few days. Is Wellington there?"

"No, Niklas. He left for Tokyo this morning and won't return until next week."

"Oh, that's funny. Azul didn't mention that. We were wondering how he's coming on the project, and since we are here, we wanted to see if we could get a peek at what he's created so far—if that doesn't seem taboo for him."

"I believe he's almost finished, but not quite there yet." Grace knew Azul was aware that Wellington was going to be out of town and wondered what he was trying to do. He knew Wellington would flip at this idea, but the contract was very important to Wellington. The thought of a quiet afternoon was quietly disappearing.

"You know how sensitive artists are about their work," Grace said. "I probably should check with him first, but unfortunately, he's on a plane."

"Well, Azul is with me, and he said he believes it is okay long as he is present."

Grace's throat tightened, and anger was rising quickly. *Azul is so devious*, Grace thought. *He knowingly set this up and is putting me in a jam.*

"Well, I suppose it would be okay." Grace knew Wellington would kill her when he found out she let them see an unfinished work. "What time would you like to drop by?"

"If it's not a bother, what about in a couple of hours?"

Grace gasped, visualizing the studio, the work required to get it in shape, and her spa appointment. "Sure. That will not be a problem, especially if Azul says it's okay."

"I'll see you at one o'clock," he said.

Grace hung up the telephone and called Spa 52 to reschedule her appointment for three o'clock. She went to the studio and began reorganizing, shifting canvases, paints, and throwing things into the

closet. She took one last look at the artwork Wellington had created
for them and hoped for the best. Before leaving the room, she pulled
the divider that separated their work space closer to the table to keep
anyone from entering her work area.

28

Secret Unveiled

Precisely at one o'clock, the doorbell rang. Grace opened the door for the Johanssons and a smiling Azul. "Hello." Grace motioned for them to come in. "I could kill Azul for doing this," she mumbled. "Please come in and make yourself comfortable," she added, pointing to the couch. Grace shot a fake smile at Azul.

"Thank you for allowing us to stop by," Niklas said. "We are in town for only two days and thought it was a perfect opportunity to see how the project is coming." He chuckled. "We are bubbling with excitement to see what he has created. We also heard the good news about your pregnancy and extend our congratulations."

"Thank you. Can I offer you something to drink?" Grace asked.

"No, we are fine. Why don't we go into the studio?" Grace stood and pointed the way.

The group followed her to the studio, and Rafa did too.

The Johanssons loved the wide-open space, large picture window, high ceilings, and modern overhead lights. Plants and painted vases were placed in different spots across the room. Canvases and paintings were spread throughout the huge room.

As they roamed from painting to painting, Azul was poking around the divider that separated her space from Wellington's space. His cell phone rang, and he stepped into the hallway to answer it.

Niklas stepped closer to the bamboo divider. "Which painting is it?"

Grace pointed to the one, and he and Laine approached it. He stepped backward to get a different view and stepped on a loose paintbrush. When he bent down to pick it up, he tilted the divider.

Grace gasped, reaching to catch the divider, but it crashed to the floor. Grace's abstract painting was exposed with its splashes of beautiful colors and a streak running down the middle, which resembled the shape of an angel.

"A-ha!" Niklas said. "You are holding out on me—just like a sweet little artist's wife would do to protect her husband." He clasped his hands together. "I should have known the masterpiece would make my heart jump when I saw it." He smiled.

"No, no! This is not the painting. The one I pointed out is the one Wellington painted for you." She pointed to the other painting.

"I do like it, but this one is amazing. Oh my God! Look at that angel. I knew he could do it. I knew he could make some magic happen." Niklas clapped again. "It is ten times better than I imagined."

Oh mercy, Grace thought. *He thinks this is Wellington's work. How am I going to break the news that it's mine? I don't think he knows I'm an artist.* "Niklas, I assure you, he's not finished with this yet," Grace said. "Besides, this painting is for someone else." She felt the baby moving. "The one behind us is for the opening."

"Oh, I see," Niklas said, taking another look. "But I love this one as well. It does not look like the sketches Wellington sent, but since when does the artist stick to that anyway?" He laughed. "Oh, please excuse my poor manners. I failed to ask what you do for a living. I know surely you are more than just the artist's wife." He smiled.

Grace's heart was beating fast. "I'm an artist and decorator. I dabble in window treatments and the like," she said softly.

Niklas smiled. "Sounds like fun. I'm sure you are good at it."

"I do what I can, but I'm nowhere near the talent of Wellington."

"This is astonishing. I love the use of his strong colors, which is totally different for him. I must have this masterpiece. Do you think he would be willing to sell this one to the gallery? I'll pay anything for the original. Just name a price. My clients are going to go crazy when they see this work."

I can't quote a price, but maybe if I do, he'll back off. "I'm not sure, but I believe it's going to be priced around fifty thousand dollars."

He laughed. "That is peanuts for my clients. I beg you to talk to Wellington about selling and sending this one to us soon. You did say it's almost finished, right?"

Grace pointed to the painting. "Look. He has not signed the work."

"Oh, yes, the signature. That is easy. When Wellington returns, have him sign it—and then ship it to us. We are leaving tomorrow evening. I will call you, and I hope you have an opportunity to speak to him."

Grace's mouth fell wide open. "Okay, let me try to reach him, but I'm not sure if I can. I can't guarantee anything. We can talk tomorrow around noon."

"You would make me a very happy man if you would do that for me." Johansson kissed her hand.

"Do what for you?" Azul asked, returning to the room.

"Talk to Wellington and ask him to send the finished painting to me next week," Niklas said.

"Wow, it didn't take long to satisfy you." Azul looked at the painting and smiled.

"All right, my lady. I think we are finished here." Niklas walked toward the door. Goodbye, young lady." He shook her hand. "You have been most gracious today."

Azul winked as they left.

Grace closed the door, and her entire body felt numb. *Thanks for what?* She sighed. *I'm in a terrible jam and have no idea how to get out of this. Why couldn't I just tell them it was my painting? That would have ended the conversation.* It dawned on her that somebody had finally recognized her work and loved it.

Grace's ego liked that. She had never felt a level of competence in her work until she started drawing abstracts. She sold many items at the shop that she painted on fabric and vases. *It could be the beginning of a budding art career. Wellington always said everyone should find their niche.*

Grace had no idea that her work would get the attention of an international gallery owner. It was just her luck that it happened like that. She really needed to clear it up immediately. It could intensify and enlarge an already huge problem. *It's Wellington's project—and not mine.* Grace decided she would nip this in the bud. Wellington would surely understand and help her get out of this mess. *God, this really must be a dream. My work is selling in the European market? Amazing Grace, how sweet the sound. Or is it Amazing Grace, how sour the thought? Whatever!*

It was leaving a bittersweet taste in Grace's mouth, and she needed to get over it. Could she blame it on the pregnancy and the crazy things going on in her head and her body? Everything felt upside down.

29

Girlfriend Reinforcement

Grace released the workers for the day, jumped into her dark blue BMW SUV, and headed to Spa 52.

Grace sat up abruptly in the middle of her massage. "Nothing is as important as my loyalty to him. I should never have compromised Wellington's privacy. Now I have a lot of explaining to do about a painting he has never seen. Something pushed me to the next level. I feel terrible. What am I going to do?"

"You're a good artist," Ellona said. "Why don't you take credit for the work? Just call Niklas and explain that it's your work. If he loved it so much, that won't change his mind."

"Yes, but his clients want Wellington's work—not an unknown artist. They are serious art collectors, girl! A name means something to them. Can't you understand?" Grace sobbed.

"Oh, so that's the problem, huh? You are a nobody. Poor baby! Why didn't you just say that from the beginning," Ellona said, handing her a tissue.

"You are so confident and have it all together. I didn't think you would understand."

"Oh, I do understand, girl. I haven't always had it together," Ellona said. "I know my business is thriving now, but it didn't start off that way. I was an awkward-looking child with lots of drama. I had to build my own self-esteem because I surely didn't get help from my parents. I made a living, but it was not an honest one. It caused me heartaches and wore my body down—if you know what I'm talking about. I don't think I ever want to see another jail cell in my life or live on the streets again. My only salvation was an older African American lady who came to my rescue one day when my man was beating me almost to death. She witnessed the attack on the streets, screamed, fought, and scared my man away. She took me in her care. I was about twenty-one. She took me to church. I found the Lord, and my life changed. I have been on a positive path ever since. I'll never go back to that world. If the desire to make fast money and that lifestyle come back to my mind, I have to fight them off."

"You? I would never have guessed," Grace said, blowing her nose into a tissue.

"It's going to work itself out, baby, but you have to be willing to look at yourself in the mirror and let the truth speak," Ellona said.

"You're right," Grace said. "Now just relax, lie down, and let me finish this treatment. Try to put the day behind you until you leave this place—or you'll spoil the reason you're here. Just focus on our saying, girl, with the sentiments of the old church folks."

They laughed and said, "It is well!"

CHAPTER

30

A Talk with Mom

Grace left the spa at five o'clock and drove to the Jones Deli to pick up a sandwich. The baby was kicking hard. She guessed it was the baby's way of letting Grace know that she was hungry too. By the time she reached home, it was too late to call Wellington. She called her mom instead.

"How are you feeling, honey?" Ruth asked.

"I'm okay," Grace said.

"Are you eating like the doctor suggested?"

"Yes, Mom. I just finished eating a turkey sandwich. I'm not good at keeping secrets."

"I know. You can't hold water, but what secret could you possibly keep from me, your mother?" Ruth asked.

"It's bigger than you think. Oh, I forgot I told Ellona."

"Great, you know that girl won't keep it very long."

"Mom, don't be so hard on Ellona. You don't know her that well. She's a good person. She's cool, and we have a special bond. She won't tell. I must get this off my chest. I'm not going beat around the bush any longer. I'm painting a picture for Wellington's birthday entitled *Artist Wife*. I don't even know where to begin. I got myself into a mess with the gallery owners from Switzerland. You haven't met them yet, but they commissioned Wellington to do the painting for their fund-raiser in the spring."

"How nice. That sounds like a big opportunity for Wellington."

"Yes, it is, but that's not the issue."

"What is the issue, child?"

"It's a long story. How much time do you have?"

"I have all night," Ruth replied.

"Okay you may want to sit down for this one," Grace said.

"I'm not liking the sound of this already."

"Mom, just listen while I explain. The Johanssons asked if they could stop by to see how Wellington is progressing on the painting. Wellington is on his way to Tokyo for an art exhibition and won't return until next week."

"Did you tell them he was not there?" Ruth asked.

"Yes, I did. Azul knew that too, but he told them to call me anyway. Azul knows Wellington does not like anybody in his studio if he is not there. Azul is so arrogant and is really pushing this deal."

"Well, didn't you know that too?" Ruth asked.

"Know what, Mom?"

"That Wellington does not like anybody in the studio?"

"Yes, Mom. I did know, but I also considered how important this opportunity is for Wellington, and I thought it would help the relationship since they came from such a long distance. I wanted to be congenial."

"Sounds like you. So, what happened?" Ruth asked.

"Well, against my best judgment, I told them to come over. They arrived at the house and were looking at the art. Mr. Johansson stumbled upon the painting I did for Wellington, and he thought it was Wellington's work," Grace said.

"How'd that happen?"

"While he was looking at Wellington's painting, he slipped on a paintbrush and fell into the divider. That exposed my painting. He did not know we shared a studio or that I am an artist." Grace grimaced.

"Why didn't you just tell him? That was your opportunity."

"Mom, he was so wrapped up in the painting and loved it so much, I couldn't spit it out. I let him believe it was Wellington's. He was so overwhelmed by it. I couldn't talk him out of it. My tongue and my hands seemed tied. I wasn't thinking straight and figured that I would work it out later. Plus, I lied even further. Thinking he would back off, I told him that the painting was for a special customer. He didn't care. Instead, he offered me a ridiculous price to buy it. Everything got crazy and out of control. Haven't you ever said something you don't understand how it could come out of your mouth? Well that's what happened to me today. I know I'm not making sense."

"Yes, and no, dear. You had opportunities to tell him and didn't. I don't understand that part."

"Mom, life events are changing me, and I discovered some things I like about myself and some I don't. I don't know if pregnancy has anything to do with it, but I'm not thinking straight."

"What about Azul? He knows you have a separate space in the studio. Why didn't he say something?" Ruth asked.

"Right before all this happened, Azul left the room to take a call. Wow! Now that I think about it, the timing seemed odd. Anyway, before Niklas left, I told him I would talk to Wellington and call him tomorrow with an answer. I have not had a chance to talk to Wellington about it. I left several messages, but he has not called back. I'll have to wait to speak to him tomorrow. I'm afraid to tell Wellington because he's going to explode when he hears that they were in his studio. It's really stressing me out."

"Now calm down, Grace. We don't want to disturb the baby. Can't you text him?" Ruth asked.

"I'd rather not. He needs to hear this straight from my mouth. It's that serious."

"Call him first thing tomorrow and tell him the truth," Ruth said. "Then call Niklas and get the matter straightened out."

"Yes, Mom. I can't believe he liked my painting! I didn't want recognition of my artwork to happen this way. It was a very confusing situation. I did not expect or invite Niklas and his wife on my own. I simply wanted to be a good wife. I didn't want to be a novice. I didn't want to be unaccommodating to his European buyers in the States on a short visit, making a request accompanied by his agent—about business! My studio had my surprise painting for Wellington's eyes only, and my painting made things more complicated while I was in the moment. I was stunned by the divider falling over and by the ecstatic reactions of Niklas and his wife to my work. All I could think of in that terrifying and terrific moment was their appreciation of my work. When I composed myself about which work belonged to whom, it made things even more complicated because they considered my painting of a higher quality in relationship with their commission to Wellington's. All I could think of emotionally and physically was it was a serious mess. I know you have always held me in high esteem and believed I was your perfect little angel. I really hate to disappoint you, but I'm not that innocent little girl anymore. I need to establish an identity as an artist too. Maybe I do have an ego. Ugh! I'm a little uncomfortable about that, but I guess that's part of the creative package."

"Nobody but God is perfect, Grace."

"Mom, stop! There you go again. You always make a way of escape for me. This time it is *different*. I messed up and made an unforgivable mistake that could cost me my marriage. Like I said before, I wish I had a sister. She would be familiar with my good and bad intentions, and we could talk about it." Grace sighed.

"Yes, but you don't. But you have me—and you have a friend in God. Have you asked him to help you out of this predicament? He's merciful, and he's willing and able to forgive and rescue you out of all circumstances. I always quote Bible verses to bring peace in your situations. When you get time, I want you to read this scripture: 'As water reflects a face, a man's heart reflects the man.' That is found in Proverbs 27:19."

"So, what does that mean?" Grace asked.

"Let your heart tell the truth because your character should be that of truth. Just look the wrong you've done straight in the face and correct it. That's the way we raised you."

"Mom, that's good advice and confirmation. Ellona said almost the same words. Thanks. I needed to hear that. I'm going to read that and sleep on it. Tomorrow, I'm going to tell Wellington everything."

"Okay, baby. Rest and remember my words. Good night."

31

Forestalling the Truth

The next morning, Grace dialed Wellington's hotel room, but there was no answer. She dialed his cell again.

"Hey, honey," Wellington said. "This place is so amazing. I think you would love it. How are you feeling today?"

"I'm feeling okay. I'm glad you arrived safely. No more issues with the plane I hope," Grace said.

"No. All went smooth once we boarded again," he said.

"Listen, I won't talk long. I have something important to tell you," Grace said.

"Well, honey, spit it out. I am short on time and running late."

"The Johanssons are in town."

"Oh really?"

"Yeah. They want to know how your work is coming for the fund-raiser. I told them good. Um, and they came over to the house with Azul."

"Azul came with them? I wish I would have been there," Wellington said. "I wish you were too."

"They said they would be returning to Europe tomorrow."

"Anything else?" Wellington asked.

"Well, nothing that can't wait until you get back."

"Cool. I gotta run now. Take care and call me if you need me. I'll see you Thursday. I love you."

The phone clicked off, and Grace slammed the phone down. *What a coward! Why couldn't I just tell him what happened? Wellington is going to be so disappointed when he hears what I did.* Grace decided right then that she would tell Niklas the truth when he called at noon.

This is the time to go ahead and tell the truth. Why? This is intriguing. Just think of the recognition you could receive. But you love your husband, don't you? Of course, you do. I know you want to make his name great, right? But you always sacrifice for somebody else. When are you going to make time for yourself?

Grace picked up the phone.

"Hello, Grace. Did you have an opportunity to speak with Wellington?" Niklas asked.

"I did," Grace said.

"Well, tell me the good news," he said.

"Wellington said he would look forward to talking to you next week."

"Right, right. But what did he say about the painting?"

"He's distracted by his exhibition and has a lot going on right now. He wants to give it more thought when he gets some time."

"Well, I guess that will have to do for now. Tell him I'll await his call. You said he'll be back next week, right?"

"Yes, on Thursday," Grace said.

"Great! I'll look forward to speaking with him. Good day, dear."

"Have a pleasant and safe trip home." Grace walked into the studio and looked at both paintings. Hers was a simple abstract with an angel driving through the middle of the canvas. How could this cause so such much trouble? *The only way out of this is to sign Wellington's name to your painting.* She never envisioned that a lie could grow so deep that it would possibly blur her vision. She had heard of soliloquies before, and this felt like Shakespeare. She felt like Lady Macbeth with blood on her hands. Grace picked up the paintbrush and was ready to scribe his signature, but her heart stopped her.

What are you doing? Don't you know that the truth will set you free? You are making a big mistake.

Grace dropped the paintbrush.

This is ludicrous, but there are other options. You could mail it to the Johanssons before Wellington returns, with a note: "Please keep this under wraps, and I'll call you in a few days. Now, now. Don't try to rationalize this thing. How will you explain the check?

This ideas her mind was conjuring were overwhelming. Grace threw up her hands, made her way back in the living room, and cried herself into a deep sleep. While asleep, her dreams became epic.

"Ladies and Gentlemen, please stand to your feet and welcome the Emerging Artist of the Year, the Artist's Wife, the lovely Mrs. Grace Holmes."

Grace approached the stage, and the usher helped her up the stairs. She approached the microphone. "Thank you. I'm at a loss for words."

The people kept clapping.

"Thank you, thank you. I graciously accept this honor. Many thanks to my dear husband, Wellington, my manager, my mother, and all those who had faith in me. I never dreamt as a young girl that I would receive this honor. I thank my Lord and Savior, Jesus, and thanks to all who voted for me."

The crowd began clapping again.

As she exited the stage, Wellington was waiting near the stairs to help her down. She reached for his hand, but he disappeared. He was nowhere in sight. Grace panicked. She ran down the stairs and started calling out his name. She bumped into several waiters, upsetting their carts before exiting the room. Once outside, the streetlights went out—and everything turned dark. She could only make out four individuals in dark clothing with wings. They were flying and running toward her. They said, "Angel in disguise." As they approached, she saw their fiery angry red eyes.

Grace sat straight up on the couch and wiped the sweat from her brow. She turned over and looked at the clock. It was only one o'clock in the afternoon. This was another weird midday dream causing her despair. Grace realized she needed to decide what she was going to do. *Sacrifice now and suffer the consequences later. I can't take it any longer.* Grace's mind won the battle. She would send the painting unsigned and figure out the rest later. She marched into the studio, grabbed the painting, and began wrapping it up.

When she finished, her mind congratulated her, her heart wept, and her body was exhausted.

CHAPTER

32

In Search of Courage

Grace was napping Thursday afternoon when Wellington pulled into the garage. He tiptoed through the house, trying not to wake her, and he couldn't resist passing through the studio to look at his unfinished canvas. He noticed some things had been moved around and cleaned up a bit.

She's at it again; moving my stuff around. He smiled, headed upstairs, and approached the bed. It was a long trip, and he was happy to be home.

"Hey, doll. How was your trip?" Grace turned over to face him.

"It was a long one, but it was very successful." He planted a kiss on her forehead and rubbed her bulging stomach. "I'll tell you all about it later. How are my two favorite people? It looks like you grew a bit since I left. What have you been doing every day while I was away besides eating?" He chuckled.

"Missing you—that's all—and eating a lot. For the most part, it's been uneventful," Grace lied. "I'm glad you are back. I have something to tell you, but it can wait."

"Good. Enough of the small talk," he said climbing into bed. "I need to catch up on more important things." He laughed, dove under the covers, and began tickling her.

"What about that dinner you promised me?" Grace asked.

"That will have to wait. I have more interesting things to do right now."

Grace would hold her secret a little longer—and when she found the courage to break his heart, she would tell him the entire story.

33

Wellington's Secret

Grace's cell phone rang and woke her at six o'clock. She didn't realize it was so late.

"Hey, honey," Wellington called from downstairs. "You looked exhausted, so I let you sleep a while longer. FedEx called and left a message saying they would be here in the morning to pick up the package. What package are they talking about?" he asked as he came up the stairway.

Oh Lord, Grace thought. *This is my time to tell him the truth.* She turned over, rubbed her eyes, and cleared her throat. "I'm returning a package of fabrics to a shop in Europe. It's the one that—"

The telephone rang, and Wellington rang down the stairs to pick it up. *Whew,* she thought. *Saved by the bell.*

"Hello. Yes, this is Wellington."

"This is a collect call from Albuquerque, New Mexico. Will you accept?"

"Yes, I'll take it," he said, moving to another room.

"Hello, Wellington. I'm sorry I'm calling you at home, but you have not been answering your cell phone. I need your help."

"What is it, Sonya?" he asked.

She began crying. "My health is failing. My mother is helping out as much as possible. I do not want to make a big issue out of this, but I need some money."

"Sonya, I'm sorry to hear you are not well. Have you seen a doctor?"

"No. That's one reason why I need money."

"I understand. Call me at the office, and I will have my assistant take care of everything. And I asked you not to call me at the house."

"Yes, I know, but this is urgent."

"Okay. I understand, but please never call me here again!"

"Okay. I'm sorry. To bother you."

"How is Javier?" he asked, lowering his voice.

"He's good and jovial as ever. He can't wait to see you again," Sonya said.

"Yes, well I'm doing a lot of traveling now. Call Marcella at the office. I'll make sure she takes care of your needs. Goodbye." He hung up the phone quickly.

"Who was that?" Grace asked from the top of the stairs.

"Oh, nobody. Just one of those sales people trying to talk me into buying something."

"You sounded pretty pissed off," Grace said.

"Yes, they have a way of doing that to me. I'm cool."

"It sounded serious to me. Are you sure it was not one of your old students, still chasing you?" Grace snickered. "Actually; come to think of it, that's not funny. All that traveling you do, I know you meet ladies who come onto you. You can tell me," she said as she walked closer to him.

"Be serious. It's nothing like that." He tried to smile. "There were a few who chased me when I was single, but that life is behind me. I guess you could call it a mystery why some women are drawn to artists. A lot of them. As a single man, we are allowed to have a little fun, and we don't feel we have to answer to anyone. When I became serious about you, I knew once and for all that I had to throw away that little black book. I couldn't take the chance of losing you. You are the only girl for me." He planted a kiss on her cheek.

"That's a sweet-sounding story, but it doesn't stop me from asking or checking on you, boy." Grace slapped his hand as he tickled her.

"Everything is good, dear. I promise. I made reservations for us at Fisherman's Restaurant at eight—so get dressed. I have one run to make, and I'll be back around seven." He pulled his topcoat from the closet. "I promise. We will talk at dinner." He kissed her forehead.

Grace hesitated a moment. *If I waited this long, I guess a little more time won't matter.*

Wellington was pulling out the driveway. She still had time to tell him the truth.

Her mind reminded her of its only option. *No, keep your plans to send it in the morning. Just do it and tell him later. Send the painting now. He was too busy to listen to you—so why make time to tell him right now?*

Grace went into the studio to check on her wrapped package. She couldn't believe her mind was stronger than her heart, especially after the lovely time she had with Wellington that afternoon. More unsettling was the thought that she wasn't following her mom's advice.

The Painting Arrives

Tyler Hamilton checked his watch as he walked toward the Johansson Gallery. He had two hours to spare before meeting his client for lunch. As he opened the door to the gallery, a FedEx man followed him in.

"Good day, young men," Laine Johansson said.

"It is a good day, isn't it?" Tyler said.

"Welcome to our gallery. If there are any items I can show you, please let me know." She signed for the FedEx package and headed to the back room.

"Thank you," Tyler said as he began looking around the gallery.

"The package from Grace just arrived," Laine said, setting it before Niklas.

He opened it with excitement. "Oh, my God," he said loudly, pulling the painting from the box. "This is more gorgeous than I remember! I can't believe it's in our hands."

Laine glanced at the painting and said, "Our clients are going to go mad over this!"

"Mad over what?" Tyler asked, peeking into the room. "Sorry. I couldn't help but overhear your enthusiasm."

"Over this painting!" Niklas said.

"Whoa, that is awesome!" Tyler said. "Who's the artist—and what's the name of that piece?"

"His name is Wellington Holmes. It's entitled *Angel in Disguise*. Have you heard of him?"

"By all means. I know him by name, but I don't believe I have any of his art in my collection. Is this for sale?" Tyler asked.

"I'm purchasing it, and I commissioned him to do another one for our spring collector's fund-raiser," Niklas said. "Isn't this electrifying and refreshing? I can't wait to show it."

"Oh, excuse my manners, young man. I was so busy with this painting that I failed to ask if I could help you with anything."

"I'm glad you asked," Tyler said. "I'm interested in this piece of art."

"What is your name?" Niklas asked.

"I'm Tyler Hamilton," he said, extending his hand. "You can call me Ty. I travel the world looking for extraordinary work like this. I just happen to be in the area for lunch and stopped in your gallery, and I'm glad I did."

"Good to meet you. I'm Niklas Johansson, and this is my wife, Laine," he said shaking Ty's hand.

"How much is this painting?" Ty asked.

"We just received it, and I have not priced it yet. I estimate around fifty thousand, but it is worth much more."

"No doubt. It's an astounding piece of art," Ty said pondering the piece. "What if I offered you seventy-five off the cuff?" Ty asked.

"Well. That is a very generous offer, but I would have to give it some thought," Niklas said. "Wellington is sending more pieces that I'm sure you might like to see."

"I could pay you in cash, and you could still show the piece at your fund-raiser," Tyler said.

"That all sounds good, but I'll have to speak with the artist first," Niklas explained.

"Tell me how you know the artist," Ty said.

"His agent introduced us while we were in New York. I fell in love with his work immediately and commissioned him to create this piece for us."

"I noticed it is unsigned," Ty said.

"I can explain that," Niklas said. "Wellington was in Tokyo, and I was in such a hurry to get it I asked his wife to send it. He will sign it when he comes to visit."

"I see. That's seems like a perfect opportunity to invite them over to my house for dinner," Ty said, scratching his head. "Maybe talking to him will help him sell it to me. I can also help your fund-raiser by asking some of my friends who are important buyers to attend your event." Ty smiled.

"That sounds wonderful. I will try to reach him and ask." Niklas looked at his wife with raised eyebrows."

"Here's my card," Ty said. "I will be in town for a few more days, but I would love to hear from you as soon as you talk to him."

"I understand. I felt the same way when I first saw it," Niklas said.

"I will be waiting to hear from you." Ty left the gallery.

After the door shut, the couple looked at each other.

"Hmm," Niklas said. "Tyler Hamilton of Berkeley Heights. That name sounds familiar. Wait a minute." He reached on the shelf for the latest issue of *Art Shape*. "Ty Hamilton was on the May cover along with his infamous dad, Paul Hamilton, one of the largest art collectors in Europe. That's where I've seen his face before!" Niklas scratched his balding head. "My God, I better dial Wellington right away. This could be the ticket we need to drive our fund-raiser."

Dinner Invitation

T he telephone rang five times before Grace could reach it. "Hello, Grace. This is Niklas Johansson."

"Hi, Niklas. Did you receive the package?"

"Yes, I did. We can't stop raving about it. Is Wellington there?"

"No, not at the moment."

"I have good news for him."

"What is it?" Grace was glad Wellington wasn't home.

"You'll never guess what happened. A gentleman was in the gallery when we opened the package and overheard our excitement. It so happens he is not a person unfamiliar with art; he's the son of a prominent art collector, and he's a collector himself. He flipped when he saw the painting and begged to buy it for an unbelievable price."

"What? Are you serious?" Grace said, beaming and holding her heart.

"Yes, he offered seventy-five thousand and wants it in his personal collection."

Oh, my God, she thought. "Do you know him well?" Grace asked.

"I don't know him personally, but I know of him—and so does the entire art community. His name is Tyler Hamilton. They call him Ty."

"I don't believe I've heard of him, but Wellington might know him," Grace said.

"I'm sure he does," Niklas said.

"Wow. I don't know what to say." Grace bit her tongue.

"He wants to meet Wellington and suggested dinner at his house."

"When?" Grace asked timidly, fearing the worst.

"Azul mentioned that Wellington has a show in France in a few weeks. Maybe you could stop here first. I can talk with Azul about it. Ty is eager to meet Wellington—and you too if you are able to come."

"Well, I'll have to discuss it with Wellington first, but I'm sure we can arrange it somehow. I'll let you know after I speak with him," Grace said, trying to sound as calm as possible.

"Ty could become a very important client."

"You think so?" she asked. "All right, I'll speak with Wellington and get back with you within a day or so."

"Oh, by the way, the total expense of the trip is on me. Talk to you soon."

Grace felt the baby kicking and punching. She was probably disappointed at the way Grace was handling this matter. Her sense of a good character was really becoming more and more questionable. *Why can't I just tell him and not postpone my misery?* She sat on the couch to relieve the load of the baby. At four months pregnant, she would need approval from the doctor to travel.

She thought more about the task of explaining her predicament to Wellington. *This is not going to be easy. The call from Niklas complicates matters even further. What a happy and delicate mess. This has become my crazy life!*

CHAPTER

36

The Tip

Detective Ramos was in London to apprehend Azul. At eleven o'clock, he peered through the tinted windows of his blue Fiat. The long working days and nights were getting the best of him, and he longed for the days of hunting down smaller criminals. However, it was the one case he couldn't shake. He wasn't letting go until he could bring justice and peace to the families of the artists.

He parked on a dark corner across from Club 300 in downtown London, on Newburgh Carnaby Street. He had received a tip that there was going to be a pickup. After putting the pieces together, he figured that was the location.

Azul's partner, Smitte, the DJ at Club 300, was throwing a party with special guests. Someone would deliver the goods to the club around midnight. He watched as the patrons entered and left the club. A dark blue C300 Mercedes sedan pulled up in front of the club.

A tall African American man who looked like a bodyguard got out of the car and looked both ways before opening the back door for Azul. He held his hand out for a slim African American woman who was wearing a short red dress with matching heels. She wrapped her arm around his as they strolled toward the club.

Before reaching the door, a man dressed in black stepped out of nowhere and placed something in Azul's hands.

Azul smiled and kept walking. The man followed him, and an argument ensued. The bodyguard stepped in front, grabbed the man, and threw him to the ground.

Azul laughed, turned, and entered the club.

Detective Ramos got out of his car and slid up against the side of the club, watching to see if anyone approached the man on the ground. Sure enough, two heavyset men came running, picked him up, and sped off in a black S-Class Mercedes with a license plate that read 2KOOL MP.

Detective Ramos approached the door of the club. He looked around for Azul but did not see him. He walked over to the bar and sat on a stool in the corner. He ordered a coke and waited.

Two hours passed with no sign of Azul. The tip proved wrong again. They had slipped out of his hand somehow. He paid the bartender and left. *At least I have the license plate number.*

37

Half Truths

At five o'clock, Grace met Wellington at the Fisherman's Restaurant for dinner. He stood and presented a bouquet of roses. "My One and Only Love" was playing in the background.

She knew it would be a bad time to dampen the romantic mood.

"For you, sweetie," he said as he kissed her on the cheek. He pulled out her chair, and she sat down. "I know my schedule is hectic with my traveling all over the world, but I want to assure you my love won't fluctuate for you."

"I know, Wellington. This is an important time, and many breakthroughs are happening for you. In fact, I got an interesting call from Niklas today."

"What did he say?" Wellington asked.

Grace cleared her throat. "A well-known art collector is interested in your work."

"Really? What is his name?"

"Tyler Hamilton. Do you know him?"

"Know him? Who doesn't. His father is a big-time avid art collector."

Lord, I need your help! She prayed silently under her breath. "He wants to meet you."

"He does?"

"Yes. Plus, I have some other news to tell you. I thought tonight might be a good time." Grace tried to smile. "After you left for Japan, Niklas called and asked to stop by. He wanted to know how the work was coming."

"Wait a minute." Wellington grimaced. "You did not let him see my work, did you?"

"Well, Azul was with him and thought it would be good for the relationships, so I humored them and let him stop by. Let me finish," she added, feeling a little winded. "When I couldn't reach you, I thought it would be okay as long as Azul was with them. Since they are special clients, I thought it would be okay to give them special treatment."

"Special treatment? You know how I feel about anyone going into my studio. Besides, I can't say I fully trust Azul's motives these days."

"I know how important this deal is to you. I figured they came a long way, so it was only the right thing for me to be hospitable. I told them they could stop by."

"Grace, get to the point! What happened?"

"Well, I let him look at a few pieces, but I did not tell him which painting it was. They liked all the work. But a funny thing happened." Grace could feel her blood pressure rising. "Niklas tripped on a paintbrush and the divider fell, exposing my studio."

"What's the difficulty in that?" Wellington asked. "I thought you were going to say he didn't like my painting."

Grace was floored. She didn't know how to tell him they saw her painting and loved it. Grace's heart sank, and she tried to continue with the truth, but it would not come out. "When Niklas was here, he took a photo of your painting. Ty came into the gallery and asked about the artist. I think that is how it happened. Ty is interested in the commissioned piece, and he wants to invite us to dinner. Niklas is ecstatic and says he will pay for the entire trip."

"This is the best news I've heard all day," Wellington said. "Of course, we'll go. Let me see. I have a show in France in a few weeks. We could travel to Switzerland first and then take a private plane to France."

"That's what I thought. I'll have to check with the doctor to see if I can travel."

"I'm sure that won't be a problem."

"You know. I would love to go to Switzerland for another important reason. I found this letter from Daniel, and I really need to reach out to Monica and get clarity about that letter. Something Daniel said hit a nerve. I know you were leery of hiring Azul as my agent, but he's been cool with me and has been making big strides in my career. I need to ask Monica some questions to find out more about Daniel's relationship with Azul because I'm beginning to question him myself."

"I'll call her and let her know we will be there and see when we can get together. It has been a few years since she left New York. Outside of reading about her team's monumental scientific developments in the newspapers, we really haven't checked on her to see how she's doing."

"Wow, girl. You are awesome. I love you more each day. You are really looking out for me." He kissed her forehead. "Remind me again what took me so long to marry you?" He smiled.

Grace wasn't smiling inside. She had failed to unload the truth again, and her disillusioned heart pulsated in distress.

"The Shadow of Your Smile" played softly in the background as they finished their dinner.

38

The Trip

The doctor gave Grace permission to fly, but he also put her on a strict diet because she was gaining a little too much weight.

Wellington and Grace arrived in Switzerland on Thursday, and Azul met them at the airport. He spoke in Spanish to a man dressed in black, and the guy disappeared without introductions.

Wellington stopped at the desk and said, "Ma'am, I want to check on a private flight to France."

"You have to go to the counter on the second level, marked Concourse International."

Grace waited in the lobby while Wellington and Azul took the escalator to the second level. "Hi, I'm checking on a private plane leaving for France tomorrow morning."

"One moment sir, let me check." The official typed his information into the computer. "Yes, it's scheduled to depart from Hanger 56 at five o'clock. You should arrive one hour before the flight takes off."

"Thanks, I'll inform my pilot," Wellington said, dialing his number. "Hi Detrick, this is Wellington. The flight is scheduled to leave at five. Now don't go out partying Friday evening." Wellington laughed. "I'll see you around four."

Azul said, "Before you hang up, let me speak with him."

"Sure. Hold on a moment, man. Azul wants to speak with you." Wellington moved over to the counter to check final details while Azul whispered into the telephone. Wellington returned to Azul's side. Something about Azul's demeanor was unsettling, but Wellington couldn't put his hands on it. He chalked it up to excitement of Friday's dinner and the big show in France.

"Let's go and meet our—I mean your—bright future," Azul said. Wellington glared at him.

CHAPTER

39

Exposed Secret

Grace appeared in the bedroom door in an inch above-the-knee light blue chiffon dress and low matching heels. "You like?"

"Yes, enough to jump into it myself." Wellington gently touched her butt.

"There is something very important I need to tell you before we go."

"What is it, sweetie?" he asked, smelling her neck as they sat down on the bed.

Grace pushed him away. "No. This is serious, and I hope you don't get too upset with me."

"I could never get upset with you, as good-looking and good-hearted as you are."

"Well, brace yourself," she said, pushing him away. "Have you noticed that I have been in my studio a lot lately?"

"Yes, you are always there, but that's not unusual."

"Well, what's unusual is what I have been doing in there. I have been working on a special painting that I was going to present for your birthday."

"Really? How sweet, but why a painting?"

"I want you to see how my artistic talents are developing, but that's besides the point right now."

"So, what is the point?" Wellington asked.

"Well, someone peeked at the painting before you. Accidentally, of course, and now … now it is bringing me a lot of grief." Grace held her hand over her mouth.

"What are you talking about? Why are you crying?" Wellington asked. "You are messing up your beautiful makeup."

"Well, what I have to say is about to bring you some grief too."

"Me? How so?"

"There is no easy way to tell you this unsettling news, so I'll just spit it out. The painting they saw at our studio and now have in their possession is not yours."

"Not mine! Well, whose is it?"

"It's mine," Grace said softly.

"Yours? What the hell are you talking about?" He jumped to his feet.

"Wellington, before you get upset, listen to me." Grace stood next to him.

"Is this some sort of trick? Did you bring me all the way to Switzerland to tell me this?"

"No. Honey, it's not a trick. Please let me explain," Grace said.

"You better do some fast talking."

"Well, … remember I told you about the day they came over?"

"Yes, keep talking."

"We went into your studio. They saw your work, and they liked the one you did for the spring collection."

"Okay. Keep talking."

"During the visit, Niklas bumped into my divider and knocked it down."

"Yes, you told me that part already."

"Well, when he knocked it over, it exposed the abstract I created for you."

"And?"

"The abstract I am painting is a surprise for your birthday. I named it *Artist Wife*. The picture also has an angel in it, and I didn't tell them it wasn't your *Angel in Disguise*. They liked it so much and were offering so much money."

"Wait! Slow down, girl. You are talking fast and not making any sense," Wellington said. *The Artist Wife*? How ironic. And this is how my *artist wife* treats me?"

"I can explain," Grace said.

"Well, start now, because I'm listening for more clarity."

"My painting is an abstract and looks very different from yours. They didn't know I was an artist or that the section of the studio was mine. They thought it was yours. I tried to tell them that it wasn't, but they were not hearing it."

"You tried to tell them? What did you say? Did you tell them it was yours?"

"No."

"Why not? That should have been easy to do."

"They were so overwhelmed."

"Overwhelmed? So, you got locked mouth, forgot all about the word *truth*, got some momentary glory, and lost your mind?"

"No, it didn't happen that way. I promise you. I tried to stall them and told them I would speak to you. But every time I tried to call you, you were too busy and wouldn't take time to listen to me. I never got a chance to tell you. I didn't want to break your heart either."

"What do you think you are doing right now? Oh my God. Are you crazy? What gave you the right to stab me in the back and possibly ruin my career? Look at this mess. We are headed to a famous art collector's home to discuss a big deal—and maybe a career boost—and he thinks this piece is mine. What a joke! You deceived the Johanssons, and now we are trying to deceive Ty? Did Azul talk you into this? I'm suspicious of him in general, and more so the way he was acting when he picked us up at the airport. Something ain't right!"

"No, he wasn't in the room at the time. He stepped out to answer his phone."

"Yes, how convenient. Did you sign my name on the painting?"

"No. I told Niklas you would sign it later, and he said that was fine because he knew you would take care of that detail while you were here." Grace was in tears.

"Oh! It's making sense now why the FedEx guy called. He was coming to pick up the painting. That was another chance for you to tell me, but you lied about what you were shipping. Grace, how could you do this? It's so unlike you. I know pregnancy can cause one to think and act differently, but this is some crazy stuff. What were you thinking? Why did you bring me all the way across the world to have this conversation? This is so embarrassing!"

"Wellington, please don't be so upset. I was doing this for you."

"It sounds more like you had yourself in mind. You always wanted someone to notice your work. Perhaps your ego got a little worked up on this one. I never figured you'd use my name to promote yourself. I guess I don't really know who you are after all!"

"Is that what you think of me? I always put you first. Everything is always about you. Your paintings, your exhibits, yada, yada, yada. I don't even have a life of my own—except planning for this baby. Between painting that abstract for you and preparing for her, it's the only way I've kept my sanity. Can't you see the stress it has caused me?"

"Well, you sure lost all of your senses when you sent them the painting. Damn it! How could you blow such an important relationship?"

"Wellington, I'm so sorry. I didn't plan on it turning out this way." Grace touched his hand. "They wanted it in a rush ... and I guess I made an emotional and irrational move."

"You're telling me?" Wellington replied. "Here. Put your coat on. Let's go!" He placed it roughly on her shoulders. "You've got some explaining to do to these people tonight, sweetheart."

Grace stood up quickly and almost fell backward.

Wellington caught her hand. "Come on," he said angrily.

Dinner at Ty's

The ride to Berkeley Heights was long, dark, raining, and foggy, and the road was full of curves. Grace felt like Wellington was trying to kill them. They didn't exchange any words until they arrived at Ty's home.

Wellington stepped out the car and opened her door. "I can't believe you would embarrass me like this and present some amateur piece of work and put my name on it." He slammed the door behind her.

"First of all, I wouldn't call seventy-five thousand dollars an amateur piece of work. Second, I didn't sign it!"

They walked up the steps to Ty's home.

"Seventy-five thousand dollars? Oh, Jesus. More drama. Did you sign it or not? I don't know if I can believe you anymore."

Ty opened the door and said, "Welcome to my home. The Johanssons and Azul are here."

The doorman took their coats.

Wellington shook his hand and said, "This is my lovely wife, Grace."

"I must admit you are a lucky man." Ty said, checking her out from head to toe out of the corner of his eye.

Grace blushed. "Thank you, Mr. Hamilton."

"Please call me Ty."

She looked over at Wellington and whispered, "I like that you added the word *lovely.*"

"Yes, but you don't deserve it—and it won't be long before he finds out about you."

"Please keep your voice down. I promise I'll fix this. Give me some time. For now, let's enjoy this evening."

"Yeah, right," Wellington said.

Grace couldn't help but notice the décor in the dining room. Accents of mauve, greens, and browns everywhere, and flowers were giving off an aroma of calmness. A silver chandelier hung over a wooden table, and natural-fiber rugs lined the floor. Bright and bold chairs had a hint of modern chic. Masterpieces hung on the walls, and there were a few large sculptures.

Pretty slick for a single rich man, Grace thought.

Dinner was roast duck with an orange ginger glaze, oyster dressing served with roasted potatoes and carrots, steamed spinach with pearl onions and almond slices, and a glazed lemon cheesecake—all topped off with chilled red wine.

Ty exchanged glances and smiles with Grace all evening. "Let's get right to the matter, shall we?" he asked. "When can I purchase this treasure of yours? I've identified the perfect spot in my home."

"Well, Ty, we haven't entered into negotiations yet. Besides, I might need a few more days to ponder some new information I just received," Wellington added, looking at Grace.

"New information? Will that affect my purchase?"

"It might," Wellington said.

Grace kept her composure, hoping Wellington would not open his mouth.

Across the table, Azul raised his eyebrows.

"Well, then, let's not spoil the evening by talking business. Why don't we just drink to a successful and lasting relationship." Ty held up his glass. "Here's to a new promising relationship."

Everyone in the room roared with laughter—except Wellington. His face was flushed with anger.

The Quarrel

Wellington and Grace arrived at the hotel at eleven. Wellington did not come around to open her car door. He went straight into the hotel without looking her way.

When Grace arrived in the room, he was in the bedroom, violently stuffing clothes into his suitcase. "Honey, what are you doing?" Grace set her purse on the bed.

"Do you think I'm just supposed to sit here while you smile and live a lie all night?"

"We were all having a good time. I didn't think we should spoil that moment. You're still mad that I didn't tell you about the painting, and now you are trying to take it out on me in another way. I promise you I didn't mean to hide this from you. Can't you just forgive me?" Grace tried to hug him, but he pushed her away.

"I'm too angry to stay here with you tonight. I'll going to get another room. I'll head to my show in France in the morning. I don't want to have to think about being with you right now. You acted selfishly, and I can't trust you right now. It appears you are trying to ruin my whole career."

"No, honey, I am not. I know the big plans you have for the school and it's going to take some big investments from other people. Can't you see I was doing it to try and help you? Niklas mentioned he is also interested in the art piece you created."

"Yes, but you should have consulted me first! Your first mistake was letting them into my studio. Now look at the mess we are in. Or should I say *you* are in? How can I face the Johanssons? What do I tell them? That my wife is a liar and that the work they have is hers? How humiliating is that for them to pick the work of an unknown artist over mine? I don't want my clients to be embarrassed or confused about the selection because this is business, Grace!

"Average? Is that what you think of my work? How can you say that about a piece you haven't seen yet? Something must be good about it for them to have raved over it and selected it. You didn't give me a lot to go on while I was in your class. That's why I dropped out of your stupid class and selected my niche as an abstract artist. As a child, I loved art and spent years developing it. You told us to find our niche, and I found out I loved painting abstracts. Now that I am on my way, you call my work average?" She threw a pillow across the room. "How encouraging is that?

"Average, because you have just begun on this journey of becoming a great artist. You don't have to take it so negatively. I have been established as an artist for years, and my body of work speaks to that. That's why the gallery chose me for their spring exhibition. I can't for the life of me understand why you tried to harm that business relationship. I don't call what you did helping me. It looks more like deception since you hesitated to clean up your mess. Why didn't you tell me this information before we left home? That would have cut down on the drama. You have broken the trust code."

"I tried to tell you many times, but you were too busy to listen. I had to make a decision."

"Yes, a costly one too."

"I want to make your name great," Grace said.

"Make my name great? I thought that was God's job."

"Well, if you let me explain, maybe you can finally hear the entire story."

"How about the truth? That's what I want to hear!"

"I told you the truth. Niklas knocked over the divider and saw my painting."

"He just stumbled—just like that?"

"I promise you that's how it happened. When Niklas saw mine, he was amazed—and so was his wife. I tried to talk them out of it, but he wasn't hearing it."

"Okay, are you happy now? Now you'll get the glory. First, you plan something behind my back, never telling me the truth, and then you smile all night with Ty—somebody you don't even know."

"Wellington, it's not like that at all. This is a future customer. He was being friendly, which is more than I can say for you. You barely smiled. Besides, you are suspicious of everybody."

"I wouldn't have to be if you did not act the way you did. I saw the way he looked at you, and you just cheesed right back in his face."

"He welcomed us into his home, and he is interested in your work, Wellington—not mine. This is a big opportunity for us."

"The way you acted tonight was like a lady without a husband! I'll leave it at that—without saying what I really mean."

"A what? You called me what?" Grace said.

"Okay, maybe not that low, but you were embarrassing," he said.

Grace grabbed his hand and turned him around. "Darling, I love you. I only have your best interests at heart."

"No, it's obvious that you have your best interests at heart," Wellington said.

"I found the letter stating you needed more money for the school, and we have a baby on the way. We could use that money."

"What do you mean?" he asked.

"A letter came in the mail about two months ago. You could lose the school property. So, after my dilemma with the painting and no easy explanation, I knew this would help. You don't communicate with me and let me know things that are going on. That's why I'm making extreme and outrageous decisions by myself."

"There you go again. Taking control and sticking your nose in my business," Wellington replied.

"No, it's our business, honey. You didn't share about financial worries, and that's where you failed to see me as partner in this relationship. You've been single for so long—"

"Grace, why are you changing on me? When I met you, I loved your honesty and loyalty, and your beauty didn't hurt either. Something obviously has changed and blinded you. What's going on?"

"If it concerns you, it concerns me," Grace responded.

"Well, concern yourself with this. I'm getting another hotel and leaving for France in the morning. I can't stay here with you tonight. We need to reduce both of our stress levels. You take care of you and the baby, and I will see you back in New York."

"Wellington, don't go!" Grace tried to grab his arm.

He released her grip, picked up the phone, and dialed the operator. "Can you call a taxi for me? Thank you."

Grace flung herself on the floor near his feet, planting her hands to hold him still. "You need to line your thinking up with God's Word."

"Yeah? What about you? The lying, the deceit? How does that line up?"

"What I did was out of love. That was my mind-set," Grace held his ankle tighter.

"Your conduct is inexplainable and out of order. You can't use the world's standards and then just cover it up with the Word of God's principles on truth. 'I just did it out of love.'"

"You are just fearful!" Grace gathered herself and stood up.

"Fearful of what?" he asked.

"That my work will be recognized and used for this big event," Grace said.

"That's not true, Grace," he said softly. He set his suitcase on the floor and placed his hands on her face. "I don't think we need to compete."

"I was not competing. I painted a gift at our home for you. And now, before you could acknowledge it and my talents, it was discovered by your clients. Now, Professor Holmes, somebody finally recognized my work."

"A-ha! There it is! I told you it was all about you." He removed his hand from her face.

"This is not a competition, and you are wrong for that," she cried. "You are right, and I am sorry. It's not about you or me. It's about us. You can't let the enemy divide us like this. He wants to cause the strife. Don't let it happen." Grace tugged on his arm, trying to get him to stay. "Think about it. Your work is great, and we are about to have a baby. Darling, please don't do this to me. Don't leave me."

"It's your selfish ambition that's getting to me." He snatched his arm away. "I have to clear my head. I have to go."

"Don't judge me or condemn me, Wellington. I'm the only one on your side who really knows you and loves you."

"What you did doesn't look like love to me. How can two people in love walk together unless they agree?"

"Wellington, you barely go to church, and now you want to quote the Bible?"

"Yes, I can. I know some of the things written in it. One thing I know for sure is that your act was done with a selfish objective, and you need to think about your actions."

"Your vision is blurred. You need to let God do this for us. Let him bless us."

"Go and call Ty and the Johanssons and tell them the truth. When I return from France, I want things to be straightened out. Do you hear me? I'll see you when I return." He released Grace's hold and slammed the door.

Once outside the room, Wellington dialed Azul's number. "Hey, everything is going as planned. I'll see you in the morning."

"Everything okay, man? You looked uncomfortable tonight."

"I'm good. My head is just full, thinking about this big show in France."

"Yes, it's going to be unforgettable for sure." Azul hung up his cell.

CHAPTER

42

The Accident

Uneasiness swept into Wellington's heart and crept on his flesh as the plane swirled and dipped. His mind focused on the last look on Azul's face before he departed. He seemed overjoyed and content to see him off and was uncomfortable at the questions Wellington posed.

The plane continued to swirl, and the pilot and copilot called, "Mayday."

Strapped into his seat, Wellington checked for his vest. He realized it was Azul's plot to take him out. He began rapid prayers for mercy: "Dear Lord, please let me live. I can't go out like this with a baby on the way and leave my wife a widower. Please, Lord, have mercy and save me!" He tried to stay calm, held onto the window, and grabbed the door.

The aircraft turned sharply, its wings becoming vertical before plunging into the sea. Underwater, his head slammed against a big metal plate that was on top of a rock. His body swayed back and forth, slamming into the next big rock until a rope wrapped around his waist caught on a larger rock. He tried to untangle it and tugged and pulled while holding his breath. It was only the grace of God that the last tug released him, and he swam upward to catch his breath. He clung to a piece of airplane wreckage and spent the next several hours in the middle of a vicious sea. His only hope was for military helicopters to fly over the area and see him.

Grace dialed Wellington's cell phone a fourth time and left a message. "Honey, please forgive me. I'm sorry for everything. Please come back to the hotel so we can talk."

It took a long time for her to fall asleep, and just when she closed her eyes, she was awakened by a sharp knock at the door. It was eleven o'clock. She slipped on her robe and walked slowly to the door. "Who it is?" She looked through the peephole.

"Sergeant Brown with the British Police."

"Yes, one moment." Grace removed the security lock. "Can I help you, sir?"

The officer flashed his badge. "Sorry to bother you, ma'am. I regret to inform you that Wellington's plane crashed in Lake Geneva early this morning."

Numb with disbelief, Grace listened as he described the news. "Oh my God!" Grace felt faint.

The sergeant said, "Are you all right, ma'am? Let me help you." He took her arm and sat her on the couch.

"Are you sure it's his plane?"

"We received word from Swiss Airways that a charter was down, and after checking the log, your husband's name was on it. Apparently, the plane got lost in the fog. A rescue team was sent immediately to the scene. The pilot was killed on impact, but they were unable to locate your husband. We are doing everything in our power to search the area and find him."

"Oh, God, have mercy." Grace sobbed. "If I had not been so stubborn, this never would have happened."

"Don't blame yourself, ma'am. You had no control over the plane. I know this is very hard for you, but I need to ask you some important questions right now. Is that okay?"

"Why, God? Why now? Please answer me!" She fell to her knees.

"Ma'am, here's a tissue," Sergeant Brown said. "Let me help you get up. I know this is a very sensitive time, but I need some general information."

"Sir, I can barely talk right now. Can't that wait?"

"Well, if you want us to find him, it would help if you could tell us what he was wearing, his height, and his weight. Do you have any pictures of him?"

Grace looked in her purse and handed a picture to the officer. "He's six foot four and has black hair and brown eyes. I don't know what he was wearing. Can you return this picture when you are finished with it?"

"Sure. Let me assure you we will do everything in our power to locate him. Have faith. Is there anyone I can call to be with you right now?"

Grace opened her mouth, but nothing came out.

"Ma'am, is there someone I can call to come stay with you?"

"I know that I probably deserve this. God is paying me back."

"No matter what happened or what you did, God isn't like that. Don't you know that he is a forgiving God?"

"You sound a lot like my mother." Grace wiped her eyes.

"Your mother is right, young lady. You ought to believe her," Sergeant Brown said. "I have a few men who could stay with you if you like."

"I would like that. I'm from New York, and I don't know many people here."

"Great. Sergeant Kendrick will stay on duty at the door. Again, my sincere condolences on your loss," he added, closing the door behind him.

Grace dialed her mother's number. "Mom?"

"Grace, what's wrong? Control yourself, dear. You are hysterical."

"Wellington and I got into a terrible argument last night after dinner. I told him about the painting, and we said terrible things to each other. He was so mad that he left the hotel. His plane left early this morning for France ... but ..."

"Grace, talk to me. Tell me what's happened?"

"It's a terrible accident. His plane plummeted into Lake Geneva. It's surreal. I can't believe this. I'll never see him again! He was so mad at me, and now I will have to pay for it. I'm sure God took him from me because of my irresponsible actions."

"What do you mean? Slow down, child, and make some sense."

"When we got back to the hotel, we had a horrible fight. Mom, what am I going to do? Wellington is my life. How can I survive without him? Why would God do this to me now? I'm so confused. I thought you said he loved me? Me and the baby can't take this kind of pressure." Grace sobbed.

"Darling, please calm down. I'm so sorry to hear this, and I know how distressing it must be for you. This is dreadful and upsetting news. Let me remind you: God puts nothing on us we can't handle. He's not the one who kills or takes away. God did not take Wellington. This was an accident. They happen. Please don't turn your back on God now when you'll need him more than ever. I promise you he'll get you through this."

"Mom, I'm trying to do everything to just stay calm. My whole body feels numb, and my head is about to explode. I need you."

"Baby, I wish I was already there. I'll get there as soon as I can. Let me check the airlines and see when I can get a flight. What's your room number?"

"Room 334."

"Have you contacted the Johanssons?"

"No, you are the first person I called."

"Give me their number. I'll call them."

"Mom I can call them."

"No, you don't need the pressure. I'll call them, and they will come and be with you."

"Mom, I feel like I can't handle life without Wellington."

"Darling, you are strong. Tell yourself that. You're gonna make it. God will help you through this storm. Remember that you have to remain calm for the baby's sake also."

"Mom, you are so right. Being frantic is not good right now. I'll try to do my breathing techniques."

"Let's pray together before I hang up. Dear Lord, my dear baby is in so much turmoil. You know the circumstances, and I know you have a listening ear and that you care for her. Lord, please help the authorities locate Wellington—and let him be unharmed. Rescue him! Grant my daughter peace as you said you would do in times of trouble. In Jesus's holy and precious name. Amen!"

"Thanks, Mom. I already feel a calm coming over me. I can't wait to see you."

"I'll be on the next plane. Have some hot tea, take some Tylenol, and try to rest before the Johanssons get there."

"Okay, Mom. I love you. Thanks."

"Love you too, dear."

Grace turned on the television, and the reports of the plane crash unhinged her. "Oh Jesus." She grabbed her stomach and ran to the bathroom.

43

Call for Support

"**H**ello, this is Ruth Green, Grace's mom. I'm calling from California. I'm not sure if you heard, but Grace just gave me some unsettling news. Wellington's plane crashed into Lake Geneva. It's awful."

"Oh my God. No!" Laine Johansson said. "That poor child."

"It's unbelievable. I just got off the telephone with her, and she is distraught. I'm calling you because she doesn't need to be alone right now. I was wondering if you wouldn't mind going over there? She is staying at the Swiss Hotel."

"Mrs. Green, I'll tell my husband. We will get right over there."

"I appreciate your help. I'm flying out as soon as I can. On top of that, Grace is pregnant and in a very delicate stage."

Laine gasped. "Oh my. That's right. We will hurry! We'll take care of her. Please don't worry."

"I'll check back later with you to see how things are. Thank you for your help. I know it's in the Lord's hands, so I'm not going to worry," Ruth said.

Niklas and Laine stopped at the reception desk and dialed Grace's room to let her know they were in the lobby. They did not get an answer. After calling twice, they explained to the desk clerk the point of urgency and asked if security could assist them.

A security guard escorted them to the third floor. They knocked on the door several times without receiving an answer. The security guard used his key to gain entrance into the room.

Laine entered first and called out to her. She discovered Grace's body on the bathroom floor with a large cut on her forehead. "She must have hit her head."

Niklas checked her pulse. "She's breathing. Call the paramedics," he shouted.

The security guard dialed the telephone, and they watched the news report on the television. "Dear God, we lost another great young artist. What's going on? This is the third one in less than two years."

"Hello, we need an ambulance right away. Yes, I'm at the Swiss Hotel, Room 334. A young lady fell and hit her head. She's pregnant. Please hurry!"

"Funny how things happen so fast," Niklas said. "Last night, we were all laughing and drinking together. God surely works in mysterious ways, doesn't he?"

"Honey, God does not work in mysterious ways. This thing we are in is called life, and sometimes it's mysterious to us, but not to him," she said. "Let's say a prayer for her. Dear God, I know you are all knowing. You said you would hear us when we pray and call to you. Please help this family." Laine grabbed a pillow and placed it under Grace's head.

Niklas sat next to Grace in the ambulance while Laine called Ruth.

"What's going on?" Grace tried to sit up.

"Please do not move." The paramedic pushed her head down softly. "We'll arrive at the hospital in minutes. Just stay calm."

"Hospital? What happened? It's not time for delivery yet," Grace said.

"Sh. I'm here with you." Laine held Grace's hand. "You fell and hit your head. We prayed that everything will be okay."

Grace began to cry. "It's all my fault … it's all my fault. This never would have happened if I had made the right decision."

Laine said, "It's going to be okay."

Grace closed her eyes and wondered, *What is God going to do next? First Wellington, and now me? Oh, God, forgive me for my selfishness. I didn't mean to put my family through this dilemma. I pray for mercy and that you will help me in this trouble.*

Niklas and Laine were watching television in the hospital waiting room. They stood up as the doctor approached.

"Is she going to be okay?" Niklas asked.

"She is resting well, but she lost the baby. I'm sorry."

"Oh, Jesus." Laine sobbed in her handkerchief and sat down. "This is too much for this young, girl. First her husband, and now the baby."

Niklas said, "When can we see her?"

"She is still drowsy, but you can visit her now. I haven't had a chance to tell her yet because she was asleep."

"Should we tell her if she asks?" Niklas asked.

"If she asks, then you can use your best judgment."

Grace's forehead was bandaged and swollen from the fall.

Laine sat on the edge of the bed.

Grace turned to face them and saw the tears in their eyes. "I lost her, didn't I?"

"I'm sorry, dear. I know this is hard news for you to hear," Laine said.

"It's all my fault!"

"Dear, please don't blame yourself."

"But you don't understand. It really is my fault," Grace said.

A nurse entered the room and said, "Mrs. Holmes, the doctor ordered another sedative for you to help you rest." She placed pills in her hand and gave her a glass of water. "Take these."

Laine nodded to the nurse to let her know Grace knew about the baby.

"I'm so sorry about your loss," the nurse said. "Your rest is imperative. You lost a lot of blood. If you need anything just push the buzzer."

"Grace, your mother called this morning," Laine said. "She's the one who called and asked us to check on you."

Grace grabbed her hand. "Thank you for being here. I don't know what I would do without you two." Grace sighed.

"Dear, try to rest. The past twenty-four hours have been rough for you. Niklas has to return to the gallery, but I'll be right here at your side." Laine kissed Grace's forehead and caressed her hair. "I'll call your mom and update her on everything. After you get the proper rest, I will make sure you speak with her."

44

Crash Confirmation

"**A** twin-engine Antonov AN-28 crashed into Lake Geneva this morning, killing two of the three passengers aboard. The official weather agency said conditions were normal. The plane disappeared from radar two minutes after takeoff. Pilot error or a technical fault were likely to have caused the tragedy. The identity of the passengers will not be released until all the families can be contacted. We'll have more coverage on the accident at noon. Deidra La'Trect reporting live from Channel 32 in Geneva, Switzerland."

Azul snickered as he turned off the television. "My plan worked smoother than designed." He laughed and rubbed his hands together. "Now Grace will have no other choice but to do things my way." He blew into his .45-caliber weapon.

CHAPTER

45

Survival of the Fittest

"**S**ources have now identified the pilot as Jared Harris from Great Britain, and he was killed instantly. Some of the official statements claim the pilot had a heart attack. The search is ongoing for the body of the only passenger, now identified by Swiss officials as Wellington Holmes, a renowned artist and former professor from New York. A police diver said the underwater search for Mr. Holmes was being hampered by low visibility and cold water temperatures, which forced divers to work in one-hour shifts and into the late evening. We also received information that the plane was owned by Ricardo Azul, Mr. Holmes's art agent from Spain, and he was not on board. We'll report more coverage on this incident as it comes in. Deidra La'Trect reporting live from Channel 32 in Geneva, Switzerland."

Dr. Monica Wolf usually didn't pay much attention to the morning news, but as they relayed this morning's information her ears perked up. She gasped, paced the floor, and thought about what to do.

Her concern for Wellington grew intensely. She could not stop thinking about the freak accidents that constantly happened to Azul's clients. It probably wasn't a coincidence. She was leery of Azul's motives. In cold water, hypothermia is the greatest enemy. With her security credentials and plethora of high-level friends and doctors, she decided to call a close associate to gather a search team to locate Wellington. She was determined that Azul was not going to get away with murder again.

Monica dialed Dr. Patel's number, requested strict confidentiality, and begged him to help. He agreed to get a team together as soon as possible and prepare for a search and medical assistance. If they located him, it was imperative that they shield him from everyone, including the police.

She prayed that—with God's help—the team would find Wellington. She jumped into her Red Jeep Wrangler and circled rocky areas around the crash, avoiding the area with all the media and police and hoping to discover him before nightfall.

Wellington lifted his head above the water and balanced his weight on a tree stump. His legs felt like lead, and he was unsure if he could reach it. He prayed, "Dear Lord, please help me. I know I'm not serving you like I should, but if you please, please save my life, I promise I will … get the message you are sending me."

The strength he gathered was outside of his natural power, enabling him to swim to shore. He couldn't recall how long he had been in the water, but he was cold, limp, and hungry. His body gave out from exhaustion.

After what seemed like eternity, he felt a warm hand on his face. He couldn't move or feel his legs.

"Please don't sit up. Stay still. I'm a doctor, and I'm checking for injuries."

"Ouch," Wellington said.

Dr. Patel said, "I want you to stay still. I need to take you to a hospital."

Wellington struggled to sit up, and he had no clue where he was and fell back down.

Dr. Patel called Dr. Wolf and said, "It was a miracle! He was just lying there, and no one was around. I can't imagine how he got so far away from the crash site. Maybe his body floated there. I know this is a gift."

"I'll be there in a moment." Dr. Wolf wasn't sure what to do next, but she prayed for wisdom. She wanted to update the authorities, but if Azul knew Wellington was alive, he'd come after them.

Wellington woke up in a hospital room surrounded by equipment.

The door opened, and a beautiful lady entered with a tray of food. "Good evening," she said. "I see you finally decided to join the living."

Damn. That confirms it. I must be in heaven, he thought. "Where am I?" He tried to sit up to reach the food. "Ouch!"

"In a hospital. You were in a bad plane accident. Dr. Patel performed your surgery and will be here in a few moments to talk with you."

"How long have I been here?"

"Three days. Tell me what you remember," Dr. Wolf said.

Wellington put his hands on his head. "I can only remember a plane and the pilot shouting for help. I don't remember anything else."

"We didn't find any identification on you," she lied. "I was hoping you could tell me your name so I can contact your family. I see you have a wedding band, so there must be a pretty wife somewhere worried sick about you."

"Married?"

"You don't have to try to remember it all in one day. Do you know your name?"

He thought for a moment and shook his head.

"My name is Dr. Monica Wolf. Do you know me?"

He shook his head again.

"I'm a doctor. I do research on animals. Dr. Patel is treating your injuries and will do his best to help in your recovery."

"What's wrong with me?"

"You suffered multiple wounds, some broken bones, and some memory loss. Your memory will return. I'm just glad we found you. Your body took a thumping. Apparently, you are in good physical shape. They say the best-equipped people to survive what you went through are fit young men. More importantly, you obviously have God on your side because you are a miracle!"

"I'm grateful for that. How long am I going to be here?"

"I'm not sure. Let's take one day at a time."

"Looks like I have little choice in the matter. I'm at your mercy. Thanks for being there for me. I owe you."

"This is what we do. You owe me nothing." She pointed to the soup. "You need to eat something." She lifted the spoon to his mouth. "Eat up before the doctor comes. I have a feeling he's going to give you some strong medicine that may put you out for a while."

The Search

In the first twenty-four hours after the crash, the Swiss border guard and helicopters surrounded the area to search for Wellington. They found the wings and other items that could hold vital clues. As the days passed, the likelihood of finding Wellington alive greatly diminished. After seven days with no results, the official search operations were called off.

After two weeks in the hospital and a few days at the Johansson home, Grace and Ruth flew back to New York. Grace needed closure, and Ruth helped organize a small memorial service at St. Paul's Baptist Church in New York.

Calls, flowers, and letters poured into Grace's home for weeks. Friends, colleagues, and several of Wellington's family members attended, taking turns to eulogize him. Grace spoke to no one for days after the service.

Ruth stayed for a month.

Grace found only a glimpse of reason to live after losing two of the three most important people in her life within such a short period of time. It was difficult learning to live without Wellington at her side. Her mom's encouragement saved her during those dreadful weeks. Her tender love and support nursed Grace back to life. Although Grace was in dire need of a good massage, she saw Ellona only once—at the service.

"Grace, you know you could move to California with me," Ruth said.

"That sounds so great, but there is so much more that Wellington wanted to accomplish. I just can't leave his work unfinished. I must press on with his vision. I'll come out and visit, but it's important that I get my act together and keep on living for Wellington's sake. You have been very helpful and instrumental in my mental, physical, and spiritual rejuvenation. I have been reading my Bible and praying—all the things you taught me as a child. I feel that God is with me and will show me what my next steps are. I have to learn to trust him more."

"Yes, dear. Trust is the key. 'Trust him with all your heart and mind and do not lean on your own understanding.' That is what it is says in Proverbs 3:5. Also, be grateful for things you have. Gratitude is the quickest way to get God's attention," Ruth said with a smile.

Ruth returned to California the following Monday morning. At eleven o'clock, Grace received a call. "Hi Grace. This is Malcolm. When I first heard the news about Professor Holmes, I tried to reach you. I'm so sorry to hear about your loss. I came to the memorial service, but you were surrounded by so many people. I decided not to approach you. I hope you are okay."

"Yes, it was rough there for a moment. It all seems a blur now. I'm still recovering. In fact, I rarely answer the telephone to talk to anyone since the service."

"Really? Then I feel special."

"You were truly a good friend to me, and I think I'm in need of one right now. My mom was a steady force for a few weeks, but she recently returned to California. Everything has been quite overwhelming."

"I know some fresh air would do you some good. Is it too soon to ask you out to lunch?"

"I actually think that might be nice. You have been a friend since high school, and I could use some company right now."

"I have an appointment on Saturday. We could meet at Eataly for a sandwich and a cup of coffee. Would that work for you?"

"Yes. I'll look forward to it."

While putting the finishing touches on her makeup, something inside of Grace was bubbling for the first time in a long period. She felt excited about getting out of the house and meeting Malcom for lunch. She figured she could talk about other things like college, abstracts, and maybe his life.

In the restaurant, Malcolm greeted her with a new look. He was striking in a tight T-shirt, cool jeans, and fancy black-rimmed glasses. He appeared taller and had a very nice beard.

"It's good to see you," he said, greeting her with a kiss on the cheek.

"Good to see you too." Grace blushed.

The waitress seated them in a cozy booth.

As they looked over the menu, Grace caught him glancing at her a couple of times. "What?" Grace asked.

"Oh, nothing. You just look so pretty," he said.

"Are you serious? I'm not feeling it at all. This is the first time I have been out in weeks."

"Trust me—you do."

"Thank you. I owe you for getting me out of the house. My couch was surely going to push me off it if I stayed there another day," Grace laughed. "So, how have you been—and what you been doing for yourself?"

"Not a whole lot for myself. I have been busy with family stuff. My mom passed some months back, and I'm getting things in order."

"I'm sorry to hear that. Was she ill?" Grace asked.

"Yes. It eventually got the best of her."

"Are you okay?"

"Yes, I'm good now. We were very close, and I miss her a lot."

"Did you ever marry?" she asked.

"No. I was in a serious relationship, but it fell apart. I'm still not sure what happened. I don't like to think about it."

"Oh sorry. I didn't mean to intrude in your business," Grace said.

"No worries. That was a year ago, and I've moved on." He cleared his throat. "I suppose it's been hard for you without Professor Holmes?"

"Yes, he was my life. But I'm recovering as well. The hardest part is talking to people. I just haven't felt like it. I knew I had to break that cycle and come out of my shell, so it was good that you called."

"I understand well. Death can be overwhelming, and the emotions start rushing in when you talk to people. The first thing they say is that they're sorry. I know they mean it, but those words bring back the sting."

Grace said, "I thank God that he helped me begin to move on. Only recently did I decide to stop feeling distraught and change my position. Now I'm thinking that I need to see if I can fulfill Wellington's vision in art and education through his school."

"Oh, good for you. I know that is what Professor Holmes would want. He was a great man. I learned so much from him. And from you too!"

"Me?" Grace asked.

"You were the one who helped me. You gave me the encouragement I needed to explore abstracts. I probably never thanked you. So, thanks."

"I think we supported each other. We were a good team. I miss that," he said looking into Grace's eyes.

"Yes, we were good friends. All those days of studying and sharing ideas was fun."

"Have you remained connected to Hope College?" he asked.

"No, I have heard a lot about things going on, but I haven't gone over there," she said. The only school I have been thinking about is the Wellington Art Academy. And incidentally, I have a meeting with the school administrator soon."

Malcolm paid for the meal and took her hand as they rose from the table.

"It is so good to see you again," Grace said.

To her surprise, he pulled her close and kissed her on the lips.

Grace stepped back in shock. "Malcolm, why did you do that?"

"Sorry, but I have been wanting to do that for some time. I guess my emotions got the best of me. I apologize. I've had a crush on you since high school, but I was too shy to let you know. I knew how you felt about Professor Holmes, so I knew I'd be a fool to think you would give me the time of day. That's why I didn't pursue you. I guess I overstepped my boundaries, and I hope my forwardness doesn't stop you from seeing me again."

"No, but I'm just a little shocked at what you are telling me. I had no idea you felt that way. All those times we spent together, and you never told me or paid me that kind of attention."

"Like I said, I apologize."

"I think it's a little too early to date or think about a relationship right now." Grace smiled to cover up the awkward moment. "I'll give you a call after I get the office together and let you know a good day for you to come see the school. I hear they need volunteers." She smiled.

"That would be great," he said as they walked their separate ways.

When Grace reached her car, she thought, *This can't be happening.* It was all coming back to her. She played back in her mind the many times they studied together—and the number of times she would catch him staring at her. She realized he had feelings for her all along, and they were now in the open.

47

A Dance with the Devil

*T*ossing and turning became the norm for Grace, and every night was filled with confusing dreams. A panel of three individuals were on a dark platform, and Grace was sitting in a chair in front of them. She could not see their faces, but she could hear their voices:

Panel: "We talked to the devil. Don't you think you should forgive him?"

Grace: "Forgive him for what? The wrong thoughts he planted in my mind that changed my life? Absolutely not. God didn't forgive him so why should I?" She sensed a thick presence of the spirit of evil approach her and knew it was Satan.

Devil: "I think God did forgive me. Look at me. He gave me the earth and all this power I didn't have before. I think I'm doing pretty good." He brushed himself off.

Grace: "You are mistaken. Although you were once his perfect angel, he didn't forgive you. He just stopped putting up with your greedy thoughts and needs, and then he cast you to the earth."

Devil: "Well, look who's talking." He laughed uncontrollably.

Grace: "Don't think you can manipulate me. My situation is different. The only mistake was sending my art, and for that I was wrong, but I have reconciled it with my Lord and Savior. I am not greedy, and unlike you, I have a God who loves me, forgives me, and forgets whatever wrong I do because I belong to him. Unlike you who wanted to compete and be God yourself. That's why he threw you and one-third of the angels out of heaven. Dude, your destination is hell."

Devil: "That's okay. I can affect people like you—and then I'm happy. I think I heard God say it gives me short-term victory. That's cool. Look at me. Am I not getting results? You are a prime example. You listened to me and see how my implied thoughts changed your life? No husband, no baby. You are all alone. This is proof I got power, and I got control. Loser. Ha!"

Grace: "The only mistake was sending my art, and for that I was wrong, but I have reconciled it with my Lord and Savior."

Grace jumped out of bed in a cold sweat. Her heart sank, and guilt filled her entire being. The emotional anxieties of losing Wellington and the baby pierced her heart. She knew it was the enemy creeping into her dreams, and she prayed for peace.

Grace washed her face and collected herself before heading downstairs with Rafa. As she passed Wellington's studio, courage and Wellington's spirit urged her to enter. She placed her hand on the doorknob and turned it for the first time since his death, knowing it was not going to be an easy task. It was her selfish act that had brought much sorrow to her life. Now she couldn't help but think about that dream and how things could be different had she not listened to thoughts that were planted in her mind by the enemy. Like her mom said, "It is the past. Stop blaming herself and move forward."

Grace pushed that disturbing dream out of her mind. Turning on the light, she touched the heart-shaped clock on the desk, which she had given Wellington for their first anniversary. Grace picked it up and brought it close to her heart. She picked up a note he wrote and admired his writing. She saw the last anniversary card he gave her next to the clock, and a tear ran down her cheek. It was handwritten and personal. He wrote a version of Ecclesiastes 3:1, 8: "There is a time for everything, and a season for every activity under the heavens … A time to love."

Grace sat at his desk, smiled, and thought about their honeymoon. *He told me he loved me because I was always there to support his mission and was a calming, steady influence on him.*

She treasured those words and held onto them when she was lonely and had no one except the Lord to hold onto. *My beloved husband—why did it have to end like this? I'm so sorry.*

Grace moved toward the window and sat in Wellington's favorite wicker chair. Rafa jumped into her lap. She kissed and hugged him. Turning her head, she saw all the honors he had received. The one that caught her attention was the honor from the mayor for the groundbreaking of the Wellington Arts Academy. The plaque reiterated Wellington's dream: "To inspire, impact, and instruct less fortunate children who desire to become artists."

Wellington did not have the luxury of having a mentor at a young age. As a result, his dream was to give back to the community by forming a center that would raise the consciousness of young artists, teach them art history and how to paint, and give them life skills and purpose. A cloud of inspiration slowly covered her head. It was as if Wellington's presence was comforting her. Encouragement filled her heart.

For the first time since Wellington's death, Grace felt the desire to paint. Perhaps it was God reminding her of her destiny. Grace felt the burden and a weight lifted off her shoulders. Grace knew the only step she needed to take was forward. It was an order given, and by faith, she received it. *Forgetting the things that are before and pressing on toward the mark—to press on with Wellington's dreams.* Grace fell to her knees and began to pray. "Lord, forgive me for my stubborn ways of not acknowledging you. For my poor choices. Please help me through this pain. I realize I need your help and can't make it alone. I've tried and tried, but it's not working. That's why I'm turning to you. I know I have ignored you, but please forgive me. Please, if you are real, hear my cry and answer me." She wept uncontrollably.

Grace eventually got up off her knees and touched the Bible on the table, which was open to Psalm 91. Although they didn't attend church often, Mom suggested years ago to keep the Bible open to that psalm. In a time of trouble, it would bring peace and comfort. The Bible and prayer were her only solace.

The sound of the telephone ring startled her.

"Hi, Grace. This is Azul. How are you doing?"

Yeah, right, Grace thought. *He hardly cared about me when Wellington was alive. Now suddenly, he is showing concern? Just like the devil. To interrupt in a time of peace.* "I'm okay, Grace replied.

"I called you several times this week, and you haven't returned my calls," Azul said. "There are several loose ends we need to go over."

"You are right about loose ends. I have been avoiding a lot of things. I apologize. Today was the first day I felt like I could take any steps forward."

"Good—because we need to talk," Azul said. "Can you meet me for lunch tomorrow at noon at Mack's Café?"

"Could we make that one o'clock?"

"Sure, that'll work."

"Cool. I'll see you then." Azul hung up without saying goodbye.

Something about him did not set well in Grace's heart and spirit. She could only trust God to reveal any secrets he was hiding from her.

Grace left the studio and went into the bathroom to assess her appearance. *Ugh.* It was worse than she thought. She really needed a good massage and some girl time. She dialed Ellona's number. It was time to get a grip on her life. Wellington would never agree to her looking like that while representing him.

CHAPTER

48

Wellington's Recovery

Dr. Wolf sheltered Wellington in her home for months. She recorded his puzzling nightmares in her diary: "The momentum is gathering and overtaking me. Inside something burst, and I began falling from the sky, and I couldn't control myself. Although I kept dropping, I never hit the ground, but my head was always in pain and hurting as if I had hit it."

Wellington had no idea why that menacing dream would ease into his consciousness in bed. For many days, he rarely slept, fearful the nightmare would return.

Dr. Patel said, "Unresolved conflict is one of the causes of the frequent terrorizing dreams. They are like episodes that trigger your anxiety and depression about your traumatic experience in the airplane."

He woke up sweating and crying each time.

Dr. Patel recommended prazosin for PTSD, but it left him drowsy in the morning if he took it at night.

Wellington picked up his crutches and hopped to the bathroom. He didn't have any idea how long he had slept, but he was tired of lying down.

Dr. Wolf had adjusted his bandaged face because it was so tight that it hurt. The medicine Dr. Patel prescribed worked wonders. The medicated bandaging performed miracles on his face, numbing the pain and dispelling the headache that had been his steady companion since the crash. The pain that lingered was in his jaw. It pulsated and made it hard for him to swallow. Summoning the courage to confront the pain, Wellington gently pushed two pills coated with olive oil into his mouth and flushed them into his system with the mineral spring water that had become a staple in his daily routine.

Dr. Wolf faded in and out of his view. She would always say she had work to do in her laboratory and would be gone for hours. She had spent a lot of time taking care of him in the past few days: feeding, washing, and talking to him. She never talked about herself—other than the fact that she was on a special mission, had lived in the United States for several years, and was once married.

Over the past few days, Dr. Wolf appeared more acutely aware of his health, devoting as much time to Wellington as she did her research and paying attention to the smallest details in Wellington's medical and nutritional chart. It was as if she was a professional trainer getting her champion ready for a title fight.

That morning, she mentioned she was going to the city to shop for food and other essentials for the lab and Wellington's care. Hearing her exit, Wellington peered down the hall, scanning the area to see if he could detect her presence. After determining she was no longer in the house, he carefully slipped on slippers and a robe and eased into the living room on his crutches.

The room had rattan furniture, plants, bold colors, and books everywhere. He hopped out the back door to get some fresh air and noticed a building in the back, which he figured must be her laboratory. He turned around slowly to make sure no one was around and tripped over a rock. He used his crutches to stand, gathered his robe and tied it securely, and moved toward the building.

He hadn't seen the sun in what seemed like months and smiled at its brightness and warmth. He was eager to see what type of work she did. He eased open the door with the tentativeness of a cat burglar and was awestruck at its massive size and organization. There were several rows of animals in cages. He moved closer. The first row were rabbits and birds of different sizes.

As he opened the cage, Dr. Wolf said, "Find what you were looking for?"

He slammed the door. "I was just curious how you spent your day. I heard you say you spent hours in your laboratory, but you never talked about what you were doing."

"That's because I told you it was confidential information for the government. Remember? All you had to do was ask. I'm glad to see that you are feeling better." She took his arm and helped him out of the laboratory.

"That bed and I have been friends long enough," Wellington joked.

She laughed. "I know how you feel. I work for the government and am involved in experimental projects to find a cure for weakened immune system caused by microorganisms in public water. It's a mysterious disease that adults have and can pass on to their children."

"That's funny. I have heard that term before."

"This is pretty intense, high-security work, so you really shouldn't be in here."

"I apologize for disrespecting your request and intruding in your classified area. I guess I am just curious about what you do day in and out. I also feel better and think I need something to do besides lie around all day."

"Can you remember if you had any hobbies?" She closed the door to the laboratory and walked toward the house.

"I don't remember."

"No worries. There is time. Remember, patience is the key." She smiled. "Let's go into the house. I've got an idea." When they entered the house, she handed him a pencil and paper. "Why don't you start by writing down some things that come to your mind? Any word is a starting point."

"I'll do it," Wellington said. "Something has got to click sooner or later."

"Sooner would be my guess," she said with a smile. "Tomorrow, I'm going into the city to pick up some supplies. Maybe you'd like to ride with me after we remove your bandages. It would be a good change of scenery."

"I don't feel good about seeing anyone in this condition."

"You've got a point there," she said.

"You have a special way with people," he said. "The depression seems to leave every time I'm near you." He touched her shoulder.

She backed off and brushed his hand aside. "Remember, you are a married man." She pointed to the ring on his finger. "Be good. Some lucky lady is coming back to claim you. Don't try any crazy moves, young man." She grinned.

"This is the first day I felt good. Perhaps my awareness and sense of humor are returning." Wellington laughed.

"That's a good thing. I think it might be time for you to start addressing me as Monica. It sounds more informal, but my relationship with you is on a professional level—as a specialist. Being a scientist, I like discovery, but it is my nature to stay alert for any attacks to the system, including isolated advancements that could be harmful and contagious." She laughed.

A Fresh Start

The Wellington Art Academy's hallway was alive with giggling, energetic students rushing to their classrooms. Grace opened the door to Wellington's school and was astounded to find everything in its place as if he were still there.

"Grace, what a nice surprise to see you," Marcella said as she got up from her desk to hug her. "You look great, girl," she added in her Jamaican accent.

"Thanks," Grace replied.

"I know how hard this is for you, and I didn't want to pressure you with school issues. I knew they could wait until you are ready," Marcella said.

"Thanks for keeping everything together," Grace said as they entered Wellington's office. "Wellington spoke very highly of you.

I have been trying to get here for days, but I just couldn't bring myself to face this moment until recently. I feel as if Wellington's spirit was directing me to take charge. I have been doing some thinking too."

"I hope you are not thinking about closing the school," Marcella said, moving closer to the desk. "Wellington worked so hard to this and for the future of the academy."

"Far from that, Marcella. I know his dream, and I want it fulfilled," Grace said with a smile. "I have been going over some of Wellington's ideas for the school, and I realize that I need an administrator who can help me manage things—someone with Wellington's high expectations."

"Who do you have in mind?" Marcella asked.

"It would have to be someone I can trust. The one person that comes to mind is you," Grace said.

Marcella's large eyes lit up. "Me?"

"You don't have to give me an answer today, "Grace said. "I want you to think about it first and then call me in a few days. You worked for him for several years, and I know Wellington shared his vision with you and the staff. I have confidence that we can all work together." Grace stood and patted Marcella on the arm. "Well, on top of that, the new administrator will receive a special bonus and a raise."

"Grace, would you consider me? That would mean the world to me. I love this work and want to partake in finishing his mission, but I don't think I'm qualified for such a position. There are many others who are better suited than me."

"Listen, Marcella. Wellington spoke of your incredible work ethic. Your name came into my thoughts and spirit while I was meditating at home. I know you are the one. You won't be alone in this mission. I'm here to guide you, and God will guide us. Please give it some thought. I'll call you in a few days to discuss it." Grace hugged Marcella. "I won't be staying long today. I just wanted to stop by to see you. When I return in a few days, I'll start going through Wellington's desk. We can talk further."

Grace turned to leave and noticed a puzzled look on Marcella's face. *She's probably overwhelmed at the thought of this new position,* Grace thought as she closed the door.

50

Blackmail

As Grace approached the table, Azul stood up to greet her. He planted a kiss on her cheek and pulled out a chair. "You look as beautiful as ever."

"Thanks," Grace mumbled.

"Would you like to order some wine?" Azul asked as he looked at the menu.

"No thanks. It's too early in the afternoon, but I'll have some sweet tea."

"I know you are not particularly fond of me, but I want to assure you that I always had—and still have—Wellington's best interests at heart."

"Well, I can't say I agree with that," Grace said.

"It's true. Just look at his beginnings and how his career developed. In fact, that's why I wanted to meet with you. My contacts from all over the art world write me daily. They want more of those abstracts that Wellington created. His works have risen in value. You know that though, right?"

The waitress approached the table, which gave Grace a moment to think before responding.

"I'll have a glass of Chablis, and the lady will have sweet iced tea," Azul said.

"Do you need a few more minutes to look at the menu—or are you ready to order?"

"We would appreciate a few more minutes please." Grace smiled at the waitress.

"No problem. I'll get your drinks and be right back."

"Now, what were you saying about the abstract and value of art?" Grace asked.

"There's a big demand for more of Wellington's work. Specifically, more abstracts like the one the Johanssons have," Azul said. "Yeah, well, unfortunately, Wellington only painted one. There are no more." Grace looked Azul straight in the eye.

"Only one?" He peered into her brown eyes.

"Yes, you heard me correctly," Grace said. "This was a new expression for him, and we did it specifically at the insistence of the Johanssons. We never realized they would fall in love with it."

"*We* did it? Really? It seems to me it didn't quite happen that way."

"What are you talking about?" Grace asked.

"I was present when the Johanssons first viewed it. Remember?"

"Yes, I remember you were there. And?"

"Well, I stepped out into the hallway to grab a call. When I came back in, it seemed peculiar that the picture was not located in Wellington's portion of the studio. Now, don't say anything that will incriminate you—"

"What are you implying?" Grace asked.

"Do I need to spell it out, my dear?"

Grace looked down at the table and wondered how much he knew.

"Grace, I've got to hand it to you." Azul clapped his hands. "You are smarter than I thought and quite the artist. What a brilliant strategy you concocted. A young, talented artist who has been working to become noticed surreptitiously uses her husband's name to achieve fame at any cost. You are starting to think like me." He laughed loudly.

"You liar! I never tried to use my husband's name to get attention or fame. Everything I did was for Wellington's sake. And I'm definitely not devious like you."

"Oh, did I hit a nerve, little lady?"

Grace said, "How did you know it was mine?"

"I worked with Wellington long enough to know his work, and there is no way he would come up with a concept like that. Besides, Wellington told me that side of the studio is yours. I've got to hand it to you, Grace. It is an outstanding piece of work you created. I didn't know you had it in you. All this time, I have been pursuing the wrong client."

A tear rolled down Grace's cheek. "I never intended for it to turn out like this. I used incredibly poor judgment, and now I'm paying for it. The Johanssons pushed me so hard that I couldn't bring myself to say no. I loved Wellington and wanted his career to take off, but I never wanted to deceive him. We were planning to tell the Johanssons and Ty the truth, but then ... the accident happened. You can't imagine the pain I have been going through this past month. It was a reckless decision. If only I had told the truth. What a fool I am!"

"Now, now, my dear. You must not be so hard on yourself." He touched her arm. "Even a fool can recover from mistakes. In fact, I wanted to meet with you today to discuss a solution to resolve this situation."

Grace jerked his hand away. "How can anybody help me now? I'm bombarded with issues and the school. I just don't know where to turn."

"Are those your only concerns?" Azul laughed. "Allow me to explain, my dear. This work of yours is hot! Galleries and owners are dying to get their hands on more of these abstracts. At this point, they don't have a clue that you are the artist. The price for his work is sky-high now that he is dead. Of course, I did not promise them anything. Just think of the millions we can make together. All you need to do is create about twenty-five more pieces. I will keep our little secret, and both of us will get wealthy—and you can carry on with your lifestyle. The good thing about all of this is that Wellington's name and legacy will continue to live." Azul rubbed his hands together and smiled.

Grace was shocked and couldn't believe the words streaming from Azul's mouth. *Is he on crack? This is nothing short of blackmail. What can I do?* "How can you conjure up such a plan? If we are caught, we will spend years in prison," Grace whispered.

"We?" He laughed. "Correction. If anybody finds out what you've already done, *you* could go to prison, my dear, for forgery," Azul whispered.

"I haven't signed the painting—so it is not forgery," Grace whispered.

"Yes, but you will." He laughed.

"My God, you wouldn't do that to me, would you?"

"Don't worry. That will be our little secret … if you cooperate," Azul added softly. "Besides, just think of how Wellington must be smiling down from heaven because you are carrying on his legacy."

Right. He probably made it to heaven, but with this corrupt plan, I'm sure to end up in hell, Grace thought.

"What do you think? Deal or no deal?" He held out his hand.

"I need time to think about this." Grace stood up. "I have a reputation to keep. Excuse me." Grace almost knocked over the drinks on the waitress's cart.

"I'll call you in a few days," Azul shouted. "Give it some thought. You won't be sorry."

"I was sorry the day I met your conniving ass," Grace said under her breath as she stormed out of the restaurant.

CHAPTER

51

Girl-to-Girl Talk

By the time Grace reached Spa 52, her eyes were red from crying and her face was flushed from her encounter with Azul. At a time when she needed some sensitivity, he displayed no sympathy, and on top of it all, he was trying to frame her. Grace didn't have a scheduled appointment, but she hoped Ellona could squeeze her in.

Ellona was sitting at the front desk when Grace walked in. "What's up, girlfriend? You look shaken."

"I am," Grace replied. "I need a girl-to-girl talk. A massage session wouldn't hurt either."

"Girl, I have been calling you for days. Where have you been?" Ellona asked.

"Join the list," Grace responded. "Everybody has been trying to reach me. I haven't felt up to talking to anybody."

"I know your body is begging for some tender loving care." Ellona stood up and hugged Grace.

"Yes, I'm feeling really fragile. I'm sorry I haven't called. You can't imagine what I've been going through since Wellington and the baby died. We need to talk. Can you squeeze in a good friend?"

"You don't see anybody waiting, do you? Come on back." Ellona grabbed Grace by the arm. "Business has been slow, and I could use some company myself."

"You? Lonely? That's hard to believe."

"You know the drill," Ellona said, pointing to the room. "When you are undressed, ring the bell. I'll be at your beck and call."

Grace wondered how much information she should divulge. Thus far, she had not told Ellona about the painting. *Tell her all of it,* Grace's heart shouted. Ellona walked in with a special fragrance in her hands. "I have the right portion to make you relax and forget all your troubles. Or at least, tell me some of them." She chuckled. "Girl, you are a mess."

Grace smiled. "That's why I like you. You know how to make me laugh. I'm overdue for that. I hope you are not using the same fragrance you used last time I was here."

"Definitely not!" Ellona started rubbing Grace's back.

"You won't believe the things I'm going through with the galleries and Wellington's school. It's so much pressure."

"Well, you know that too much stress can kill you. Oops! Excuse me, honey. That's so insensitive of me. I didn't mean to say that. Please forgive me."

"No problem. I understand what you mean."

"Keep talking, girl, and release those negative thoughts and chemicals so we can get some results," Ellona said.

"Well, one good thing happened today. I made a decision to move on with Wellington's vision for his art academy. I'm appointing his assistant as the new administrator."

"That's a good thing, girl," Ellona said. "Wellington was such a fantastic artist and a good person. You know how much he loved art and teaching children."

"Yes, he was. Unfortunately, I was unable to give him a namesake," Grace added sadly.

"Now, girl, you must let that go," Ellona said. "Your life isn't over. You are young, and one day, you will meet somebody else and have children."

"Girl! It's just not that easy, Ellona. I can't fathom being with or loving another man. It's too soon!"

"Girl, with all these fine men out here, believe me, in time, your heart will heal, and you will move on. Let the right one come around, and you'll change your tune. Okay, maybe I'm being too insensitive. I just want you to try to move on with your life. Look at you." She touched Grace's waistline and patted her butt. "You are letting yourself go. You are gaining weight and not taking care of yourself. I sure hope revitalizing Wellington's dream will help you. He would want you to continue on."

"I realized that when I was in his studio the other day," Grace said. "It was the first time I went into the studio since his death. I felt a spirit in there that chilled me to the bone."

"What do you mean?" Ellona asked.

"Have you ever had a spiritual experience with God you couldn't explain?" Grace asked.

"Yes, I did after I changed my lifestyle. That was a deep spiritual experience."

"Well, for me, it was like Wellington's spirit was in the room and ... then overtook me. It's hard to explain, but peace I haven't felt before invaded the room, and it has remained in the house."

"Girl, I don't think I ever heard you talk about God. I think this is a good time to shout, 'Hallelujah!'"

Grace said, "Girl, quit playing. I'm serious."

"Okay, I'm sorry. Go on. Tell me more," Ellona said.

"I guess one of my fears is how to deal with Wellington's art business." Grace sat up. "What if somebody tries to blackmail me?"

"Girl, you are talking foolish. That'll never happen. I think you have been watching too many movies."

"No, I'm not kidding. Wellington's work was selling well around the country. Since his death, the price for his work has skyrocketed. People are calling, and some of them are smooth talkers. They all want to make deals. I don't know who to trust."

"Send them to me—and I'll handle them. In fact, you need to hire me. I've dealt with criminals in my past. If anybody knows slick when they see it, I do."

"Okay, Miss Slick. You don't know anything about art though."

"Yes, you are right, but I've dealt with some shady characters— and I have street sense."

"I may just take you up on that," Grace said.

"You should," Ellona said with lifted eyebrows.

"Girl, you are so crazy. Why would you do that for me?"

"Just because," Ellona said.

"Because what?" Grace asked.

"Girlfriend, you have been through a lot already. You don't know boo about the streets. Somebody needs to protect you. Besides, you are my good friend."

"I'll owe you big-time for this," Grace said.

"Girl, you will owe me nothing but to continue to be my friend. You don't know how many times you have come in here when I was feeling low—and you encouraged me with just one positive word."

"I know my time is up, but let's continue this conversation. I really appreciate having a friend like you. Thanks for the treatment today and for listening." Grace smiled as they finished the session.

52

Wellington's Restoration

"The Lord is my shepherd. I shall not want," Wellington read out loud from Psalm 23:1.

"That is the truth." Monica set down a cup of tea on the table near Wellington's chair.

Wellington closed the Bible. "I don't remember reading this book before."

"The Bible?" Monica asked. "It's not new. It's known as the 'world's best seller.' It's been around for ages—since the beginning of time."

"Somehow it seems foreign to me."

"Maybe you didn't have a Christian background—or you didn't study it," Monica said.

"I can't remember. Today I read about Lazarus and how Jesus raised him from the dead. I can relate to that because that's really what happened to me. It made me believe there really is a God who cares about me."

"After your experience, I would think you would not hesitate to believe there is a God in heaven who loves you and saved your life. He's got something special planned for you," Monica said.

"I believe that. Thank you for sharing this Bible with me," Wellington said. "It has been a daily strengthener in my recovery."

"I knew it would be. That's why I put it there for you to read anytime you want. When I lost my husband a few years back, I turned to God. This book gave me the hope and strength to go on with my life. It gave me such a peace."

"What happened to your husband?"

"It's a long story. Maybe one day I'll tell you. It's still very painful to talk about."

"I'm sorry. I didn't mean to upset you."

"I'm okay. No problem."

"I appreciate your prayers for me. They're working," Wellington said. "Pieces of information and memories are starting to come back every day since I have started reading and praying. In fact, the bad dreams have stopped—and I'm dreaming in color. I can't make it out, but bright colors keep surfacing. I use those pads you gave me to write these things down, but something weird happened this morning."

"What?"

"While I was writing, I started doodling. I formed some shapes and images. They probably aren't much of anything, but I had so much fun drawing them."

"Can you show them to me?"

"Yes," Wellington said, getting up to grab the pad.

"Wow, these are interesting," Monica said. "My husband was an artist."

"Really?"

"Yes, and quite talented. Art is a good form of therapy during recovery. When I'm in the city tomorrow, I'll pick up some art supplies for you."

"I would like that," Wellington replied.

"Count it done." She smiled. "We are going to put more fun in your life."

Love at First Sight

Niklas said, "I'm sorry, but I can't get Grace on the telephone. I have been trying for the past two weeks."

"There's got to be a way to reach her," Ty said. "This is a difficult time for her. I would like to give her my personal condolences."

"I guess I could try her mother," Niklas said. "She contacted us after the accident."

"No, no, you don't have to do that. I realize this may not be the time to inquire, but I am very much interested in more of Wellington's paintings."

"Grace and I agreed to put the sale of the original on hold for now, but Azul is anxious to sell it," Niklas said. "I don't understand what is going on, but in the past several years, artists he's represented have died."

"I know. All mysterious accidents too," Ty said.

The door of the gallery opened, and Dr. Wolf walked in.

"Hello, young lady," Tyler said. "Don't I know you from somewhere?"

"Oh, that familiar sorry line again?" She gave him half a smile.

"No, seriously, you look like someone I know. What is your name?"

"Dr. Monica Wolf."

"I'm Tyler Hamilton." He extended his hand. "Do you live around here?"

"I have been here a couple of years."

"Are you a collector?"

"You sure ask a lot of questions," she replied, moving around the gallery.

"I'm sorry. Please excuse my bad manners."

"No, I'm not a collector," she replied as she walked toward the counter.

"Can I help you find something?" Niklas asked.

"Yes. I'm looking for some art supplies. I need some paper, brushes, and paints."

"You will find them on the shelf to your left." Niklas pointed and walked her to the spot.

"Thank you." Dr. Wolf picked up some Canson paper and found some paintbrushes and several tubes of paint. When she returned to the counter, Ty smiled at her. "Do you work here?" she asked.

"Now look who's asking the questions."

"That will be $25.11 Swiss francs," Niklas stated.

She paid him, said thanks, and began walking out of the gallery.

"I think you left something." Ty placed his card in her hand. "You may need this."

"I told you I'm not in the collecting business." She put the card back into his hand.

"Wait," he said. "I remember your face now. Your husband is Daniel Wolf, the artist who was killed in New York."

"Yes, that's correct."

"Sorry. I didn't mean to be so forward. I was just telling Niklas how sad it was to hear about another artist's death. I'm trying to get in touch with Wellington's wife."

"Oh, really?" she said, stopping in her tracks. "She was a close friend of mine when I lived in New York. I heard about the accident, and I also have tried to reach her."

"I knew your husband as well, and I collected his work. I met Grace and Wellington in New York, and they were here the weekend of his death, visiting with Ty and me."

"Oh, yes. That makes sense now," Dr. Wolf said. "These are the gallery owners Grace spoke about when she first contacted her about their trip."

Niklas went into his office and returned with his address book. "I have Grace's mother's number if that would help. Tell her I gave it to you."

"Thank you so much. You'll never know how much this means to me," Dr. Wolf said as she left the gallery.

54

Dr. Wolf's Diary

*M*onica sat down to recap the week in her journal. She couldn't believe how her life had changed so drastically. Just a month ago, her life was simple. It was now complicated with secrets. It lurked with danger, especially if Azul found out Wellington was alive. She understood the danger of playing this secretive game, but considering the heartache she went through losing her husband, she was willing to take the risk to help save Grace's husband and her friend.

Wellington appreciated the art supplies, and they uplifted his spirits. She prayed that it would trigger his artistic abilities and that his memory would return quickly.

Wellington's memory was beginning to return slowly, but he didn't remember that he was married. It was refreshing to have some company since she has been alone for so long. They shared playful conversation and laughed a lot. She was anxious to contact Grace, but the timing had to be just right.

Dr. Patel recommended a PET scan to track and record which memory centers were stimulated in Wellington's brain tissue. He suggested hypnosis to help retrieve the traumatic memories without being overwhelmed by them.

Monica prayed that the therapeutic sessions would work—and that God would restore everything Wellington had lost.

55

Rekindled Vision

Grace looked in the mirror and touched the black bags that had formed under her eyes. Even though she had got very little sleep, she felt invigorated with a new mission at the school. Swinging back the closet doors, she searched for her new clothes: a plain black skirt with a design at the bottom and a white lacy blouse. She grabbed her fluffy white robe and headed for the shower.

The ringing phone stopped her. "Hello, Grace. This is Marcella. Listen, I gave your offer some thought. I humbly accept."

"I'm so excited. I knew you would do the right thing," Grace said. "You must have read my mind. I was going to stop by the school to convince you. I'm so glad you agree. I'll see you around ten."

"Yes, ma'am. See you then."

Grace sat in her black BMW and admired the old brick building. Wellington had purchased this building and renovated it to hold six classrooms. The school's current enrollment was forty students with five staff members. Wellington had big dreams of a new building in uptown Manhattan. Until his death, when he was not traveling, he would teach during the week. His passion for art was contagious, and the emerging artists at the academy were between eight and eighteen.

"Good morning, Marcella," Grace said.

"Good morning, boss," Marcella answered.

They both chuckled.

"Let's go into your new office, shall we?" Marcella opened the door.

The office was neat, airy, and spacious. A large oak desk in the middle of the floor was surrounded by plants, a large window, bright walls, and rattan furniture.

"First things first," Marcella said. "There is a lot of mail that requires your attention. The files on the right contain personal information. The files on the left are business matters."

"Do you have the key to this drawer?" Grace asked.

"Wellington is the only one who had a key to those files. I have not been able to locate it. I can call a locksmith and have him open it. The business files are unlocked."

"Thank you, Marcella. I appreciate all you have done to keep this place running smoothly."

"So glad to finally have you here," Marcella said. "If you need me, I'll be in the other room."

Grace pondered the pile of papers on the desk, not knowing where to begin. She sat down and looked at a picture of Wellington on the desk. Tears welled in her eyes, and she forced them back down into a private place of unrelenting mourning, her own personal sea of grief. She began shuffling through the pile. There were bills and letters of condolence. Grace made separate piles and began organizing the papers in order of importance.

In the desk drawer, she found two keys on a keychain. "I wonder what these are?" she said, holding the keys up to inspect them.

"I am not so sure myself," Marcella said. "I tried them, but they didn't work. I thought you could use a cup of peppermint tea."

"Yes, that's perfect. Thank you," Grace said.

When Marcella left, Grace opened the drawer and began looking through the papers. She came across a file folder with confidential written across the top. It was dated July 10—almost a year earlier.

> Staff, tomorrow we are going to have a celebration for the student I selected as my protégé. As you know, out of twenty-five students from underprivileged families, I chose an individual with exemplary talent and one who I could mentor throughout his growing years. His name is Javier Morales. He is eight years old and from Albuquerque, New Mexico. His tuition will be fully funded through the school year. Please join us in the cafeteria tomorrow in the Cafeteria at eight for the presentation. Wellington.

Wow, how nice. Wellington had a mentee.

He never shared that with her, but he kept many things about the school to himself. Grace walked over to the window and noticed the children painting in the yard. How she longed for life to be as simple as the picture she witnessed.

Marcella entered the room and said, "Here's the mail."

"Wellington had a beautiful view of the kids from here, didn't he?"

"Yes, ma'am. Often, throughout the day, he would stand there and observe the students.

A tear fell from Grace's face.

"I'll let you finish your work, Grace. Let me know if you need me."

Lord, I know you are here with me. Grace wiped her tears and headed back to the desk. *Thank you for giving me the confidence to press on—despite my heart's condition. I'm ready now. Use me to perfect Wellington's unfinished vision. I need your help!*

The Letter

By the end of the week Grace had completed looking through six file drawers but still had not touched the credenza behind the desk. She opened the mahogany cabinet and found several bills tied in a bundle, along with two separate letters that were unopened. She opened the first one.

> Wellington, I hate that it has come to this point, but you continue to disappoint me in the lack of support of our son. Javier barely sees you at school and has no personal time with you. Up to now, I have respected your request not to get your family involved, but I'm in need of monetary help and support. This leaves me no other recourse but to file for child support.

I'm also taking him out of the school immediately and moving back to Santa Fe with my mom. You know where you can reach me. Sonya.

Grace gasped, placed her hand over her mouth, and fell back in the brown leather chair. *My God! A son! Wellington never mentioned him to me.* She knew something was bothering him, but she never figured it was this.

Grace thought her own secret about the painting was deep, but this was of a different magnitude. *When and how did this happen?* If he supported the child, she would have known. She thought back to that mysterious phone call that he brushed off as a bill collector.

She went over to the file cabinet to look for more evidence. She pulled out drawer after drawer, dropping papers everywhere and slamming drawers, but she found nothing. Hurt entered her heart first—and then anger. She shook the personal file drawer that had no key. Finally, she slumped down in the chair and began to cry.

Wellington had showered with her so much genuine love that she couldn't see how he found time to spend with another family. Her mind flashed back to his constant conversations about having children. "God, why?"

Marcella rushed into the room. "Are you okay? What's wrong?" Marcella picked up the letter it and began reading.

"Did you know about this?" Grace asked through sobs.

"Yes, ma'am. I did. Wellington made me promise not to tell you. He said he was going to tell you. I'm so sorry you had to find out this way. I figured you knew by now."

"This is embarrassing. My own husband tells somebody something as private as this—but doesn't share it with me? I'm still recovering from all the other drama in my life. I don't even know where the child is or how to contact him."

"Grace, don't worry. I can locate him. He was a student."

"Was he Wellington's protégé—the one the school and staff celebrated?" Grace asked.

"Yes, he was," Marcella said. "Wellington figured it was a way he could help support him. He moved Javier and Sonya to New York to attend the school. Something must have happened because Sonya pulled Javier out of the school about a month before Wellington's death. Wellington was afraid to tell you because he thought you might leave him, and he didn't want to lose you."

"He's right," Grace said. "I was so caught up in my own drama that I failed to observe what was going on in my husband's life."

"If it will help dull the pain in any way, please know that he met her way before he knew you—and it was just a one-night affair."

"Wow, you really know more than I do. How is it that he confided so much in you?"

"I was his mother's best friend, and I served as a mother figure to him when she passed. It was like therapy for him to talk about his life, and I just listened."

"That's one thing I used to be good at."

"I hope you will not lose your trust in me," Marcella said. "You can understand, can't you? This was not my call, and I asked him on several occasions to tell you. I was sure he had shared it with you."

"No, Marcella. He didn't. I'm so confused right now. I'm not holding you responsible. I think I just need to be left alone to sort this out."

"All right. I'm so sorry you found out this way. I can help locate Javier and his family for you." She left the room.

Damn it, Wellington! Grace picked up the picture, threw it against the wall and sobbed. *What else will I uncover in these files? More women and children?*

Wellington's Transformation

Wellington stood up from the doctor's table and faced the mirror. "Doc, what a marvelous job. You made me look handsome." He turned his face from side to side.

"I think the plastic surgery went well," Dr. Patel stated. "Some discomfort after facial scar-revision surgery is normal. You will also have some swelling, bruising, and redness, which is generally unavoidable. I want to explain the procedure I performed on your right hand. The radiograph and MRI showed an extreme ligament tear. It was damaged so severely that it caused a dislocation of the joint and required immediate surgery to realign the bones back to the normal position. I treated it with a splint. You may experience some stiffness and pain. We will schedule a follow-up visit for two weeks and follow that up with hand therapy to maximize recovery and restoration of your hand function. If all goes well, we won't have to do reconstructive surgery." Dr. Patel touched Wellington's face. "Your nose and cheek give your face a rounder and fuller look. I like the new haircut. It makes you look younger."

"Yes, finer too," the assistant added, touching Wellington's shoulder as she pranced by.

"Don't mind her," Dr. Patel said. "You've got to watch out for young ladies these days. They are aggressive."

"Doc, stop teasing me." The assistant blushed and left the room.

"All right, Wellington. I'll see you back in my office in two weeks."

"Thanks, Doc. I owe you, man. You'll never know how much I appreciate you."

"Monica told me about the art therapy she added to your schedule. She said you were quite talented."

"I don't know if I have any talent. Right now, it's just fun trying to use my left hand."

"The beauty of recovery is not to be afraid to make any adjustment that will help you accomplish healing. In that process, you also discover something unique within yourself. I want you to start an exercise program. Exercising regularly for three months will increase the blood flow to the hippocampus, which is responsible for memory. This also leads to the production of new brain cells."

"Doc, I'm so glad you are looking after me. You seem to know everything."

"No, man. I'm continuously studying and learning so I can stay sharp and help restore good people like you back to health. Take care of yourself and keep painting, man. I'll see you in two weeks."

The assistant gave Wellington a card with his next appointment on it and winked at him as she slipped her phone number into Wellington's hand before he exited.

CHAPTER

58

Grace's Search for Truth

Grace headed home to look in Wellington's office for more clues. When she entered the studio, the same serene spirit overtook her and transformed her ruffled emotions. She envisioned Wellington painting or writing at his desk and could faintly hear the melodies in the corridors of her mind coming from his guitar. As much as she detested the screeching sound, right then, she missed it.

Grace opened the shades, and sunlight filled the room. She had never gone through Wellington's personal belongings in his desk. She opened the drawer and pulled out a small blue notebook containing client contact information. A folded letter fell to the floor. Inside was a picture of a cute little boy with big black eyes and black curly hair. Grace began reading and was shocked to see the letter was addressed to her.

Grace:

The only way to describe you is the words of Solomon found in Proverbs 31:10. "Your worth is far above jewels." Honey, know that my love for you is strong, and I never want to do anything to hurt you. There is one thing though that may leave you confused or bitter and bring a wedge between us. I don't know why it has taken me so long to share this with you. I guess I'm waiting for the right time. I haven't found a way to express it in words out of fear of losing your trust. I'm so happy we are expecting a child, which means so much to me. The surprising news is I already have a son. Yes, I know this is a shock. This is a picture of my son, Javier, who is six years old on this picture. I know what you are thinking, but please let me explain. This was a one-night incident that happened before I met you. I was in Santé Fe and met a young lady. It was a physical attraction only and one I wished I would not have succumbed to. This one-night stand changed my life and now will change ours. I know this is hard for you to bear, but I'm asking for your forgiveness for not telling you sooner. I probably don't deserve it, but I feel like I deserve you. Javier is a sweet kid who also deserves our attention. I'm hoping you will accept and embrace him in our lives. I'm going crazy and the level of anxiety of all of this is

Grace flipped over the letter, but it was unfinished. On the back was a name and a number: "Call Detective Ramos about Azul (011 41 489 43 82799)."

Grace thought back to an incident that transpired between Wellington and Azul. When they were traveling and having dinner with Azul, Grace excused herself to go to the restroom. When she returned, Wellington and Azul were entrenched in a heated conversation. Grace had never seen Wellington so upset. He was fuming. He stood up, shouted a few distasteful words, and threw his drink in Azul's face. He grabbed her hand, and they left the restaurant without dinner. When they arrived home, Grace asked him about it, but he went straight to his studio and refused to talk about it. So, Grace left it alone. After that night, every time Grace mentioned Azul's name or whenever Azul was around, Wellington became edgy—but he continued to work with him.

Grace set the letter on the desk, looked at Javier's innocent face, and wondered if their family was aware of Wellington's death. The funeral service was held for close family members and a few friends, but she couldn't recall everyone that was there.

Grace's situation with Azul was consuming her. She needed somebody she could trust and share information. She didn't want to open a closed book, but she could use Ellona's street knowledge. Grace dialed her number.

"Hey, Ellona. What's up?"

"Nothing, girl, just chilling."

"Girl, I need a big favor from you," Grace said.

"Anything for you sis, what's up?"

"Remember Wellington's agent?"

"Yes."

"His birthday is coming up, and I'm thinking of giving him a certificate to the spa. I need more to come out of that treatment."

"What are you talking about, girl?" Ellona asked.

"I want you to get into his head."

"Really? Why?"

"Stop thinking dirty, girl," Grace laughed. "This is a serious matter. I think he's trying to blackmail me."

"A-ha. I get it. That's what you were trying to tell me the other day."

"Yes. I just didn't know how to say it. I may be in trouble and need to confide in you. I need to trust you with this. You can't share this with anybody."

"What do you mean?"

"I have an idea," Grace said.

"Okay. Tell me about it," Ellona said."

"I need you to use your gift of gab and your soothing hands on him. You know you have a special way to break any man down." Grace laughed.

"Yes, I am gifted in that way."

"Azul's birthday is next week. I plan on purchasing a gift certificate to the spa, and the idea is to get him to like you. I know he'll fall in love with you, but you can't fall in love with him. Do you think you can help me?"

"Is that your goal? So, when is this supposed to take place?"

"Friday is his birthday. How does your schedule look on Thursday?"

"Three o'clock is open," Ellona said. "What does he look like?"

"Believe me, you'll like him. He's about five foot nine, dark hair, fair, slim, and a sharp dresser," Grace said.

"Sounds like my type."

"I'm not asking you to do this because he's your type. This is business. I'll call him and set it up," Grace said.

"You gonna owe me for this one, sista," Ellona said.

"No problem, girl. I just need your help. Thanks again." Grace tucked the letter and the picture in her pocket. She needed to tell her mom about the new addition to her life, but she needed to rest first. She had enough surprises for the week.

59

Mom's Counsel

"Hello, Mom."

"Hey, baby. I haven't heard from you lately. How have you been?"

"I'm stressed. I have several new developments and unanswered questions."

"Is it about Wellington? Did they find him?"

"Not yet, Mom. I'm dealing with some personal information about Wellington. He has a secret life I didn't know about."

"What do you mean?"

"I uncovered some information that shocked me and will also surprise you. Brace yourself, Mom. You have a grandson."

"What do you mean?"

"This may be hard to believe, but Wellington has a son I didn't know about."

"When did you find out?"

"Yesterday, while cleaning out his desk. I was so hurt and confused. All he had to do was tell the truth and trust me. I'm afraid of other stuff I might find."

"Grace, it appears you both had secrets."

"I know. This is messed up though."

"You have been through so much. This is some hard news to swallow. Are you okay?"

"I'm going to be all right. It just hurts."

"Child, you are letting him off the hook. He should have told you!" Ruth said. "Why didn't you call me yesterday and tell me?"

"I'm sorry, Mom. I'm on edge and didn't mean to raise my voice."

"It's okay, sweetie. I understand. I just don't want you to face these difficulties by yourself. I know this is upsetting. Maybe it will help to meet Javier and get to know him. That's what Wellington would want, right?"

"I'm a little apprehensive about meeting him. I asked God to prepare my heart, but I'm nervous about the whole thing!"

"I can only imagine, but it's the right thing to do," Ruth said.

"I agree. Marcella said she can contact them."

"Great. That's what you should set your mind to do."

"Mom, you are right again. You always know the right words to comfort me. I miss you so much. I have been praying more like you suggested. It is helping me deal with all these issues that are piling up."

"You deserve some peace, and I know God will grant that."

"Thanks, Mom. I'll call you next week and let you know how things work out."

"Okay. I love you, and things will get better soon."

As soon as Grace hung up, the telephone rang again.

Malcolm said, "Hey, Grace. I hope I didn't catch you at a bad time."

"No, I just got off the phone with my mom. What's up?"

"I haven't heard from you and was wondering if you were still upset with me."

"I was never upset. It was that kiss. It caught me off guard. We are still friends—so don't sweat it over a little kiss. I know I told you that I would call and invite you to the school. I have just been so busy. As a matter of fact, I'm meeting the class on Wednesday for the first time since Wellington's passing and it might be a good time for you to come. It's time to talk with the students to lift their spirits and assure them all is well with the school. It's not going to be easy, so I welcome your joining me. It would be a great source of support."

"I would love that," he said. "Mentoring and volunteering are things I've recently gotten involved in, and I'm finding out I enjoy it."

"Great. Do you know where the school is?"

"Yes," he replied.

"Plan on meeting me there around ten. I'm going to speak at ten thirty," Grace said.

"Sounds like a plan. I'll see you then."

Grace's stomach rumbled with nerves as she thought about Wellington's mission and what she should say to the students.

Lord, I'm going to need your help again. So much is happening, and I feel unsure of my next steps. I know you are able and that nothing is too hard for you. I know one thing for sure; your grace is sufficient and will give me the strength to get through all these crises. You are constant, and you always come through when I need you. I need you now!

Malcolm Visits
the School

"**G**race, Malcolm is here," Marcella said from the office doorway.

"I'll be right there," Grace replied. "Good to see you Malcolm," Grace said with a smile. "I'm so glad you came. Did you meet Marcella?"

"Not officially," he said turning to her. "Good to meet you."

"Malcolm and I attended the same high school. Little did we know that we both selected Hope College. Malcolm was also one of Wellington's students."

"That's pretty cool," Marcella said. "It's always nice to keep up with friends. I'm glad you could participate today."

"My pleasure, ma'am," Malcom said.

"Let's go into my office to go over the plan for today," Grace said as she walked toward her office.

"Wow. This is nice," he said.

"Thanks. I'm beginning to feel more comfortable despite the big shoes I have to fill. I'm so glad you came today."

"You know I wouldn't miss this chance to help you." He smiled.

Grace gave him the outline for the day, and they headed to the classroom.

As Grace addressed the students, her love for the arts and her husband oozed from every word that came out of her mouth. She mirrored Wellington's tenderness and concern for the student's learning and future as artists. She was a genuine example of a devoted artist's wife by promoting and upholding her husband's vision. Despite battling her own hurts and losses, she was sensitive and responsive to the student's emotions concerning the absence of their adored teacher. She assured the class that the school's program would not be interrupted despite the changes that were being going to be put in place.

"Class, I want to introduce to you a friend and one of Professor Holmes's students at Hope College: Malcolm Jenkins. Please show him some love," Grace said. She stood in the back and listened as Malcolm interacted easily with the students. He had a simple manner of teaching and captured their attention with his humor. That's what she liked about him.

After his presentation, Grace caught him looking at her again. "What?" she asked.

"You took a brave stance back there. You faced a demanding situation and handled it fearlessly. I'm so proud of you."

"Thanks, Mal. It sure was not easy. My heart was jumping out of my skin."

"You handled it well, and I know you are going to be a great leader."

"I'll do my best. I'm dedicated to the long-term development and success of the students, and I'm optimistic about the future of the school. I know—with God's help—it will be done."

"I hope you invite me back again. I would love to teach a class and support the vision," he said.

"I can make that happen." Grace smiled. "Thanks again for coming. It means a lot to me. Just like the old saying goes, 'It takes a village to raise a child.'"

"Just know I'm just a call away." He squeezed Grace's hand and left.

CHAPTER 61

Surveillance of Azul

"That's him," Detective Ramos said.

Detective Mendez snapped a picture of Azul crossing the street. "Let's keep our distance."

Azul entered the Bonet Café and sat down near the window across from a man in his twenties.

Ramos and Mendez crossed the street but remained out of sight.

"Hey, man. I almost didn't recognize you in those dark shades and that slick New York hat," Azul said.

"Dude, I'm trying to keep a low profile."

"I got a call from Jake last night. He's in Barcelona. A big shipment is coming in next week, and he needs someone to pick it up. Can you handle it?"

"How much?"

"The usual."

"Man, I'm risking my life just to make a few bucks. I'm going to have to raise my prices soon."

"Boy, don't get greedy on me. If you didn't have me, your ass would be on the streets. Just shut up and give me your answer."

"I'm knee-deep now. I guess I don't have any other choice."

"That's my boy. I need that merchandise, and I don't want any surprises. You got that?"

"I got you."

"I'll arrange everything and get the information to you. Don't try to call me. I'll contact you. Want something to eat, man?" Azul passed him a menu.

"No, I'm straight."

"Okay. I'll be in touch."

Ramos took a snapshot of them shaking hands and another of the license plate when the man got into his 450 Mercedes. "When you get to the office, see what you can find on this guy."

Azul's cellphone rung as he got up to leave the café. "Hello?"

"Hey, Azul. It's Grace."

"Hey. Have you given my proposal some thought?"

"Yes. I apologize for the way I acted at lunch. I didn't mean to be so confrontational. I have been under a lot of pressure since Wellington's death. I did some thinking. I need a plan to support myself and believe we can work something out."

"That a girl. I knew you would come around."

"I understand your birthday is around the corner."

"How do you know that?" Azul asked.

"I saw it on Wellington's desk calendar the other day. To make up for my bad behavior, the least I could do is purchase a gift certificate for you to my spa. I'm sure you could use a stress reliever."

"Wow! You've got a point there. I have been pretty stressed out," he said.

"Spa 52 is on the Lower East Side. I checked with my masseuse, and she's available next Thursday at three o'clock, which is a day before your birthday."

"Let me check my schedule," he said. "I'm free."

"Good. I'll make the arrangements and text you the address."

"Cool. I appreciate that, little lady. I can't believe you are thinking about me."

"Yes, it's the least I could do." Grace smiled.

"You're a smart lady. I knew you would come to your senses about the paintings. Let's hook up next week and talk about everything in detail."

"Okay. Enjoy your spa treatment."

Azul Visits Spa 52

Detective Ramos and Detective Mendez followed Azul to Spa 52.

Detective Ramos said, "I don't remember him going to this location. Let's wait and see if he comes out quickly—then we'll know if he's there for a spa treatment or on business."

Ellona wore a peach and white striped sarong, scandals, and a tank top. Her shoulder-length brown hair was pinned up in a neat french roll. She had applied the right amount of perfume to stimulate Azul's senses.

"Hi," Azul said. "I'm here to see Ellona."

She flashed her best smile. "You must be Azul. Can you follow me?" She added a little extra swag in her walk. *Wow! He's more handsome than Grace said*, she thought.

His eyes stayed fixed on her perfectly round butt. The scent of jasmine candles streamed down the narrow hallway, which led to the room filled with the jazzy beats of Herbie Hancock.

"Undress to the level of your comfort, and I'll be back in a short while," she said, flashing him a temptress smile before closing the door behind her.

The aroma mesmerized him as he stretched out on the cot with a thin sheet covering his well-chiseled body.

Ellona entered the room and began mixing her oils. She started rubbing his back and touched a sensitive spot that made him cringe.

"Wow. That is tantalizing. What are you doing to my body?"

"I'm reshaping a canvas. That's all," Ellona responded, gazing at his exquisitely crafted body.

In a very short time, Azul was sound asleep.

"That's it for the day," she said, giving him an extra slap on the butt to wake him.

"Wow! That went so fast. I was dreaming that somebody was beating me," he said as he sat up. "Does this have to end now?"

"Well, it doesn't have to. You can make another appointment," Ellona said handing him a towel.

"Do I have to leave?" He looked straight into her eyes.

"Yes. I have another customer arriving shortly."

"Do you have plans for tomorrow?" he asked. "It's my birthday, and I would love for you to join me for dinner."

"Tomorrow won't work for me. I already have plans."

"Okay, what about Saturday?" he asked.

"Okay," she said.

"Have you been to Alfredo's on Forty-Seventh Street?"

"Yes, and I love Italian food." She smiled.

"Perfect. I'll make dinner reservations for seven."

"Cool. I'll see you then. And have a great birthday tomorrow." She grinned.

Azul gave her a huge tip and left.

Detective Ramos snapped a shot of Azul as he got into his Mercedes and sped away.

An Alarming Visitor

*E*llona arrived at Alfredo's a little before seven, and Stoney Johnson—an ex-boxer turned street hustler for whom she had worked in the past—was sitting across the table from Azul. They were laughing like old buddies. She quickly ducked into the ladies' room and peered through the door. Her hands shook like a leaf. *What in the hell is he doing here? I thought he moved to Europe two years ago after he spent several years in prison.*

The men exchanged business cards, and Stoney left the restaurant.

Ellona waited a moment before she approached the table.

Azul stood up to greet her and pulled out her chair.

"Thank you." Ellona sat down. "Sorry I'm late. I noticed a guy just left your table. I hope I didn't interrupt anything. Is he a friend of yours?"

"Not really. We were acquaintances some time ago, and he noticed me as he was leaving."

"Oh, I see. He looked familiar, but New York is so huge. Everybody starts looking alike."

"I know. I haven't seen him in years."

"You look lovely tonight," Azul said.

"Thank you."

"Did you have a good birthday?"

"Not bad at all. A few of the boys and I went out, but it would have been better if I had spent the evening with you," he said, touching her hand.

"Grace told me you represent artists. Who are some of your famous clients?"

"I represent a few locals and some international artists. Most of them are emerging artists on their way to the top."

"Yes," she said. "It was sad to hear the news about Grace's husband. I feel so bad for her. It was unfortunate that they never recovered his body."

"Yes, that was disappointing," he said. "Can you excuse me for a moment? I'll be right back."

Stoney had left a business card on the table. She turned to make sure Azul was out of sight and picked up the card. *Mark Dutton? That's not his name! I wonder what those two are up to.* She wrote down his number and placed the card back in its original position.

Azul smiled as he approached the table. "You ready to order?"

"I can eat," Ellona said with a smile.

After dinner, they had a few more glasses of wine before he walked her to her car. He planted a small kiss on her lips before departing.

Once he sped off, she dialed Grace's number. "Girl, you didn't tell me that the man was that fine. I almost lost control while working on his body the other day. You know what I mean?"

"You are crazy, girl. He's handsome, but cute ain't everything."

"How did it go?" Grace asked.

"He loved the massage and then asked me out for dinner tonight. I just left the restaurant."

"Girl, what did you do to him?" Grace asked.

"Just my usual. A little pampering, ya know?"

"I asked for your help, but I didn't know you were going to move this fast," Grace said.

"We had a good time tonight, but I saw him talking to someone from my past. Stoney Johnson is not someone you would want as a friend. Back in the day, he went to prison on drug charges and attempted murder."

"Murder?"

"Yes, girl."

"Did Stoney see you?"

"Oh, hell no. I hid in the ladies' room until he left. He would remember me, and that would crush any opportunity to obtain information from Azul. Azul played it off. I could tell there was more to the relationship than he revealed, but I didn't push it. I feel like I'm a lamb among wolves."

"Are you afraid?" Grace asked. "I don't want to put you in danger."

"Girl, with all the stuff I've been through, I can handle this."

"I have some more news."

"Girl, adventure is becoming your middle name," Ellona laughed.

"Stuff just keeps happening huh? Anyway, while I was reading one of Wellington's letter, I came across a number that may be important. A special agent reached out to Wellington. His name is Detective Ramos."

"Really?" Ellona said. "I know that name, but I hope he doesn't know me."

"I haven't called him yet, but he's watching Azul, which means he's watching us too."

"Girl, what are you getting me into?" Ellona asked.

"Relax, you have a legit business. If you stick to the plan, I see no problem. When are you going to see Azul again?"

"He said he would call me next week."

"I want you to be careful, girl. You could get caught up in something dangerous, and it'll be my fault. I can't have blood on my hands again."

"Don't worry. I've got this. You asked me to do this for you, didn't you?"

"Yes, but you don't know Azul. If he sees something he wants, he goes after it. I'm talking about you."

"I'll be careful. I'm also going to dig for more information about Stoney. Are you going to call Detective Ramos? He might have information that can help—and calm my nerves about him watching me."

"I plan on doing that," Grace said.

"Do you own a weapon?" Ellona asked.

"Are you talking about a gun?" Grace asked.

"Yes, a gun! The class of people we're dealing with don't play. I see you have zero street knowledge. I'm going to have to get you up to speed on how to play this game. You're going to need protection."

"Wellington has one, but I don't like having it in the house. My life hasn't had a need for guns, and I hate the thought of it."

"If Azul is trying to frame you like you said, you might want to give it some more thought, girl. You can start by telling me the truth about what's really going on with you and Azul. What are you hiding and why?"

"Okay, okay. How much time do you have?"

"How about meeting me at the spa tomorrow at two. We can talk. The massage will be on the house for introducing me to Azul."

"You may be thanking me too early," Grace said.

"I don't think so. There is something that draws me to him."

"Yes, danger. That's all—and you said you were through with that!"

"Don't worry your pretty little head. I told you I've dealt with slick folks before. I'll be careful."

Dr. Wolf's Disguised Call

Dr. Wolf tried dialed Grace's number. "Hello. Can I speak to Grace Holmes?"

"This is Grace."

"Grace, I have some important information about your husband that you need to know."

"Who is this?"

"I can't reveal my identity right now, but you are in danger—and I can help you. It is imperative that we talk. Can we meet on Tuesday at Sam's Bar at six?"

"Why should I trust you?" Grace asked. "I don't even know you."

"You are right. I know how you feel, but you can't afford not to meet me the way things are going on in life right now. I promise I'm not going to harm you, and I will help you to restore everything you have lost. I will be sitting in the back of the restaurant. I'll be dressed in black and have a large black hat with sunglasses. Please don't bring anyone with you or speak to anyone about this call. It's important. Just come!" Dr. Wolf hung up and threw the burner phone in the trash.

Grace's life was being consumed with darkness and skepticism. It was really pushing her up against the wall. Ellona's suggestion of owning a gun was sounding better by the moment. Grace had learned how to shoot one, but it was totally outside of her parameters to fire one. Her life was becoming more dangerous by the day. She couldn't imagine who else besides her mother, Ellona, and Azul knew her secret.

Dr. Wolf closed her suitcase and propped it upright on the bed, contemplating her travel arrangements. She checked her passport and ticket and weighed her impending flight to New York, which would depart in three hours. She had hired a nurse to stay with Wellington while she was away. He was improving and spending most of his days occupied with painting.

"Hey, you. You didn't tell me you were going on a trip," Wellington said.

"I'm headed to New York on a research trip. I won't be gone long. While I'm there, I will meet with my old boss and visit a special friend."

"I will miss you."

"I'll miss you too. I'll call when I arrive in New York. I expect you to behave yourself," she said.

"I will." He pulled her closer. "I watch you every day that you come into my room and wait on me. You are so beautiful. It's getting hard to ignore you." Wellington smelled her neck.

"I look at you only through the eyes of a concerned doctor and friend—and nothing more." She pulled away. "And remember that there is still a lot to uncover about your life." She pointed to his wedding band.

He drew her near again and kissed her on the lips.

She touched her lips and moved away slowly. "Like I said, behave yourself."

CHAPTER
65

Grace Meets Dr. Wolf

Grace got in the car and backed out of the driveway. Her mind was preoccupied with the mystery woman. Grace questioned why she should trust someone she didn't know. She was desperate.

When she arrived at Sam's, she wondered how she had ever navigated the streets and traffic. She was jostled out of her private world by the valet. She failed to notice the car that had been following her since she left home. It parked and assumed a surveillance position as she entered the restaurant.

In a trance, she marched to the rear of the restaurant. She scanned the room, and a slim woman in dark attire and a hat motioned to her.

Grace sat down.

"Thanks for coming. I know this is hard for you with all that is going on. I didn't give you much information because I have to keep us as safe as possible."

"Us? Safe from who? What are you talking about?" Grace asked.

"I have news about your husband's plane that nobody—not even the police—knows, and I want to share it with you."

"How is that going to help me? They never found him."

"I have good news. Wellington's plane was sabotaged."

"Sabotaged? By whom?"

"I think you know the answer to that. Do you remember Daniel Wolf?"

"Yes, he was a good friend. His death was so mysterious and sad, and I don't think they ever solved it."

"Yes, it was a mystery to some, but not to me. I believe he was murdered."

"Murdered? Why do you think that?"

Dr. Wolf removed her glasses, and Grace looked directly into her eyes.

"Oh my God. Monica? You changed your hair?"

Monica put her hat and glasses back on. "Yes, it's me. I had to come in disguise and be discreet about our meeting. I guarantee you, from this point on, we will be watched."

"It's so good to see you, but I don't understand how you are involved in this."

"Let me explain. I believe Azul had something to do with Wellington's accident too. I was going to meet you two in Switzerland. My house is not far from the lake where Wellington's plane went down. I heard the crash that morning and saw the smoke. When I heard that Wellington was on the plane, I knew I had to get to the crash scene. When I arrived, the area was surrounded with police and reporters. They made everyone stand back. I noticed something on the ground and picked up a note with Azul's handwriting. I didn't tell anyone. There's more, but I want to share the good news first."

"Good news?" Grace asked.

"Hold your breath," Monica said. "Wellington survived the crash!"

"He did?" Grace let out a small scream that made everyone in the restaurant turn and look at them.

Monica said, "Nobody can know it yet."

"Oh my God. He is so good!"

"Yes, he is, girl!" Monica said.

"Why are you risking your career and life for us? Aren't you scared?"

"Yes. I'm terrified, but it's worth the risk. You are good friends, and I can't let what happened to my husband occur again. That's why it is crucial that we keep this secret between us until the time is right."

"How did you find him?" Grace asked.

"I engaged a team of friends to help me search for him. They found his badly bruised body. We put him in the car and took him to a private hospital for surgery. He is recovering well."

Grace stood up and hugged Monica. "Oh my! This is unbelievably great news. I needed this today. Thank you so much for saving my husband's life."

Monica said "We have to be careful about being too friendly. They released a national report about the incident. Did you see it?"

"No, I must have missed it. What did it say?"

"I brought the *New York Times* with me."

> The National Transportation Safety Board investigator revealed that a faulty carburetor made the engine completely cut out shortly after takeoff from the airport causing the plane to plunge out of the sky. It is concluded that Wellington Holmes's body was never recovered.

"Something bad happened when that plane crashed. Wellington doesn't remember who he is. He suffered several broken bones and a major concussion. He recently underwent reconstructive surgery on his face. His memory is returning, and we are hopeful for total restoration."

"Oh my God, what are we going to do?" Grace asked.

"The only thing to do is trust God. We are taking it one day at a time and believing for the best. He has the best doctors in the country. Wellington doesn't remember that he is a famous artist. I am working on that portion with him. I told him his name in the hopes that it would jar something in his brain, but it didn't. I'm also trying art therapy. He has started showing signs of artistic ability and expressed his love of drawing. I went to the Johanssons' gallery to buy him some art supplies. They don't know Wellington is alive. In fact, no one knows except me and Wellington's doctors."

"Monica, this must be God! You are like an angel in disguise," Grace said.

"What do you mean by that?" Monica asked.

"It's a long story, but the short of it is that you came to his aid when needed. It's the title of a painting Wellington was working on, and it is just what I needed right now."

"What is it that worries you?"

"Wellington does not remember the last terrible thing that happened between us," Grace said.

"What are you talking about?"

"Can I trust you not to tell anyone?"

"Well, yeah. I think I'm trusting you, aren't I?" Monica said. "It seems to be a fair exchange."

"I made a terrible decision that caused a bad argument between us. Wellington stormed out of the hotel in a rage. That's the last time I saw him. I was under so much duress after Wellington's death that I lost our baby. And then there's the devil himself—Azul."

"Azul? What about Azul?" Monica asked.

"He's trying to blackmail me."

"What? Why would he want to blackmail you?" Monica asked.

Grace explained what happened with the painting. "Azul is demanding that I paint several more abstracts and push them off as Wellington's."

Monica said, "Please don't cry. We need to be very careful. I believe we can find a way to entrap Azul. He can't keep winning by killing all the great artists! I'm very sorry to hear about the baby. Don't worry, Grace. Azul won't have the victory in this situation. God is good, and he will not let him prosper. He will reveal the steps that we need to take. Only believe!"

"I do," Grace replied. "This incident has changed my life and brought me closer to God. I couldn't have made it through this horrific period without him."

Monica looked at her watch and smiled. "I didn't know you were painting on that level, girlfriend."

"Yes. I guess I've learned—and I'm improving. I upped my skills a little and started dabbling in abstracts. I found something I really enjoy. It's nowhere on the level of Wellington's work though."

"I wouldn't say that. It got the attention of the Johanssons, didn't it?"

"Yes, but I wasn't trying to make an entrance into the art world like that."

"I know. No worries. Here's what we're going to do. I have a meeting in an hour. I'll pay the bill. I'm going to go the restroom, and then I want you to leave right away. Don't try to contact me. I'll call you. The name I'll use is Essetta. Not a word of this to anyone, you promise?"

"I promise. When can I see Wellington?"

"I'll arrange it at the right time," Monica said.

"I really miss him and can't wait to see him."

"Just hold on and pray." Monica slid out of her seat and headed to the restroom.

Grace exited the restaurant and Detective Ramos watched as she sped away in her car.

Ellona Hears the Truth

Grace sprawled out on the massage table, and Ellona laughed. "Girl, sounds like you stepped into some you-know-what."

"Yes, I did." Grace told her about the plane crash—but left out the part about Wellington's rescue.

"Girl, you are crazy. It sounds like the stuff I used to do. What were you thinking?"

"For a moment, I had a brain freeze from hearing that someone liked my work. It took precedence over the truth. I got so much joy out of it. At Ty's dinner, I should have told everyone the truth and set the record straight. Instead, I flipped the script. There was so much to explain in the moment that I didn't know where to start. So, it's all my fault."

"Grace, I'm so sorry. I had no idea all this was happening in your life. Why did you carry this burden so long without telling me? That's what friends are for."

"But that's not the end of the events. With Azul blackmailing, I can't live this lie any longer. I could go to jail. I need money to run the school, but I don't want to do this illegally. That's not the way to uphold Wellington's name. That's why I need your help."

"I will help you out, girl. You can look out for me another time. What are you going to do?" Ellona asked.

"I have a plan. I'm going to contact Detective Ramos."

"Girl, you know we need God's help. Have you tried that?"

"I have prayed," Grace said. "How do you think I've gotten through the deaths and this blackmail attempt? I believe God uses people to work out these situations. He's not coming down from heaven to work out life situations for us."

"I was just asking," Ellona said. "I'm sorry if I sounded insensitive. I know you don't talk much about spiritual things."

"Well, I've changed. I know I didn't mention much about my relationship with God before, but after Wellington's death, I searched my soul. I realize I need him a lot more than I thought. My mom always encouraged me to get to know him better, but I didn't. After going through this ordeal, I understand how much I need his guidance."

"I hear you. When I was going through my tests, I gave everything to him—and he turned things around for me. When you cry out to him for help, he'll answer you."

"That's what my mother said," Grace replied.

"You ought to listen to her."

"I have lately. I'm just so scared and confused right now."

"I understand. Here. Take my hand. Let's pray. You have to invite him in," Ellona said.

"I'm ready." Grace knelt down. "I'm tired of all these lies. I want to be armed with the truth. I feel so guilty about all of this. How could he ever forgive me?"

"He is forgiving and full of mercy and grace. Believe me." Ellona smiled.

"Wait." Grace stood up. "While I'm spilling my guts, I might as well tell you one more issue."

"Don't tell me more." Ellona chuckled. "I don't think I can handle it."

"I have to get this one off my chest," Grace said.

"Okay, go ahead. What else could top that?" Ellona asked.

"Believe me—this takes the cake." Grace told Ellona about Javier.

"Girl, you've got so much going on. I can't imagine how you are keeping it together. I have some issues you don't know about. It's been such a long time since I had a man friend. Azul seems like such a nice man, but he is cunning. Now you have told me this crazy stuff about him, I can't allow my heart to swell up over him," Ellona said.

"You better not. That's why I told you to watch yourself."

"Grace, you released all your troubles. I think it is a good time to tell you a little more about me. In my line of work, I'm in a position to listen to others talk, but I never share my story. I think you should know my full history and know why I'm qualified to deal with people like Azul. Most of it is a distant memory because God has put it under the blood.

"At fifteen, I was a mess. My mom is Native American, and my dad is African American. I was raised in a dysfunctional home with five brothers and sisters in a very poor, rural area in Idaho. There was a lot of tension in the house—and lots of abuse and fighting. That's why most of my siblings sought different escapes from our home in our early teens. It's still a mystery how I came through that trauma. It was not without some bruises and turmoil. I looked different with fair skin, high cheekbones, and straight black hair. I was drawn to older guys and had very low self-esteem. That was the basis of my problems.

"My life started spiraling downward. I was looking for love in all the wrong places, and I inflicted pain on myself. I started drinking and experimenting with drugs. The next thing I knew, I needed money to keep up with those habits. So, what did I do? At eighteen, I got involved with a guy who talked me into selling my body. I'm not proud of it, and I encountered some painful lessons.

"I was young and dumb, and after a while of working the streets, I got tired and fed up with my life. The problem is you are not allowed to just walk out of that situation without some backlash. I felt there was no hope for me. Ava saw me crying and came to my aid. There was something so soft in her eyes and face. It was almost angelic. She convinced me to listen to her. I was twenty-one and desperate for that life to end. She invited me to her church and had a plan of escape, which I didn't know she was implementing right then and there. I accepted. Her plan worked, and I accepted God's plan for my life.

"My life was in shambles, and I needed help. I ran from some troubling things like my home life and the streets and bumped into something good. God gave me another chance, and I'm so grateful. I had to forgive myself and others, and I never returned to that life. Without his love and grace, I don't know where I'd be. Something inside of me changed drastically. The void I had is now filled with love and hope.

"Ava was instrumental in getting my massage career started. She enrolled me in a school and has been a great support. I didn't know I had healing hands, but I discovered it was a big part of my recovery and a way to heal others who have gone through the same experience. I am now a volunteer at a shelter for girls. I give free massages to girls who are caught up in this system. I was given a second chance, and now I'm able to help others, which is so rewarding and adds value to my life. That's my testimony."

"Whoa! Girl, that's heavy stuff. That life sounds so dangerous. God really dipped you deep in the water of baptism and cleaned you up, huh?"

They laughed.

"I know. It infuriates me when people are trying to take advantage of others. That's why I know I can handle Azul and his world."

"Ellona, I appreciate you more than you know. God used your experience so you can help others redirect their paths. It's designed to strengthen you each time you help them. I'm so thankful to have a friend to talk to you like you." Grace smiled.

"I'm far from perfect and still have flaws, but God isn't through with me. One thing that Ava shared with me that I hold onto is Jeremiah 29:11: 'The plans God has for me; to prosper me, give me hope and a future.'"

"Amen to that."

"Don't worry, girl. Everything is going to work out. We are going to seek counsel right now!" Ellona knelt in prayer. "Merciful God, help!"

Hitting the Spot

"**T**hat feels so good." Azul rolled over on his back on Ellona's spa table. He grabbed her hands and brought her on top of him until their lips were inches apart.

"This is not part of my professional job," Ellona said, removing herself from his embrace. She stood up and moved toward her small table of oils and creams.

Azul sat up. "I apologize for my actions. I got overexcited and couldn't stand it any longer. You are one hot lady."

"I understand, but this is not the place for such playfulness. You know what I mean?"

He moved behind her, put his hands on her shoulders, and turned her around. "Does it make me a naughty boy because I'm attracted to you?"

"No, nothing like that. I prefer to keep this part of my life on a professional level." She removed his hands from her shoulders. "I suggest you put on your clothes, and I'll meet you out front." She moved past him and closed the door behind her.

She blew a sigh of relief, fanned her face, and headed to the front of the salon.

He walked up to her and said, "Can I see you again, like tomorrow evening?"

"What do you have in mind?" she asked.

"There is a play at the Windy Creek Theater that I'd like to see. It's called *Too Much, Too Little*."

"You don't seem like the type who would like plays."

"Don't judge a book by its cover."

"What time is it playing?"

"It starts at eight, but I'd like to pick you up at six. We could get a bite to eat first."

Ellona said, "Yeah, I'd like that. Pick me up here at the salon. I'll be ready by six. By the way, that treatment was on the house."

"Thanks. You better watch out—I could get really spoiled." Azul turned to leave.

Ellona knew he would be eating out of the palm of her hand in no time.

Grace Meets Javier

Grace stayed awake all night and thought about what she would say to Javier and Sonya. She knew very little about them, which made her edgy and fragile, but she was enthusiastic about the opportunity to embrace and connect with a person who meant so much in Wellington's life.

On the flight to New Mexico, Marcella filled Grace in on the things she knew about him. He was an only child. He was small for his age, which made him withdraw from the crowd at times. His mom sheltered him with close family and little interaction with others. Wellington helped with that by having him interact with the children at school. He was athletic and loved soccer and baseball. He had Wellington's artistic talent.

Although Wellington didn't share that part of his life with her, Grace decided it had no weight on meeting him now. It was up to her to find a way to connect with Javier.

The small brick house on the southeast edge of the city was enclosed by a broken-down fence and covered with graffiti.

Grace's heart fluttered as she climbed the narrow steps, wondering how the family would receive her. She rang the doorbell and waited with Marcella.

No one answered.

Grace peeked through the window and rang the bell again.

A lady in her fifties answered the door. "Buenos Dias," she said.

"Buenos Dias," Marcella replied.

A young boy with big brown eyes came running from a back room and said, "Hi. Grandma doesn't speak English. Who are you?"

"I'm a friend of the family," Grace said. "Is your mother home?"

"No."

"Hey, I know you." Javier pointed at Marcella. "You work at the school with my dad."

Marcella and Grace glanced at each other.

"Yes, dear, I do."

Grace nodded to Marcella.

"Is it okay if we come in?" Marcella asked.

Javier spoke to his grandmother in Spanish and motioned for them to go into the tiny house. The grandmother followed. The house was very neat.

The grandmother motioned for them to take a seat on a brown couch with a makeshift box table in front of it.

"We were hoping to speak to your mom. Do you know when she will return?" Marcella asked.

"She should be back any moment." He smiled at Marcella.

"I want you to meet your father's wife, Grace," Marcella said.

Javier's eyes got big, and he translated for the grandmother.

Grace reached out to shake his hand. "Nice to meet you."

He nodded.

The front door opened, and a thin woman with a long black braid walked in. "Hello, Marcella. So good to see you." She set the groceries on the table.

Javier ran to her side.

She hugged him and told him to go back into the room.

"Good to see you too. Thank you for letting us come by," Marcella said. "Sonya, I want you to meet Grace, Wellington's wife."

They shook hands.

"I'm sorry for your loss," Sonya said.

"Thank you. I'm glad to finally meet you."

Javier was peeking in from the other room.

"Does he know about Wellington?" Grace asked.

"No. I haven't told him yet. I'm waiting for the right time. He is so young and was so close to Wellington. I not sure how it will affect him."

"It was quite a surprise when I found the letter you wrote to Wellington. I didn't know how to approach you, but I knew that it was the right thing to do. Marcella was kind enough to help me connect with you. I know it would be Wellington's desire for me to continue supporting his son. I really want to get to know him."

"Wellington was good to us. Most importantly, he showed my son real purpose for his life and acknowledged his talent. He is going to be so hurt to find out his father passed."

"For sure," Grace said. "Whatever I can do, please let me know. If he wants to return to school, I would welcome that."

"This is all so overwhelming. You are so kind to receive us," Sonya said.

"For now, we will continue to send you the monthly allowances," Marcella said.

"I would be most gracious for your support. I am going through some health issues." Sonya held her stomach and moved slowly on the couch.

"What's the problem?"

"The doctors aren't sure. I'm undergoing some tests, and they said it's something with the blood—some rare disease. I have more tests next week, but they leave me feeling so weak. That's one of the reasons I wrote the letter. Javier was tested and also has the trait."

"Oh no!" Grace said. "I could seek medical help for him too."

"I love my son, and he is my joy. I can't imagine living without him," Sonya said.

"I want to assure you that it is not my goal to take him from you, Sonya. I could make sure he has the best doctors."

"I also believe God is our helper," Sonya said.

"I agree. I feel he led me here to help you, and I hope you will consider letting me do that." Grace smiled.

"I appreciate it. Thank you," Sonya said.

"I'll pray for you and Javier." Grace got up from the couch. "Our plane leaves for New York tonight, but I'll call you in a few days."

"I'm sure it was shocking for you to discover us at a time like this," Sonya said. "Wellington was a lucky man to have you as his wife. I never knew our meeting could turn out so well, but I'm glad it did."

"Me too," Grace said.

Grace and Marcella turned to leave, and Javier came out of the bedroom.

They waved goodbye and shut the door.

When Grace reached the car, she felt relief that a part of Wellington was still alive. It was evident in Javier's face. She knew exactly what she meant when Sonya said that she couldn't let him go. Grace needed a part of Wellington to help her through her grief. Grace couldn't wait to see Javier again.

CHAPTER
69

Javier's Visit

Sonya's health was decreasing quickly, which left little energy to care for Javier. After several months of Grace's requests for a visit, she finally agreed to let him go to New York for a weekend visit. It would give him an opportunity to see the school, keep his dreams alive, and a chance to bond with Grace.

Grace spoke with Javier, and he coughed through the entire conversation. Grace hoped to take him to a doctor for tests to determine the extent of his condition and the treatment needed.

Grace spent the week redecorating the baby's room to amuse Javier with toys, action figures, and art supplies. She headed to the airport two hours before Javier's arrival to avoid traffic. She obtained an escort pass to enter the gated waiting area and watched anxiously as the plane pulled up. The palms of her hands were sweaty, and her heart was beating fast.

What will he call me? Grace wondered. *I think Miss Grace would be appropriate.* She prayed quietly as the passengers exited the plane. "Lord, give me wisdom to guide and love him as much as Wellington."

Javier approached the door with a stewardess, and his warm smile eased Grace's nerves.

"I'm Grace Holmes, and I'm here to pick up Javier." Grace presented her identification. "Hi, Javier." She planted a kiss on his forehead.

His little arms embraced Grace's body, and for the first time since Wellington's death, she felt comforted. "I know you have not been to New York in a long time, but I'm going to show you a wonderful time."

As they walked toward the baggage claim, Javier said, "Can we go see my friends?"

"I'm not sure who your friends are, but we can talk about it and see if we can contact them. Are you hungry?"

"Yes, I can eat." He laughed.

Grace sensed that they were going to be good friends, which released all of her worries. She knew God was looking out for her by placing this child in her life. Having Javier with her was the beginning of Grace's healing process, and she wasn't going to worry about his future. "Do you want to take a selfie?" Grace smiled.

The Studio

Grace dropped the paintbrush in disgust. It just wasn't working. She had no desire to paint. There were too many distractions. And how could she paint and pass it off as Wellington's work. She picked up the telephone and dialed Azul's number.

"Hello? I'm trying to dial out. Who's this?" She kept hitting the button to clear the call.

"Hi, Grace. This is Essetta. Our lines must have crossed."

"What a surprise," Grace said. "I'm so glad you called. I can't do this!"

"Can't do what?"

"There is too much going on. I can't focus long enough to paint. What am I going to do?"

"Calm down!" Monica said. "It's not so deep that we can't figure it out. Let's meet and talk about it. I have a plan."

"I'm glad someone does. Mine isn't working. Are you in town?" Grace asked.

"No, but I'll be there next week for a business meeting. I'll text my information to you in a day or so."

"Is our friend coming with you?" Grace asked.

"No, it's still too early. Stay patient. It'll work out."

"I really need to see him. I'm think I'm losing my mind."

Grace was trying not to think about the many days that Monica was spending alone with Wellington. He didn't remember who he was, which meant he didn't know he had a wife. Who knew how he was feeling in the presence of a beautiful lady like her. Grace reminded herself that the insecurity she felt in the past was just not true. She made it a point to squash the negative thoughts and focus on the present. The long and short of it was Grace knew Monica had their best interests at heart and could trust Wellington in her care.

"You've got be patient, Grace. Know that I'm not keeping him from you on purpose. He's still recovering, and the healing process requires that his memory be restored before we introduce anything that could trigger a setback. There are times when there are no quick answers, but we have been making significant progress. I asked God to give you the strength to hold on. I'll text you our meeting place and time. It will be a different location."

"Okay. I'll do my best to hold on," Grace said.

"See you soon."

A Clandestine Meeting

Grace waited patiently at the back table in Chino's restaurant for Monica to arrive. The glass door opened, and a humpbacked middle-aged woman walked in. She was wearing weathered clothing, and streaks of gray lined her matted hair. She approached the table and took a seat.

Grace laughed. "I think you missed your calling."

"What do you mean?" Monica's smile put a crack in her makeup.

"You should have been an actress or a makeup artist."

"Really? Never thought about that. I'm on a mission, and it does feel like I'm in a movie. How have you been, my friend? I would hug you, but I don't want to look obvious."

"I came across some information that may help in Wellington's memory recovery," Grace said.

A waitress took their order, and they waited until she was out of earshot before finishing the conversation.

"There is a new development that could help Wellington. I was going through Wellington's things in his office, and I found an important letter he wrote me." She told Monica about Javier and Sonya.

Monica touched Grace's shoulder. "That is shocking. Life really throws some ugly curves, doesn't it?"

"Yes. This one is enormous. I didn't know he was keeping this secret."

"There are always surprises in relationships. That's life!" Monica explained.

"Javier is the spitting image of Wellington."

"Is that right?"

"Yes. Sonya and Javier both have a rare disease. They got it while visiting her sister in California and swimming in the Pacific Ocean. When they returned home, they started feeling sick. The doctor confirmed gastrointestinal illness, and their immune systems were compromised. Nothing seemed to kill off the microorganisms— not even antibiotics. The outbreak developed in the South Pacific, spreading from untreated medical sewage in the hospitals. Many people have died. Sonya has lost a lot of weight and is scared."

"That's the type of research I'm doing," Monica said. "I can check into it for you if you like."

"Would you please? That would be a blessing for both of us."

"You know how I feel about you and Wellington. Besides, medicine is not only my profession—it's my passion."

"I know, but you are already doing so much for us."

"It's what I find pleasure in doing, dear." She smiled.

"I would like to try to help in Wellington's recovery if I can." Grace pulled a picture of Javier from her purse and handed it to Monica. "Maybe if you show Wellington a picture of Javier, it'll jog his memory. What do you think?"

"He is gorgeous," Monica said. "It is worth a try. Do you have a picture of you?"

"Yes."

"I believe the one with you will suffice for now. Wellington is showing daily signs of healing and rejuvenation. Just last week, he painted a small canvas, which I brought along to show you. I think you are going to be amazed." Monica pulled a package from her bag and handed it to Grace.

"Oh, my God. I don't believe it. He hates abstracts, and now he is painting them? These aren't colors he uses at all. Bright blues, greens, and red? He never liked them. He loved darker colors."

"He doesn't know that. He is just having fun," Monica said. "Since I picked up the art supplies, he paints around the clock. It is critical for his healing."

"This is absolutely breathtaking."

"I have an additional thought, too," Monica said. "Why not take this abstract and present it to Azul as one of the paintings he asked you to do. You see that Wellington signed it. It looks a little different, but Azul would not expect your signature to be exact."

Grace laughed. "I can see where you are going with this."

"Yep, entrap him in his own scheme, and that will get you off the hook as well. After all, the original has not been sold or signed, right?"

"Correct. Girl, now you are thinking. This is good! Like I said, you missed your calling," Grace laughed.

"I know. Wellington is recovering fast, and it's just a matter of time before he begins putting the pieces of his life together. We will have to construct a good plan and execute it before his memory returns completely."

"Now I know for sure you are in the wrong profession. You would make an excellent detective. I'm so glad you came. I need this breakthrough, and I need to laugh. I want to clear Wellington's name, get on the right page with the gallery, and continue to build his legacy. The bottom line is to make Azul pay for stripping our community of good artists. Did I tell you that I'm working with my masseuse to extract information out of Azul?"

"No."

"Ellona does wonders with her hands and is a charm with men—but it's a very dangerous game we are playing."

"It could grow into a toxic relationship—so be careful."

"There's more. On the back of the letter was a telephone number for Detective Ramos."

"Detective Ramos? He was the officer who investigated Daniel's death. Have you tried to reach out to him?"

"No. I don't know to explain everything to him, especially the painting."

"You've got a point there, but you didn't sign the painting."

"I know, but the evidence could still point to me. Azul has a cool exterior, but he's conniving and would spin the situation to divert attention from himself."

"We need to involve Detective Ramos if we want to bring about justice," Monica said. "For now, let's think about our approach. I say we go with getting the painting to Azul. That way, we can show intent to redeem you. I see you and Ellona have also been busy testing your own detective skills." Monica smiled. "I feel there is good teamwork happening. All these developments, if executed sensibly, can work on our behalf. I'm headed back to Switzerland tomorrow and will stay in touch." She winked.

"Be careful, angel. You hear?" Grace said.

"More importantly, watch your back!" Monica said.

Detective Ramos took note as Grace walked to her car and sped off.

The Phone Call

Grace dialed Azul's number, and it went to voice mail. "This is Azul. Leave a number, and I'll get back with you shortly."

"Azul, this is Grace. Call me. I have a package for you."

Azul smiled as he listened to the message. "That's it, baby. Come to Daddy."

Ellona turned over and touched Azul's chest. "Did you say something, honey," she asked with a fake groggy voice.

"No, you are just dreaming, dear. Go back to sleep." He kissed her forehead.

Ellona turned over and smiled. She had heard Azul's response and tried to put his lovemaking out of her mind and concentrate on the task at hand. It was not going to be as easy as she thought. She had to make sure her attraction to him did not obstruct her vision and complicate the mission.

The Painting

Azul held the painting up to the light. "Damn, girl, you rocked this one. I like the colors. I may keep this one for myself."

"I have another one too," Grace said.

"Whew, we are in business." He laughed and reached over to kiss her.

She held up her hand and backed away. "Don't. We are not partners—so hold your excitement. I'm in this just to fulfill the quota, and then I'm out."

"You are one fine lady when you get mad." He smiled and touched her chin.

"Who are you selling these to?" she asked.

"That's my business. You just concentrate on painting," he said.

Grace knew she had to be cool. "That's okay. I don't need to know," Grace said.

"When do you think you'll have more paintings?"

"I can't say. It has been an emotional roller coaster since Wellington's death, and it's very hard to focus. Hopefully in three weeks," Grace said as she walked him to the door. "I'll call you."

"Don't make it too long," he added, tucking both paintings under his arm. "By the way, that little friend of yours from the spa? Thanks for introducing me. I haven't had this much fun in a long time." He grinned.

"I'm glad I could add some excitement to your life," Grace said.

"Yes, Ellona is making sure of that," he added. "I think I found someone who could be around for a long time."

Not if my life depends on it, Grace thought.

Ellona's Disclosure

"**G**irl, I was at Azul's house the other night when you called," Ellona said. "I stayed still as a possum, and he didn't know I was awake."

"You heard me?" Grace asked.

"Yes. He let the call go to the machine."

"Please tell me you are not sleeping with the enemy," Grace said.

"No, he's sleeping with me," she said with a smile. "It's a part of my investigation. You gave me leverage to work—so let me do it."

"Girl, you are playing in the lion's den with a dastardly criminal, and I'm not so crazy about that."

"Grace, you are always so serious. Lighten up. You need to relax and have some fun."

"How am I supposed to have fun or relax with all the madness that is going on? Oh, never mind. You wouldn't understand. How can I trust you to be on my side if your emotions are getting in the way?"

"I know. It's just my flesh that is weak. I'm going to get this under control because it doesn't make me feel good to be attracted to him—but he is amazing." Ellona smiled.

"I thought you were going to be careful," Grace said.

"I am trying, but one thing led to another. You know how that goes."

"Well, you need your mind, your body, and your heart to line up with what we want to accomplish. Azul is a seedy monster and can hurt you when he is through with you. Just like the devil, he'll throw you away."

"I don't plan on that happening," Ellona said. "When you called, it was like he was drawing you in. His expression was creepy and evil."

Chills went up Grace's spine. "I'm counting on you to keep it together, Ellona."

"My bad! I know you are right. My heart is in the right place, but the enemy wants to keep me tied to things in the past. I'm making up my mind to press forward, and I promise I'll keep my mind on the mission."

"There you go! Next time you get tempted, just remember what's on the line. This is serious, and I don't want you to get hurt." Grace hugged Ellona. "Remember what I told you about Detective Ramos. I know he is watching you too."

"Oh God! I forgot," Ellona said.

"That's why I'm mentioning it again. He may be watching all of us."

"He probably thinks I'm in cahoots with Azul," Ellona said.

"Exactly. You don't need to start imagining or freaking out about it though. I haven't called him yet. I'm asking you to be careful. That's all."

Maybe we should call him and cover our asses," Ellona said.

"We have to be smart and wait for the right time to call. We'll take it one day at a time."

"Who is we? You make it sound like you got some extra help."

"We do—the Lord. Just trust me on this okay? Better yet, let's trust God!"

Ellona's Plan

*E*llona gracefully walked down the spiral staircase, took out two champagne flutes, and filled them with Dom Perignon. After slipping a capsule in one, she walked back upstairs. She touched her heart, took a deep breath, and headed to the lavish bedroom.

Her sexy red lingerie from Victoria's Secret commanded his attention. She handed Azul the glass in a sensual manner and kissed his lips. "This is a toast to the future."

After they took a drink, he placed his glass on the nightstand and rolled over on her.

She laughed as champagne spilled on the covers.

They kissed and rolled over a few more times.

Within moments, he was out like a light. She pushed him aside, slipped on her robe, and cleaned up the glasses. It would be a few hours before he would be awake, and she had to work fast.

She headed down to his impeccably neat office, opened the french doors, and turned on the desk lamp. She opened the desk drawer and started looking for clues. Fumbling through papers, she found nothing. She straightened the papers and closed the drawer. She went over to the file cabinets, but they were locked.

She looked at the bookshelf. She pulled books out and opened them, looking for loose papers. Still nothing. Trying to think outside the box, she looked at the desk again. She noticed that the light on the answering machine was flashing and picked up the receiver.

"You have two calls waiting. First call: "Hey man, this is your boy Stoney. Where are you? I'm waiting for your call. You said you would meet me at the Grove at ten o'clock. You know we have a hard deadline to deliver those items to Spain. Don't let me down, man. Get back with me in a short. Call me." Second call: Azul, this is Francine. Hey, darling, I miss you. I handled that small matter for you in San Francisco. I can't wait to see you this weekend."

Ellona gasped. *Oh my God! Stoney is delivering the paintings? Francine? Hmmm. I didn't know he is seeing somebody else. Silly of me to think I'm the only one attracted to this fine specimen.*

She saw Azul's phone book on his desk and found Francine Booker in San Francisco. Anger tried to rise up in her, but she had to let that go and concentrate on the task at hand.

An idea flashed in her mind, and she decided to get creative. She looked for a book that was out of place. One stood out like a sore finger, and she pulled it out. In the middle, there were photographs, a timeline for projects, and several articles on the artists who died. There were pictures of Wellington's paintings and an article related to the crash.

She froze. There also was a picture of Grace at the graveside. Azul was talking to someone in the background. *This is getting scary.* She shut the book and placed it back on the shelf in the same position.

She had to find a way to copy some of this information without Azul finding out. Maybe she could sneak back into his house while he was away with Francine. She didn't have a key and was not sure how to make that happen.

She hurried back upstairs, jumped in the bed, tossed her hair, and waited until he woke up two hours later.

"What kind of magic did you put on me, young lady?" He rolled over on top of her and smiled.

"The real question is what you did to me." She rubbed his chest. "You put me out like a light."

"Then I accomplished what I set out to do."

They both smiled.

"We could do this again this weekend if you like," she said.

"I'm going out of town on Saturday for business." He jumped out of bed.

"Where are you going?" she asked.

"To San Francisco. My boys have new projects to discuss."

"Oh, I see. You and the boys again? What day are you coming back? Maybe I can cook a nice dinner for you."

He finished dressing and kissed her. "Let's talk about it tomorrow."

Ellona didn't push him any further.

Caught in the Act

On Saturday morning, Ellona knocked on Azul's front door, knowing that only the maid was there. "Hello, Miss Ellona," Gabby said with a smile.

"Is Azul here?" Ellona asked.

"No, ma'am. He left this morning for San Francisco."

"Oh, I was trying to catch him before he left." Ellona smiled. "I seem to have misplaced my earring the other night. Do you think I could come in and look for it? I will be very quick."

"Mr. Azul told me not let anyone in when he's not here."

"Yes, I understand. I promise I will hurry. I just need to look around. Once I find it, I'll leave."

"I don't believe it would hurt," Gabby said. "Okay—but please don't mention this to him, ma'am. He will be very angry with me."

Ellona entered the house and made her way upstairs. As soon as Gabby disappeared into the kitchen, she rushed back down to Azul's office. She took some pictures of his playbook and was on her way upstairs when the front door opened. Her mouth dropped, and her legs buckled. There was no time to hide.

"What are you doing here?" Azul said.

"I ... I just came by to find my lost earring."

"How did you get in?" he asked.

"Gabby let me in."

"I told her never to let anyone in when I'm not here. Where is she?"

"She's in the kitchen. It's my fault, Azul. I convinced her I wouldn't take long. Please don't take it out on her."

"What's in your hand?" he asked.

Ellona stepped back.

Azul came forward and raised his hand as if he were going to hit her.

Ellona ducked.

"I wasn't going to hit you—at least not yet. You keep up with these tricks, and I'll kick your ass. Nobody, do you hear me, nobody enters my house without my permission!"

"I didn't know you had another girlfriend. You could have told me about Francine."

"How do you know about Francine? If there is one thing I can't stand, it's some bitch trying to get in my business."

"You don't have to call me names! Maybe I was fooled by the special attention you were showing me—as if I was the only one. You did make me feel like—"

He snatched her arm, and Ellona pulled away.

"You don't own me, boy. Watch how you handle me."

"I'm sorry," he said. "I didn't mean for it to turn this way." He pulled her closer. "It's just that I was surprised to see you. I'm very private and don't like anyone snooping around my house. You can understand that, right?"

"Yes. I'm sorry. I guess I just got a little jealous. I thought you said you were going to San Francisco today? When I came into the house, the answering machine went off, and I overheard Francine's voice. That's why I was in your office."

"I *am* going to San Francisco, and that's still no business of yours," he said. "My plans changed, and I'm not leaving until later. That still doesn't give you the right to spy around my house."

Gabby entered the room, and her eyes almost bolted out of their sockets. "Oh, Mr. Azul, I thought you were gone. Ellona wanted to find her earring, so I let her in."

"You know my rules, Gabby."

"Sorry, Mr. A. I won't let it happen again. I promise."

"You know I don't play like that. Now go and get us some drinks!"

"Yes, sir. Right away."

Ellona checked her purse for the camera.

Azul approached her and started kissing her neck.

She chuckled and said, "I don't think you are going to have enough time for *that*."

"I know, but it sure makes me feel good." He smiled.

Gabby returned with the drinks, and they talked for half an hour before he had to leave.

Ellona couldn't wait to get out of the house. She desperately needed to move on to the next phase. Things were getting too tight for comfort.

As Ellona pulled away from Azul's house, Ramos made a quick note on his pad.

Ty's Request

Grace dashed to pick up the telephone, hoping it was Monica. She had promised to fill her in on the meeting with Detective Ramos.

"Hi, Grace. This is Ty Hamilton."

"Hey, Ty."

"You sound disappointed."

"Sorry. I was expecting a call from somebody else. It's good to hear from you."

"I have been trying to reach you for some time now. I hope you received my flowers."

"Yes, thank you so much. They were so beautiful."

"How are you doing?" he asked.

"I believe I'm over the rough part. There are still challenging days."

"I can only imagine. The Johanssons told me you put the sale of the painting on hold. I'm still very interested in buying it though."

"Yes. I thought it was best to put everything on the back burner for now. I'm sure we can talk about you purchasing it at some point."

"Whatever is best for you right now. I have to admit that I also have a selfish reason for calling."

"You do? What is it?" Grace asked.

"I actually bought a few of Daniel Wolf's paintings some years ago, and I would like to get in touch with his wife."

"Really?" Grace said. "I don't usually make a habit of giving out telephone numbers without getting the person's approval."

"I met her at the Johanssons Gallery and I can't seem to get her off my mind. Would you mind doing me that favor?"

"She must have really left an impression."

"She was snippy with me, but I liked her fire," he said.

"I can't promise you anything, but I'll see what I can do."

"Is there anything else I can do for you right now? Just name it."

"No, I'm fine. I finally got enough strength and motivation to pick up the pieces where Wellington left off with his academy."

"I didn't know he had a school," Ty said.

"Yes, the Wellington Art Academy in Brooklyn is for students ages six through eighteen. He had plans to move into a new building, but the funding is at a standstill."

"Well, maybe I can help with that," Ty said.

"I couldn't ask you to do that. You barely know me."

"I know, but I want to help. My family is big into philanthropy. We support and help build communities. The arts are right up our alley."

"I'm in the infancy stages right now, but we are looking for donors. It would be beyond my wildest dreams to have your support."

"Dreams are good. Without them, we have little to live for."

"Yes, I seem to have a lot of them. Some are good, and some are not so good."

Ty said, "When you get a chance, will you let me know Monica's response?"

"Sure. Thanks again for calling and for the offer to support the academy. I'll get back with you as soon as I speak with her," Grace said.

He laughed and said, "I'll be waiting with bated breath."

A Trusty Source

Dr. Wolf was befuddled and questioned the timing of making a call to Detective Ramos. The sickly odor of death and senseless murder of her husband five years ago was still fresh in her mind. She nearly passed out at the thought. It was a hollow reminder of the loss of companionship and the hate that gripped her heart every time the memory resurfaced. The thought also gave credence and motivation to her desire to keep Wellington alive so that he could live to be a thriving artist. Azul had successfully cut Daniel's career short, and now that the opportunity for justice had presented itself, she wasn't going to let it slip away.

Detective Ramos's phone rung multiple times before he picked up.

"Hello?"

Dr. Wolf froze, forgetting for a moment what she wanted to say. "Hello. Is this Detective Ramos?"

"Yes, it is. Who's calling?"

"I'd rather not disclose that over the telephone. I would prefer to meet with you in private."

"For what reason?" he asked.

"I'm calling about Wellington Holmes's accident. I have some information that could be beneficial to you."

"So why don't you go directly to the police?" he asked.

"From what I understand, you are investigating Azul, his agent. I was given your name as someone I could trust," she said.

"Help me understand. Are we talking about two different things?" he asked.

"I'm talking about information I have about Wellington Holmes and Azul."

"Okay. What kind of information do you have?"

"Information that the police don't have," she said.

"And you do?"

"Yes, I most certainly do."

"Why should I trust you?"

"You don't have to. It's totally up to you—but it could help your case."

"Do you know where Sam's Bar is on Forty-Sixth Street?" he asked.

"I can find it," she replied.

"Meet me on Friday at five o'clock?"

Dr. Wolf panicked. "No! That is not a good day or a good place to meet. How about City Winery in Soho on Saturday at three?"

Detective Ramos agreed and said he would sit in the back booth.

Dr. Wolf got out of her car and dropped the burner phone in the garbage can. With so much at stake, she couldn't risk anyone tracking her calls. She took a new telephone out of her purse and made airline reservations to go to New York.

Back in Europe

Monica stepped into the workspace she had designed for Wellington and watched as he stepped back from his canvas with a big smile. As he put the final touches on his new abstract, she knew there was something special about his painting.

From the moment she showed him pictures of his family, his disposition had changed dramatically. Bits and pieces of his memory were returning rapidly. He expressed a new motivation for living and regularly asked when he would see his wife and son. He did not show any emotion when she told him about his life as an accomplished artist or about his wife. She even bought up Azul's name to see if it would trigger a response. Without telling him everything, she also explained why she was protecting him and concealing him.

"Wow, that is absolutely phenomenal," Dr. Wolf said.

"I feel a special tingling inside, and it feels familiar," he said. "It's a feeling of accomplishment. That's why I named this piece *Amnesty*. I feel free."

"I'm going to New York next week," Dr. Wolf said. "Would you like to go see Grace?"

He turned with a distressed look on his face. "I would love to go. I feel a little nervous, but I'll never know unless I take that step."

"Great," Dr. Wolf said. "I have friends who can help arrange for your passport under an assumed name. They will also arrange for us to fly through a special carrier and avoid unwanted attention. This trip will be secure for you."

"I would love to give this painting to Grace as a gift," Wellington said. "Dr. Patel suggested the title, and that's what prompted me to create it."

"I love it. Now all you need to do is sign it and put the title on it." Monica envisioned Wellington giving the painting to Grace as a gift. Grace would give the artwork to Azul in the final delivery. Because it contained Wellington's original signature, it was a solution to Grace's predicament.

Dr. Wolf was nervous about Azul getting his hand on this masterpiece. *God, I thank you for protecting this work. The enemy will not triumph over us in this ordeal.*

Keeping Hope Alive

Monica dialed Grace's number. "Hi, Grace. How are you feeling?"

"Every time I hear your voice, it's a welcome fresh breath of air that brightens my day," Grace said.

"You'll be glad to hear that Wellington is making big strides. In fact, to our amazement, showing him your pictures and sharing some of his background increased his expectation of things returning to normal. It gave him hope. He recently painted an amazing abstract."

"What? Are you kidding?"

"No, I'm not. It is breathtaking."

"We are coming to New York in two weeks. He wants to see you and give you the painting. Please don't tell him I said this. He wants to surprise you."

"Wellington is coming too?"

"Since he's a little nervous about seeing you, I don't want to extend the visit for too long. I'm going to give you and Wellington a few moments alone, but you know I've got your back for that intimate date in the future."

They both laughed.

"I have an idea about the painting, but we'll discuss that later. I also plan to meet with Detective Ramos."

Grace giggled. "I'm probably more nervous than he is. While I have you on the phone, I wanted to talk to you about something else. Tyler Hamilton called me the other day. He wants to talk with you."

"I don't know. Since losing Daniel, I've been guarded. Okay, so now you are a matchmaker?" She laughed.

"Don't be silly. I'm just saying stay open. He's a nice guy and not bad-looking either."

"Okay, I'll give it some thought, but I can't promise you anything," Monica said.

"I don't need a promise. Just give yourself a chance to enjoy your life, my friend."

"You are right." Monica sighed. "I'll take that thought into consideration."

"So, it's okay to give him your number?" Grace asked.

"I have his card. Let me call him. That way, it can't be tracked," Monica said.

"I'll call you soon to give you our arrival date," Monica said.

"I can't wait to see Wellington," Grace said. "Don't forget what I said about enjoying your life."

"I will," Monica said before disposing of her burner phone.

CHAPTER
81

Reunited in New York

The palms of Grace's hands were sweaty, and perspiration dripped from her forehead. Grace was unsure how seeing Wellington again was going to affect her. It was almost seven months since that ugly day they argued. They met at Greco's on Fifty-Seventh Street. The moment they entered the door, Grace thought her heart was going to fall out.

Wellington's black hat covered his face. He was much thinner, and his tanned skin against the black clothing made him look like a *GQ* model.

A full grin broke out on Grace's face as the love of her life strutted toward her.

He greeted her with outstretched arms and planted his warm lips on hers. The soothing smile on his face said it all. Love was fresh in the air and in Grace's heart. Tears flowed uncontrollably. Grace couldn't believe that God loved them so much and had reconnected them. They stared at each other without exchanging words.

Monica left them alone, and Grace said, "Seeing you inflates my heart. You look great!"

"It's so good to see you again." He squeezed her hand. "The picture you sent gives no credit to your beauty. I can't remember what I did to deserve you." He smiled.

"We have so much to talk about. I don't know where to begin," Grace said. "I'm so sorry for all you went through. I know you had a rough time with the many surgeries, but I'm thankful to God you are alive."

He put his finger to her lips. "That's all in the past and overshadows all the issues we face right now. Monica has filled me in on a few issues you are struggling with. You have been through hell and back. Thank you for keeping the vision alive."

"It's only with God's grace and help that I'm able to press forward," Grace said. "Thank God for that."

"Thank you for contacting Javier. I know that was not easy for you. I'm so sorry you had to find out that way. It was in my heart to tell you, and I didn't want to hurt you."

"I understand. It's behind us now."

"Monica told me we both grew closer to God—so that's a good thing," Wellington said.

"Yes," Grace said. "I think we should go slowly, enjoy this short time together, and not get ahead of ourselves."

"Monica mentioned that to me too. I understand there is still danger with anyone knowing I'm alive. I don't understand it all, but I'm learning about my life." He pulled a mailing tube from behind his back. "This is for you."

"What is it?" Grace asked.

"A surprise. Something I painted for you."

Grace grinned widely as she opened it. "Is this your new work?"

"Yep. It's entitled *Amnesty*. I want you to have it."

"Wow, I'm so impressed."

Monica came back to the table and said, "Besides having an opportunity to see Wellington, we thought this would be the highlight of his return. This painting contains his signature." She winked.

"Monica, slow down."

"This is a masterpiece, don't you think?" Monica asked.

"Yes, definitely," Grace said.

Monica said, "It would be nice to add it to the spring show with the other paintings Azul is providing, don't you think?"

"I'm overwhelmed and so grateful." Grace kissed Wellington's cheek.

"Grace, can I talk to you for a moment," Monica asked. "This painting is the answer to our prayers. It has Wellington's signature, which means you can give it to Azul as one of the paintings he's waiting to receive from you. I asked Ramos to meet me, but I didn't give away my identity. We are all on the same page when it comes to getting Azul off the streets. This may be our best shot."

Grace laughed. "Girl, you have my head spinning."

"I'll call you after our meeting and let you know what he says."

"Are you sure it's time to do this?" Grace asked.

"I thought about it and prayed on it. Too much is riding on Wellington's recovery and getting his life back to normal. We can't hide him forever. It's better to be forthright with what we have. The timing is now, and we must not be afraid."

"I just want to make sure it's handled with care—and make sure nobody gets hurt."

"I understand," Monica said. "When we return to Switzerland, Wellington will go to a safer location where there is ample protection. I will bring him to see you again soon."

Wellington said, "Honey, I wish I could stay here with you, but I have to return to Switzerland."

"I'm sure we will figure out a way to talk and see each other again soon," Grace said.

"Now that I have you in my grasp, I don't want to be without you. I love you, sweetie." He kissed Grace's full lips.

"Javier is doing well. He looks so much like you. He doesn't know you are alive," Grace said. "It's best that he doesn't know because it's too dangerous."

"Be careful, you hear?" he whispered as he left.

Grace brought her hands up to her nose to enjoy the lingering smell of his cologne. The thought of his arms wrapped around hers made her perspire.

Meeting with Detective Ramos

Dr. Wolf rehearsed her lines while waiting for Detective Ramos at City Winery.

"Are you waiting for someone, miss?" he asked.

"Depends on who's asking," Dr. Wolf replied.

He stretched out his hand and held out his card.

"I'm your lady," Dr. Wolf answered.

"May I?" he asked, pointing to the chair.

"Yes, please sit down."

"You look quite familiar, but I can't place your face," he said.

"I have one of those faces," she replied.

"So, what's this all about?"

"The best way to tell you is to get straight to the point. But first I have to be assured that I can confide in you."

"That's a little strange for you to ask of a detective."

"I know, but my news is life-changing and will affect the safety of a few people, so confidentiality is critical."

"Do you want me to sign an agreement or something?" he asked.

"Yes, that would be great too, but it's not necessary," she replied. "It's about Wellington Holmes, Azul's client. I uncovered some information about the plane crash and his death."

"I believe that case is closed," Detective Ramos said.

"It may be closed, but it's not solved. Wellington was a good friend of mine, and I'm doing everything to protect his name."

"What do you mean by that?" he asked.

"When I heard the news of the crash, I went to the scene of the accident."

"You did? Do you live in Switzerland?"

"I was there. I found a letter that Azul wrote to Wellington."

"What did the letter say?" he asked.

"Not so quick, Detective. I have to know I have your word of trust and confidentiality."

"You have my word."

"Are you wearing a wire?" Dr. Wolf asked.

"Are you?" he asked.

"No, but I thought about it. Wellington's wife might be in danger. I have to protect her and Wellington."

"What do you mean?" he asked.

"This is not easy to explain. Wellington is alive."

"Wait a minute. You know he is alive and have not reported it to the authorities?"

"Keep your voice down—or the entire city will know."

He straightened his back. "You could be in big trouble for withholding this information."

"I know, but I can't tell anybody yet. That's why I needed to meet with you," she said. "My mind flashed back to the scene of my husband's death and that's when I suspected foul play by Azul."

"Are you Dr. Monica Wolf?"

"Yes, I am. I couldn't introduce myself until I explained this whole predicament. I only recently told Grace that Wellington is alive. You have to help us! I'm desperate to stop this attack on innocent artists. With all my heart, I believe Azul murdered my husband and others."

"Wow. Azul is involved in something that is driving this entire issue."

"What are you talking about?" Dr. Wolf asked.

"Art smuggling. He and a syndicate of white-collar art smugglers have been under surveillance for years. We have been unable to tie him to any of the cases. He has such great connections with the Mafia and other underworld types. These people are rich, powerful, and dangerous."

"The one thing they have in common is that they are greedy and evil," Dr. Wolf said.

"You've got that right."

Monica said, "Wellington was suffering from dissociative amnesia as well as brain injury trauma amnesia. Discovering that he was the only survivor was very traumatic. His treatment included therapy—both physical and mental—but prayer was our truest source of strength.

"With dissociative amnesia, the memories are deeply buried within the mind and cannot be recalled. However, the memories might resurface on their own or after being triggered by something in the person's surroundings. The experience of committing his paintbrush to canvas was a return to the basics. His art was key to his breakthrough. We used it to bring back his recall of his present life, which opened a window of unlimited possibilities to recovery. It's a miracle that he is painting again and better than ever. Grace told me about your calls to Wellington, but she has not mentioned it to anyone else. That's why I didn't reveal it to you until now."

"I understand, but that still doesn't make it right or lawful."

"You are correct in saying that. I took it into my own hands, and I'll take full responsibility, especially if it will result in putting Azul behind bars. Did Wellington ever call you?"

"I spoke to him only once, and our call was brief."

"Grace said the messages sounded urgent.

"Well, now you know," he said.

"We need your help in putting an end to all of this madness."

"Looks like you have been doing all the heavy lifting, and I appreciate it. Have you ever thought about being a detective?"

"Yes, I always wanted to be one, but my dad wouldn't hear of it. He drilled me in math and science, and he wanted me to follow in his footsteps as a doctor. End of story!"

He laughed. "Well, it's not too late to consider a second career."

"We've got to solve this matter first," she said. "Then I might give it some consideration. My day job pays very well." She smiled and explained their plan to present Wellington's painting to Azul.

"You hit me with a whammy. This is getting twisted, but I think it is good idea. It could help with the entrapment allegations. I could also write up a release that she could have Azul sign, which will help get her off the hook. I have been following Azul, and I have seen him with Grace a few times. I've seen him with Grace's friend from Spa 52."

"Yes, she is involved in the plan. She's cool," Dr. Wolf said.

"Now that you've given me this information, I'll keep a closer eye on these connections. Continue to stay low key—and do not discuss this with anybody else."

"I've kept it this long, haven't I?" she said.

"Yes, you did well. Where is Wellington now?"

"I have him in a safe place. He is ready to testify if need be."

"Perfect. Contact me once Grace delivers the painting, and we'll go from there. I'm hot on Azul's tail right now on a smuggling ring in Spain and close to catching him. This may be the link to bring him down."

"We pray that it will," Dr. Wolf said.

CHAPTER

83

A Turn of Events

M onica called to brief Grace on her meeting with Detective Ramos. He agreed that Grace should deliver *Amnesty* to Azul. Monica told Grace that it was time to turn the tables on Azul and force him to sign a document that would release her from producing additional paintings. She also informed her that Detective Ramos would meet with Grace before she met with Azul, so she could be wiretapped and provide a release for him to sign, which would serve as evidence. In addition, Monica informed Grace that she would be returning to New York in a few weeks with Wellington, and she promised they could spend the day together—alone. To Grace's surprise, Monica finally called Ty and agreed to see him. He would be in New York that same weekend.

Grace called Azul and asked him to meet her in the office on Thursday.

Detective Ramos called Grace the day before Azul's meeting to talk about everything Monica had explained to him. Detective Ramos arrived at Grace's office at ten to wire her, and he provided the release document for Azul to sign, along with instructions. As noon approached, Grace checked the wiring on the back of her black lace bra and made sure the painting was turned backward against the wall.

Azul arrived at noon in a brown Armani suit and brown suede shoes.

Marcella escorted Azul into Grace's office.

"When I sent the painting, it was not signed," Grace said.

"Yes, I know. But you gave it to them under the pretense that it was Wellington's."

"I merely sent them a painting to use for their fund-raiser. I also told them to put all transactions related to the painting on hold until further notice."

"Yes, I heard, and I'm not happy about that because it interrupts my business regarding selling further paintings."

"Well, the good news is that Ty Hamilton purchased *Angel in Disguise* and is interested in more of Wellington's work."

"Yes, what of it?" he said.

"I painted an abstract you asked of me that can be presented as one of Wellington's creations. I hate to say so myself, but it's a masterpiece that your buyers are going to love. It will surely command big bucks and can also be included in the fund-raiser."

"But we have *Angel in Disguise* for the fund-raiser," Azul said.

"This one is much more refined!" Grace said.

"Well, where is it? I want to be the one to approve it—not you."

"Not so fast," Grace said. "I need to clarify some things first, and perhaps this would be a good time for us to negotiate."

"I didn't come here to negotiate anything with you," he said. "We both know you are perpetrating your art as Wellington's."

"Excuse me! My case is nowhere near your tricks and illegal art dealings."

"You know nothing, young lady."

"Well, I have something in my hand that proves I know more than you think." Grace laughed. "I found letters that indicate you are under investigation for smuggling art." She waved a letter. "I don't know why Wellington never shared it with me, but it doesn't matter now. It's out in the open. Besides you can't trap me in anything because I never signed the painting." Grace laughed harder.

"Yeah, you never signed it, but your actions will set you up."

"No, sir. You are trying to set me up by asking me to paint pictures and pass them off as Wellington's," Grace said.

"You can call it a setup if you like, but you owe me."

"I don't owe you anything, but I am willing to present this last painting to you with the promise that this is the end of it. It can all be consummated on one condition."

"What condition?" he asked.

"That you sign this release." Grace handed him the sheet of paper.

"This is bullshit. I'm not agreeing to any of this." He slid the paper across the desk.

"You need to lower your voice. Everything we do moving forward hinges on you signing this piece of paper."

"You wanted to meet with me just for this? I can't believe it. Are you trying to say you can't trust me?" he asked.

"Exactly! Now sign." Grace pushed the paper back to him, walked toward the *Amnesty,* and turned it around.

Azul's mouth dropped open.

"Let me make this clear. This is your final delivery!"

Azul walked over to the painting. "You did this? Girl, it looks like you have talent after all. The buyers are going to go crazy over this. You outdid yourself this time."

"Did you hear what I said? This is your final delivery. I want out!"

"Girl, it looks like we are just getting started. Why would you want to quit now?"

"Because what you are doing is illegal. You are selling this way above value, and then you have your boys steal it back from the owner, then you sell it to millionaires in Japan for twice that amount. You want me to be part of that illegal ring? No way!"

"Girl, you are talking out of the side of your head. You don't know a thing about the art business."

"I know right from wrong."

"Did you consider right from wrong when you sent that painting?" He laughed.

"Yes, and I'm on the path to straighten that situation out."

"So, when can I take this pretty little piece with me?" Azul asked.

"I was going to let you have it today, but I'm not sure I can trust you. I need your agreement that this is the very last painting—and that you will stop framing me. And I'm not your dear."

"Calm down, little lady. You don't have to be angry. I'll sign your little piece of paper, but we both know even after this baby sells, you will still owe me."

Grace thought about slugging him with her fist. "Sign here," Grace said.

He signed the release, and Grace reluctantly handed over the painting.

"I want you to tell your clients that this is Wellington's best painting to date," Grace said.

"So, you agree to play along, I see?" He smiled.

"Yep, to the very end." She smiled back, knowing Detective Ramos had recorded the entire conversation.

CHAPTER

84

Payback

Detective Ramos followed Azul to Azul's warehouse where he stored paintings and laid out his dirty illegal deeds.

Azul said, "Hey, buddy. Long time, no see. You wouldn't be following me, would you?"

Detective Ramos said, "That's what I do. You lead, and I follow. You should be used to this routine."

"Old Ramos—ever the steady one. That why we used to call you Ramos the Rock?"

"Well, we do have a history Azul. I see yours hasn't changed. Still crooked as ever."

"Now, now. Everybody can't shoot straight from the hip like you, can they? Some are predators, and some are prey. Such is nature." Azul laughed.

"You could be right. Like wolves and deer, lions and antelope. Hey, what did I just say? What was the guy's name in the lion's den? Oh yes. Daniel wasn't it? And what about those wolves? Is this an epiphany—a straight-out revelation from God."

"What the hell are you talking about?" Azul replied.

"Daniel Wolf. Does that name mean anything to you? Does it ring a bell?" Ramos said.

"I paid you a compliment by saying you shoot from the hip, and now you're saying what you'd like to say. I've been questioned before about the untimely death of my friend Daniel."

"Friend? Do you even know what the word *friend* means?"

"Now you're pissing me off, Ramos. You're a big man with that gun and badge. What if it suddenly disappeared—and you had to stand there alone. Just you and me. You know you want to."

"I thought you'd never ask." Ramos unbuckled his holster and set his badge on top of his gun.

All hell broke loose—flying furniture, blood slinging, eye gouging, and ungodly groans. The two men were kicking the hell out of each other.

When the smoke cleared, Detective Ramos slowly buckled his hip holster on and attached his badge while Azul struggled to pull himself up from the cold cement floor.

Ramos left the warehouse, slightly limping and exhausted, but he was pleased to have opened a can of whoop ass after all those years.

85

Return to New York

$\mathcal{M}$onica dropped Wellington off at the Marriott to spend the day with Grace and then proceeded to Ty's flat on Eighty-Fourth Street.

Ty said, "I know I was a little pushy the last time I saw you, so I was shocked that you accepted my invitation." He smiled.

"Wow, what a great place you have," she said stepping into the sunk-in living room. "Very warm. I love your colors. The beige, yellows, greens, cantaloupe. You have good taste."

"Thanks. All the credit goes to my sister. She is an interior decorator."

"Can I get you a drink?" he asked.

"No thank you." She took a seat on the cantaloupe love seat.

"Are you hungry?" he asked. "I thought we could have a little lunch at this outdoor café about a block from here."

"Yes, I am. That sounds like a good idea."

He walked past her to close the window, and she got a whiff of his cologne. Something about him caused a tingling within her and created enough excitement that this meeting might be more delightful than she imagined. She smiled and reminded herself to thank Grace.

Grace sat at the foot of her bed and stared out the window, nervous about spending time alone with Wellington. She had no clue how she was going to fill the day with conversation. Deciding what to wear took a while, but she selected a simple flowing sleeveless violet crepe dress by Jason Wu with black flats.

She went downstairs, walked past the studio, and paused at the door of the studio where all the drama had taken place. When Wellington returned home, things would be back to normal.

Grace was half an hour early to the Marriott Hotel. She felt like it was a first date. The palms of her hands were sweaty, and perspiration was dripping down her bosom. She walked over to the elevator and pushed the button to the eleventh floor.

She knocked on his door, and his smile lit up her morning. Wellington presented her with a bouquet of tulips that brought tears to her eyes. They were her favorite. She wondered if he remembered, but she didn't ask. She tried to hold back the tears, but she couldn't.

He kissed her and swooped her up in his arms, kissing her ever so gently with his soft lips. The kiss turned on the fire, and next thing she knew, he was unbuttoning her clothes—and she was unbuttoning his. "I've been waiting for this moment," he whispered. "You are mine, and I'm going to make sure you never get away again."

At noon, they ordered lunch and spent the rest of the afternoon laughing, playing, and relaxing in one another's arms. They talked about how much they missed each other.

It was the best day of Grace's life, and for a moment, the memory of that awful day was erased.

At five o'clock, their perfect day ended. His plane would leave for Switzerland at ten o'clock.

After he left, Grace stayed in bed, savoring his aroma, but unsure of how much longer she could stand to be without him. It was going to take extreme discipline to keep her emotions intact. The time was nearing where they would end the secret meetings, but her patience was running out.

86

Confirmation

After the third trip to the bathroom, Grace's stomach and system were completely depleted. Her breasts were swollen and tender, and fatigue overtook her daily.

Dr. Harding confirmed that she was pregnant. That explosive, powerful night with Wellington proved to be satisfying in more ways than one. She couldn't wait to share the good news with him.

Grace called her mom as soon as she left the doctor's office. "Hi, Mom. Something good has happened, but I must tell you in person. Can you come to New York?"

"I haven't heard this much excitement in your voice in months. What's going on?"

"You'll understand when I explain it to you. I'm bursting at the seams with the good things that are happening in my life. I want you to make reservations today."

"Sure, I can put everything on hold and see what my little girl needs."

"Mom, you are being sarcastic."

"I am, huh?" She laughed. "There's nothing that will stop me from coming to see you. I have been waiting to hear that joy in your voice. It means so much to me."

"The news I have is going to light up your world as much as it has mine."

"I'll make the reservations and let you know the details."

"Good. We are going to celebrate big-time. I can't wait to see you," Grace replied.

"You too, dear. I'll call you soon."

Grace picked her mom up at the airport and during dinner at the house they talked. "Mom, I want you to remain calm when I share the latest developments."

"Honey, you know that's my middle name."

"I know, but this may disrupt your cool. There is no easy way to deliver this news other than just say it. Wellington is alive!"

"What do you mean?"

"The authorities confirmed his death. It is a very delicate situation, and we had to keep it confidential. It wasn't my choice. I'm in shock too. It hasn't been long since I found out. Monica and a team of friends found Wellington on the bank. She believes Azul is behind this. Aside from the many injuries, Wellington suffered memory loss. Only with God's help and Monica's therapy was his life restored back to normalcy. Monica is an angel in disguise."

"Thank God for her," Ruth said.

"I know I'm talking fast but try and follow me."

"Go on," Ruth said.

"We have knowledge from a private source that Azul is involved in criminal activities. Monica met with him because we need someone we can trust. He is the only person besides the doctors who knows that Wellington is alive, but he is very close to capturing him. That is why we are being very careful about what we say and do. Azul thinks he is getting away with this, but God is not going to let him. The miracle is that God allowed Wellington to live. That's the blessing!"

"Yes, dear. I'm so happy, but I'm still so confused. Where is Wellington now?"

"He's in a safe location."

"Grace, this is complicated and sounds dangerous."

"I know these are highly unusual circumstances, but I need your support—and I need you to pray. Please don't worry."

"I know honey, but you are my only child. I don't want anything to happen to you. I'm so surprised that you are mixed up in all of this. What's happening to you?"

"To be truthful, it's a surprise to me too. We were victims of a dangerous art dealer."

"Two artists living together can be creative madness."

Grace said, "I was not prepared for all the other stuff that followed. It temporarily paralyzed my thoughts and actions. I was baffled, out of sorts, and seething with resentment. This transformation forced me to grow up fast, and it has freed me from a lot of the fears I didn't want to believe about myself. Fear of not making it as an artist, fear of loneliness and now, free from knowing I don't have to do this alone. This journey has been like starting a blank canvas. You don't really know what you are going to get, but you try different mixtures of colors and ideas. You may even have to scratch what you initially started with and start all over. In the end, it can turn out to be a masterpiece. There's a silver lining in this story. Once I surrendered to God, I felt safe. He gave me peace. I persevered through the danger zone, and with his grace and help, I will win this battle. This is my husband's life we are talking about, and I'll go to the ends of the earth for him."

"I understand that, dear."

They went to the kitchen.

"Baby, girl, this is some heavy stuff."

"I know, Mom. I'm concerned about Monica getting in trouble for concealing Wellington. She could spend time in prison for this. My relationship with the Johanssons and Ty could also be compromised. What gives me peace though all of this is your wise counsel to seek God. I have a renewed relationship with him now, and I'm not afraid to face the future. After Wellington's accident, I didn't think I'd recover or be happy again. It was a trying time in my life. It was only after my many days of depression that I began to spend time on my knees and in prayer. Now that I know Wellington is alive, I have hope. All I can think of is being with him again. As soon Azul is put behind bars, he will no longer have to stay in hiding. That leads me to the next good news." Grace smiled.

"Wow—how does one digest all this?" She put her arms around Grace. "I'm sure God understands, and I know he will help. Just tell me what you want me to do."

"First of all, I don't want you to worry. It's going to be okay. God is healing Wellington daily, and his memory is returning."

"I'm so happy for you. All I can say is God's grace is amazing!"

"I still haven't told you the best part," Grace said.

"Should I faint now or later?" Ruth asked and placed her hands across her face like she was in despair. "I don't know if I can handle more."

"Mom stop acting." Grace grinned. "I'm pregnant!"

Ruth jumped to her feet and hugged Grace. "Child, how could you save that for last? Oh my God. I'm going to be a grandma!"

"Mom, I'm so excited. It happened when Wellington came to New York, and we spent the day together. Our time together was so special that it produced life."

"Well, I'm stunned. This really sounds more and more like a page out of a mystery book and not your life." Ruth smiled. "I don't know how you could work with Azul—let alone trust him."

"It hasn't been easy. I managed by God's grace and the thought that I'm doing it for Wellington. He has a legacy to fulfill and a school to continue to build. My prayer is that God is going to work everything out. Mom, I have more courage than I ever had in my life, which helps me deal with these matters."

"What did Wellington say when you told him?"

"I haven't had a chance to tell him yet. It's not safe to talk to him, but I can't wait to tell him in person."

"This is exciting news, honey. I'm going to visit you often because you don't know the first thing about raising a child."

'You are right about that, but I have a great mother who does." Grace smiled. "Try not to worry. God won't let anything happen to me, Wellington, or the baby. Promise not to worry?"

"I'll try," Ruth said as she smiled.

"Now let's go get some ice cream and celebrate."

87

Ellona and Grace Catch Up

Ellona took her cell phone out of her purse and dialed Grace's number. "Hey, girl, I got something for you." Ellona said.

"What you got?" Grace asked.

"Some evidence that can help you."

"How'd you accomplish that?" Grace asked.

"That's unimportant right now. I don't want to share this information over the telephone. Are you busy right now?"

"I'm on another line," Grace replied.

"Well, open your front door, girl. I'm standing right outside, and we need to talk now!"

Grace switched lines and told Monica that she had to go. "Girl, you are something else showing up like this. Come on in."

"Here's a list of people Azul is in bed with." Ellona displayed information on her phone.

"How'd you get this information?" Grace asked.

"It was not easy, and I almost got caught."

"I told you to be careful. You are playing with fire," Grace said. "Yes, I know that after seeing the look on Azul's face."

"Ellona, I thought you understood this game. Girl, you are letting your heart lead—and that is going to get us in trouble. You promised you would keep this on a business level."

"Yeah ... well I'm sorry. I didn't plan on this. He is just so sexy. I guess it just happened."

"Lord, what am I going to do with you?" Grace said.

"I thought it was about to get ugly—and I would have to resort to my old fighting days—but he calmed down when I played the jealous card. He was so busy trying to cover for his lies that he forgot about everything else. That's why I know he cares for me."

"Because he didn't hit you? Girl, let me tell you something. Azul cares about no one except himself. Wake up and get real!"

"I hid my phone and came right over here to see you. Girl, that scared me to death. If he finds out what I'm up to, I could get killed!

"I'm tired of playing cop," Grace said. "Azul is dangerous, and he has no qualms about taking anybody out. It definitely doesn't need to be us."

"I'd still like to believe Azul has feelings for me," Ellona said.

"Girl, stop kidding yourself. It's all lust. You may need to back off seeing him."

"But he'll get suspicious," Ellona said.

"So? Why not make up a good excuse?"

"Grace, I never knew you to be heartless. What has happened to you since Wellington's accident?"

"You wouldn't understand. My behavior will be more understandable once this is all over, but for now, let's stick with our plan," Grace said. "We don't need any foul-ups. I'll make sure Detective Ramos gets the information you send me."

The Risk of Love

A week after Monica returned from her first date with Ty, a bouquet of flowers appeared on her front steps. The message read: "I request your presence for dinner this Thursday at my place: 59 Hampshire Place, Lake Geneva, Switzerland. Please say yes!" Chills shot up her spine. She didn't understand it, but Wellington did.

Any emotions that may not have expressed themselves after the plane crash returned to him, and he felt a touch of jealousy. "Who sent the lovely flowers?" Wellington asked.

"They are from Ty Hamilton." She smiled.

"A-ha, so he did make an impression? What does the card say?"

"He invited me to his home for dinner on Thursday." She blushed.

"Sounds intimate. Are you going to accept his invitation? It's time for you get out of this house and have some fun." Wellington smiled.

"It's been a long time since someone paid this kind of attention to me. It's a good feeling."

Wellington laughed. "You didn't answer the question."

"I know. I need to stop playing so hard to get, huh? My anxiety is that I'm rusty at dating. I guess I'll never know if I don't try. It's such a risk, putting my heart out there."

"Exactly—but you won't find love again if you don't seek it," Wellington said. "It's been a long time since Daniel passed. You've got to be willing to let go."

"You are right, my friend. I'm protecting my heart and denying myself a chance to live. It's so hard, but there's something about Ty that's irresistible. I liked him the moment I saw him, and that's probably why I'm putting up such a fight. I can't deny that there are many qualities about him that I'm drawn to."

"So, what's holding you back from accepting?"

"The fear of falling in love and getting hurt, I guess."

"You've got to stop hiding sometime—so why not make it now?" Wellington said.

"Okay, okay. I get your point," Monica said with a smile. "I'll accept."

Hint of Love

Monica picked up the phone and dialed Grace's number. "Hello?"

"Hey, Monica. I'm so sorry I had to hang up so quickly. Ellona was at my door with some outlandish news. You left off telling me something exciting. I want to hear more,"

"You'll never believe what happened to me."

"What?" Grace asked. "It's Ty Hamilton. Girl, he is so smooth and charming. I feel so comfortable with him. It's crazy! I hear myself laughing out loud. I haven't felt this good and relaxed with someone since Daniel. I feel giggly like a teenager."

"Ah, I think you like him." Grace laughed.

"I told you. All you had to do is get to know him. It all starts with being a friend," Grace said.

"I want to thank you for persuading me to call him. Since moving to Switzerland, I haven't had a friend to confide in, and it's been a little lonely. He makes it so easy for me to talk to him. I'm telling him stuff I would never tell anyone. He just listens and is nonjudgmental. I like that about him."

"Sounds like something is developing," Grace said. "When are you going to see him again?"

"I'm having dinner at his house next week. I almost can't wait that long to see him again. It's a strange tingling feeling."

"I'm so happy for you. You deserve it."

"I'm so nervous. What should I wear?"

"I think you should go for the sexy look. Don't be afraid. I'm not talking sleazy—just very tasty. Just enough to whet his appetite."

"You got me blushing. It sounds like you are setting me up, but I think I can work that."

"How is my husband doing—and when will I see him again?" Grace asked.

"Detective Ramos wants us to be very careful and keep him out of the spotlight. The less he is seen in public, the better."

"I understand, but I still miss him. Tell him I asked about him," Grace said.

"I will. Thanks for being patient. I know it's not easy. I'll call you after my hot date." Monica laughed.

"Okay, enjoy yourself. And remember to have fun."

They both giggled.

After hanging up, Grace realized telling her about Ellona's predicament would have spoiled her moment of happiness. She would share that next time—and she hoped Ellona would stop playing cop.

The Dinner Surprise

Ty couldn't believe his good luck. He met a lovely lady who took his breath away, and he received a call from the Johanssons about *Amnesty*. Ty wanted to be the first to view any of Wellington's paintings that came into Europe. The moment he saw it, he fell in love with it—and he purchased it for a large sum of money. His first thought was to give it to Dr. Wolf, but it might be too soon to express his feelings for her with a gift of that magnitude.

Ty stood back and observed the masterpiece on the wall. It was astounding and a thing of beauty to behold. *Wellington was not known for painting abstracts, so this was surely going to turn heads once he made it public,* he thought. A touch of sadness entered his heart and mind at the thought of Wellington's untimely death. *Such a talented artist to die so young, but it seems to be happening to the talented ones more frequently each year.*

The doorbell rang, forcing him back to reality. His date was at the door. He checked himself in the mirror. His baby blue silk shirt gave him a soft boyish look and highlighted his brown skin.

He opened the door and saw approval in her eyes.

He said, "Good evening. Would you like a drink—water, coffee, or wine?"

"I'll have whatever you're drinking."

"Okay, wine it is." He poured two goblets of Cabernet. "Let's toast, shall we?" He raised his glass. "To the beginning of a beautiful friendship."

"I thought about it long and hard and almost did not come," she said after taking a sip. "I was so unkind the first time I met you. I felt guilty about receiving such beautiful flowers. My behavior was almost appalling."

"Yes, you were so mean." He smiled with a strange delight. "That calls for another toast: to a changed attitude."

They both laughed.

"You are beautiful, brilliant, mean, intriguing, honest, and deeply captivating. That's why having you here right now seems like a dream," he said.

"You said you would let the mean thing go," Monica said with a smile. "This may come off wrong, but it's like a dream for me too. I want and need a new life. I shouldn't be by myself when I could enjoy new friends who God puts in my life. Okay, this is getting deep. Let me stop rambling."

"Yes, it's getting deep all right. Dinner is ready if you are ready to eat. Shall we go into the dining room?" He took her hand.

Monica almost tripped over her own feet when she saw the painting on the wall. "Oh my God!" She stopped in her tracks.

"What's wrong? Are you okay?"

"It's the painting. It's so ... beautiful."

"Do you like it?"

"It's stunning."

"Isn't it though? I was fortunate enough to snatch it before anyone else saw it. It's part of Wellington's collection. It's entitled *Amnesty*. I was hoping you would like it. It reminds me a lot of you."

"How did you come across it?" she asked.

"I purchased it this week. You are the first to see it."

"I'm in awe. I didn't know Wellington painted abstracts."

Apparently, his agent has some unseen works of his."

"It took my breath away. I think I may need another glass of wine."

"Here you go," he said.

"Daniel and I were very close friends with Wellington and Grace. I guess my emotions overtook me," she said.

"I can understand." He touched her hand. "We can have dinner in the patio if you prefer."

"No, I'll be okay. You have set up this room so beautifully. I wouldn't spoil this moment for anything." She smiled.

"A toast to dreaming," he said.

Monica thought that it was too much of a coincidence—or it truly was Providence. She decided to take a leap of faith and find a way to tell him everything, including the mystery behind the painting. The timing had to be right. First, she would speak to Grace. That could be the turn of events they needed. It looked like a better opportunity had presented itself.

The Amnesty Plan

The telephone rang multiple times before Grace picked up. "Hello?"

"Grace, it's me."

"Hey, Monica. How are you?"

"I'm doing well. How did the delivery of the painting go?"

"He was so happy. I couldn't believe I did such a good job."

Grace laughed. "The joke's on him. I haven't heard back from him since I gave it to him."

"That is so cool," Monica said.

"I saw the *Amnesty* at Ty's, and I almost fainted," Monica explained.

"You didn't tell him what is going on, did you?" Grace asked.

"Of course not. Not yet anyway, but I want to. He may be the person God uses to help us, and we may need to take the risk."

"Is that what you think?" Grace asked.

"I think the best thing to do is run it by Detective Ramos first. He's the investigator, and it would be a call I want him to make. We are at a serious crossroads, and we wouldn't want to mess up the investigation."

"I agree," Grace said.

"I will call him," Monica said. "I may need to lay low with Ty until we get a plan in place."

"I don't think you should interrupt a good thing. I think you will be okay," Grace said. "Ellona did a little investigating and almost got caught."

Monica said, "That's all we need is an amateur trying to be an investigator and messing up everything."

"But it may be useful. You never know," Grace said. "I told Ellona to lay low until I get back with her," Grace said.

"Will she do that?" Monica asked.

"I don't know. That's another prayer," Grace said. "I'm so happy that you and Ty are hitting it off. You deserve to be happy."

"It's about time," Monica smiled. "I'll call you soon." She dropped the burner phone in a trash can.

"Hello, Detective Ramos. This is Dr. Wolf. I have a few issues I need to discuss with you as soon as possible. Are you in New York?"

"No, I'm traveling, but I can meet you in Switzerland if you like."

"Next week would work," Dr. Wolf said. "I'll arrange a place to meet. In the meantime, be very careful."

"I will—I promise," Monica said.

92

Trusting Instincts

Dr. Wolf looked around the café and noticed Detective Ramos sitting in the back booth. He nodded, and she moved toward him. "Thank you for meeting with me," she said as she sat at the table.

The waitress approached the table. "Can I get you a drink, ma'am?"

"Yes, I'll have some peppermint tea," Dr. Wolf said.

"Okay. I'll be right back with your drink."

"You ladies have been quite busy making my work even more seamless," Detective Ramos said. "I have eyes everywhere on this investigation."

Dr. Wolf said, "I have some bugs out there, but everything seems to be moving so fast. I believe God knows how it's all going to turn out, but I still worry. I'm trying to stay calm, especially for

Wellington's sake. I can't tell him a word about what's going on, and keeping secrets from him is consuming me."

"Is he doing well?" Ramos asked.

"Yes, he is doing remarkably well. Every day he's creating beautiful pieces. Since he had an opportunity to see Grace, he's getting a little restless and wants his life to return to normal. It's weird. Grace and I have never experienced anything like this, and we don't know what to do."

Ramos said, "I recorded a conversation between Grace and Ellona at Grace's house."

"Man, you are on it. I had no idea her house was bugged."

"I'm just doing my regular work. Attentiveness is part of it. I need to capture anything that is said in the house, especially if Grace and Azul have a conversation."

"Have you been watching me too?"

"I'm in New York most of the time, but I do have someone who's keeping an eye on you. I don't know many details. I'm not trying to interfere with your relationship."

"It's okay. I need someone to help me shoulder this burden. It's becoming too much, and it's dangerous."

"Young lady, I believe we can work out a good plan. Let me give it some thought. For now, don't mention it to anyone. We need to position this just right. If you trust Ty, I want you to tell him the entire story. Give him my telephone number and ask him to call me. If Wellington paints another masterpiece, you should give it to Grace. Azul will take the bait and want to sell it to the Johanssons right away. Maybe we could set it up for delivery to Ty's home. Don't mention anything to the Johanssons. Let's keep them out of this until we capture Azul. The fewer people we get involved in this plan, the better."

"What should I tell Grace?"

"Tell her you will deliver another masterpiece to her. Her job is to call Azul and tell him she is working on something new. Even though she had him sign the release, the news of another painting will keep him happy and off her back. Call me after you talk with Ty."

"Thank you so much, Detective Ramos. I feel a great sense of relief after speaking to you. I will call you soon."

93

Secrets Revealed

*M*onica called Ty and said, "Are you busy?"

"No. I'm never too busy for you."

"I need to talk to you. Is it okay if I stop by?"

"Wow, I like the forwardness," he said.

"I don't mean to be forward. I seriously need to talk to you."

"I'd love for you to come, and I'm anxious to hear what's on your mind."

"I can get there by seven o'clock."

"You don't waste any time, do you, pretty lady?"

"This is serious. It's not what you think."

"Yes, please come. I'll be waiting to see you," Ty said.

There was a knock at the door, and he opened it.

"By chance, you weren't standing right here waiting for me, were you?" She smiled.

"As a matter of fact, I was. Come right in." He took her jacket. "You look stressed. Would you like some wine?"

"Yes, I'm going to need it—and you will too."

"I'll get it." He came back with a bottle of red wine and two wineglasses. "What's going on?"

Monica took a large swallow and said, "I can't hold this secret any longer. It's paralyzing me. I know I haven't known you long, but I feel I can trust you with some complex information because you are also part of this situation and my stress."

"I'm part of your stress?"

"It has to do with *Amnesty*."

"What could be wrong with it?" he asked.

"Nothing is wrong with the painting. It's what is behind the scenes of the creation of the painting. I need you to promise not to judge me or tell anyone else about it, including your parents."

"Okay, boss lady."

"Azul is a dangerous manipulator and is causing some very serious problems for my friends—"

"I'm not the least bit surprised. I know him better than you think."

"He tried to kill Wellington!"

"Wellington was pronounced dead."

"Azul tried, but he didn't succeed. Wellington is still alive!"

"What?" Ty jumped up.

"Yes. Only a few people know, but you are going to have to take my word for it. It's a miracle that he even survived the crash. A few of us believe Azul tried to take him out! We have Wellington in a safe place, and it is imperative that we keep this under wraps. Our lives depend on it. "It's a dangerous game, but we are not alone. Thank God."

"This is some heavy information, Monica."

"You have no idea the weight of this thing."

"Okay, I think I need another glass of wine." He reached for the bottle.

"Pour one for me too please." She held up her glass.

"Detective Ramos has been following Azul for years. He tried to reach Wellington before he went to Switzerland, but Grace didn't know that. She called him, and they started putting the pieces together. We are working on a strategy to trap him."

"Really? What help do you need from me?" he said.

"More than you realize." She led him back to painting. "This painting jolted me the last time I was here."

"I'm still not sure where you are going with this."

"Azul is trying to blackmail Grace with this painting. Did you know that she is an artist too?"

"No, I didn't."

"There are so many moving parts to this story, but the main part is blackmail, which is causing Grace outrageous emotional pain and stress."

"This is really twisted." He rubbed his chin.

"Wellington was almost dead when we found him."

"You found him and helped him? That's amazing!"

"After he recovered, he painted *Amnesty*. Detective Ramos suggested that we have Grace deliver it to Azul as one of the paintings he requested from her. Azul sent it to the gallery, and that's how it landed in your hands. Imagine how shocked I was to see it in your home. Detective Ramos agreed that it would be good to tell you what's going on. The Johanssons will let Azul know that you own the painting. We are not telling them anything about this matter. We will provide another original painting by Wellington, set it up for Azul to deliver directly to your home, and tape the conversation. Detective Ramos wants you to call him to work out a plan. That's as far as we got."

"That's a mouthful."

"I know, and I'm tired of talking, but I feel relieved that you know now." She took another sip of wine. "I refuse to let Azul continue to destroy lives."

"Well, you aren't the only one with secrets. There is much you don't know about my past and some of it isn't good," Ty said. "Since we are sharing, you need to know more about me. I had many dealings and run-ins with Azul, but it wasn't about smuggling art. I grew up in a privileged environment. I have a very supportive family, but I was an irrational, wild teenager who didn't want to listen to logic. I did some absurd things that spilled over into my young adult life and disappointed my parents. However, they never turned their backs on me. They always bailed me out. I was so tired of that life, and I decided to give up that senseless life of drugs and crime. I asked God to help me because I was going down the wrong path and sinking fast. He rescued me and removed some very dangerous people from my life. I understand how they operate and can run with the best of them. I can help you with Azul—and will be very happy to do so."

"Ty, I need you. I don't have anybody else to turn to. I feel like you are a man of integrity despite your past. I really want to trust you. I am so overwhelmed right now." Tears welled up in her eyes.

"No worries." He pulled her into his arms. "This is getting quite complicated."

"I'm in way over my head."

"That may be the reason God has put us together," Ty said. "You might be my angel in disguise—and my amnesty." He smiled.

Monica hugged him and rested her head in his chest. "I trust God, and if he is using you, then I'm trusting you too."

"You have done most of the grit work—and good work." Ty held her hand. "He'll do it for us." Ty pointed toward the ceiling. "Just trust him."

"I will. Are you still comfortable with me after all the crazy stuff I just told you?"

"Yes, I want you next to me."

He smiled and pulled her closer. "That's good to know."

"I could use some comforting. Since Daniel, I have isolated myself and pushed people away. I've been afraid of getting hurt or letting anyone get too close."

"I'm here for you. You can confide in me."

"After Daniel passed, I went into a little bit of depression. Okay, maybe a lot. I was on the list as a suspect in his death after the way things went down. Azul left me implicated. I could have gone to prison. It was absurd! God and my therapist helped me through that ordeal. An opportunity to move to Switzerland came up, and I took it. I couldn't wait to get out of New York. I buried myself into my work and closed my heart to love. After meeting you, I no longer want to be without love in my life. When I saw you in the gallery, I panicked. Avoidance was my defense."

"So, you were resisting me? Are you saying it was love at first sight?" He smiled.

"I didn't say all of that, but some of that is behind me now." She grinned.

"Now I'm the one who is stunned. This is getting better by the minute. Tell me more." He squeezed her tightly.

CHAPTER
94

The Confrontation

Ellona removed her shoes and tiptoed into Azul's office. She turned on the desk lamp and pointed it down so the light could not be seen through the window. She opened the desk and pulled out Azul's little black book. She opened to the page that read "Artist List" and fingered down the crossed-out names on the list. She paused and squealed when she saw Wellington's name. She moved her finger down the page: "Finish job in Switzerland."

She jumped at the sound of her cell phone.

"Hey baby, what time are you picking me up?" Azul asked.

"Let me see." She caught her breath. "At eight o'clock, right?"

"I'm going to save you a trip. I got in early and will be seeing you soon," he said.

"How soon?"

"Sooner than you think," he said, touching her and breathing down her neck.

"Whoa! Ellona jumped and dropped the book. "You scared the shit out of me!"

"Were you expecting someone else?" He picked up his book.

"No," she said. "I just didn't expect you to come back so soon."

"I can see that." A wrinkle formed on his forehead. "And what are you doing in my office with my black book?" He tapped the book.

"I … I was just looking for some—"

"Yes, bitch. You don't have any words. I have been watching you sneak around for a few weeks now. I thought I'd arrive early and see what you were up to." He grabbed her hair and pulled her into the living room.

"Stop!" she screamed.

He pulled harder and pushed her to the ground.

"Why are you being so mean to me?" she asked.

"Who the hell are you working for—and what are you looking for?"

Ellona straightened her skirt and her hair. "I'm checking up on you because you are not telling me the truth about Francine. I don't want to waste my time if you are not serious about me."

"You're gonna use that sorry line? That's not going to fly with me. You better come cleaner than that."

"That's the truth. I promise you. I have no reason to lie."

"I don't know about that. Isn't there some information about your past that you haven't shared with me?"

"What are you talking about?"

Stoney walked into the room. He was smoking a cigar.

"Remember him? He's one of your old friends."

Ellona gasped. "Yes, I know him."

"Stoney happened to see a picture of you and me on my cell phone and asked about you. Seems you have some explaining to do, little lady."

"I don't have any explaining to do about him. I never asked you about your past, and I don't know why my past with him needs to be explained to you now."

Azul moved closer. "That's exactly what I want to know." He grabbed her chin. "You are going to tell me something right now."

Ellona said, "I don't have anything to say. Our relationship started when you came to my spa. You are the one that came to my spa, remember? We seemed to hit it off, and I thought we were building a close relationship and that you had feelings for me. Everybody has some bad stuff in their past. I know you do too. I'm a changed person, and that part of my life is buried. It has nothing to do with us."

Stoney shot her a mean look and blew cigar smoke in her direction.

"I've cleaned my life up, and I'm not involved in the type of activities I did in the past. Those were my young and wild days. I was trying to find myself. I've since established a reputable business with a very high-profile clientele. I don't know if I can say the same about him."

Stoney smiled, revealing a gold tooth.

Azul said, "That is irrelevant to why you were meddling in my office."

Stoney shouted, "We should kill her on the spot. Get rid of her like the others."

"Naw, man. We can't prove she's done us any harm."

"She was always a liability to me," Stoney said. "In Las Vegas, she blew my cover. She made the mistake of trusting the wrong people and gave me up to the feds."

"That's history, Stoney, and that was not my fault," Ellona explained. "You had a plan that just didn't work."

Stoney said, "Yeah, but I trusted you. I spent several years in prison for that, and you owe me,"

"Shut up, man! You talk too much." Azul walked over to Ellona. "I've grown to like you a lot, but this unfortunate development puts a damper on our relationship."

"What are you gonna do?" Ellona asked.

"I need to think about that," Azul said. "We did have a little something going on until I found out that you are nosy and can't be trusted. I think we are going to take a little ride while I clear my head." He dragged her outside to his Mercedes.

"What about my business and my clients?" She bumped her head as he forced her into the car. "I know people are going to miss me and start inquiring."

"I'll handle that too. Shut up!" He closed the door behind her.

Stoney got in next to Ellona and tried to put his arm around her.

Ellona swung at him, and when he placed a blindfold on her, she began to cry. "Grace is going to—"

"Going to what? Going to try to find you?" He laughed. "I knew you two were up to something. Her days are numbered too—trust me. I have some unfortunate plans for her." Azul started the car and sped off.

Ellona could not believe how things were turning out. Grace's voice in her head was reminding her not to let her heart lead—but it was too late.

CHAPTER

95

The Warehouse

Azul rode around what seemed like hours before coming to a stop.

Stoney opened the door and dragged her out.

Ellona heard a large door open and close behind them.

Detective Ramos parked midway down the street and called for backup.

In the warehouse, Azul pushed Ellona into a chair, took the blindfold off her eyes, and shoved a cell phone into her hands. "Call Grace and tell her to meet you here. Give her the address on this piece of paper and tell her to come now! And tell her to come alone!"

Ellona hesitated.

"Just do it!"

"All right, you don't have to shout at me."

Ellona dialed Grace's number.

"Hello?"

"Hey, girl," Ellona said in a shaky voice. "I need you now!"

"What's up?" Grace asked. "You don't sound right—and whose phone are you calling from?"

"Right. I have a new development, and I need you to meet me at 6720 Marshall Road as soon as possible. Come alone."

"Is that my signal?"

"Yes, that's right, new information," Ellona said.

Azul snatched the phone, hung it up, and slapped her across the face. "I don't know why I trusted you. I should have known you and Grace were in this together from the beginning. What are you two up to? Don't lie to me."

"She introduced you to me to receive a spa treatment. I had no idea it was going to lead to all of this," Ellona said.

"We'll see what lie Grace tells when she gets here," he said. "She's gotten pretty good at being late too."

CHAPTER

96

Adjusted Plan

G race's mind played back the many warnings from Ellona. *Ellona is in trouble because of me, but she needs me to come to her rescue. God, this is getting more intense by the moment. Where do I turn? I can't be stupid enough to go there and fall into Azul's trap. He's probably prepared to kill both of us.*

Grace dialed Detective Ramos and said, "Ellona just called me. I can tell that something isn't right. She wasn't making sense. She asked me to meet her as soon as possible."

"I'm there already. I followed them from Azul's house, and I'm outside the warehouse."

"Who are they?"

"Azul and another fellow. This could be very problematic. You must do everything I say—or someone could get hurt."

"I'm listening," Grace said.

"We have enough evidence on tape to trap Azul. Say as few words as possible and don't show any signs of fear. Do you own a gun?"

"Yes, we have one."

"Good. Go get it. Do you know how to use it?"

"Yes, Wellington taught me, but I haven't shot anyone before."

"If I can help it, you won't have to. I want you to be prepared for anything that may happen. You need to hide it in a boot or somewhere."

"I have a pair of boots I can hide it in. I'm really not trained for this kind of encounter," Grace said.

"I know it's a radical departure for you, but I have faith that you can handle whatever happens."

"I'm not afraid to say I'm scared to death!"

"Grace, you have demonstrated your resilience. This is just another courageous act that I'm confident you can do. I'm here for you, and backup is on the way. I'm not going to let anything happen to you or Ellona. You have been unflinching up to this point. You can't stop now. We are so close. We must rely on our instincts now. Stay calm—and don't do anything stupid. Everything has been set up for this moment. Don't blow it by getting emotional. Ellona is wired, and I'm listening in to the conversations."

"What should I say to Azul?" Grace asked.

"Don't confess to anything."

"Should I say anything about the paintings?"

"That's a good idea. Tell him you have another painting in the car. That could be my signal to move in, but we will play it by ear."

"Okay, wish me well. Or better yet—pray for me," Grace said.

CHAPTER

97

Showtime

When Grace rolled into the warehouse parking lot, there was an odious denseness to the steamy air. It clung to her body like a Mississippi Delta day, but grave doubts churned around in her head. She kept saying, "Our doubts are our traitors; no weapon formed against me can prosper; every tongue that arises against me will be condemned."

A man opened her car door and said, "He is expecting you. Follow me." He jammed a gun into her ribs.

At the door of the warehouse, another huge man said, "Put that damn thing away!"

The first man dropped his hand and pushed her forward.

Grace noticed all the artwork in the room and spotted one of the paintings she had given Azul against the wall. There were huge boxes and a battery-operated lantern. A man was sitting at a table, and Ellona was tied to a chair.

Azul appeared out of the shadows and said, "You are right on time."

"What's going on here?" Grace said.

"Looks like a party now that you've joined us." He laughed.

"I don't understand. Ellona called and told me to meet her here. I didn't expect to see you."

"Well, your little friend has just got herself in some deep shit. This is the second time I caught her snooping around my office. I don't know who she is working for, but I can only suspect it's you."

"Me?" Grace cried out. "Ellona is my friend. She doesn't work for me."

He laughed. "You think you are slick, but I have your number."

"I don't know what you are talking about. The only business between me and you are the paintings, and I just happen to have the next masterpiece in my car."

"What? Are trying to distract me?"

"No, I'm just doing what you asked. Even though you signed the release, I know you want more, right? Azul, I don't know what you are contemplating right now, but you need to think about it before you do something you regret. Ellona is a good woman. That's why I purchased the spa treatments for you. I hoped you would experience an improvement in your body and in your spirit and mind."

"Yes, she is good at massages and gyrating those hips in bed, which makes this situation even more difficult. She also appears to be too inquisitive for the good health she is promoting. If there's one thing I hate, it's a nosy heifer. I figured you probably had something to do with it."

"Absolutely not! She really cares for you. She told me so. When she found out about your other lady friend, she was hurt. What's your reason for getting me here—and why are you pointing that gun at me?"

Azul's partner moved closer, and Grace noticed a sharp instrument in his hand.

"I can get rid of you and her, and no one will know."

Ellona squirmed wildly in her seat.

Azul walked over and patted Ellona's head. "Now look what you have done. You got your BFF in harm's way." He laughed loudly.

"Azul let her go!" Grace said. "This is not what you want to do. If you let her go, I promise I'll do more paintings." Grace touched his hand and softened her eyes.

He laughed louder. "This lady is a real piece of work. Other than her beauty, I don't know what Wellington saw in her because she has no brains." He and Stoney laughed uncontrollably.

Grace reached in her boot and pointed her Smith & Wesson .357 at Azul. "Drop the gun. Drop it now! And what were you saying about no brains?" Grace said with a smile.

Azul's face turned white.

"Now who's doing the laughing?" Grace moved closer to Ellona and pointed to Stoney. "Untie her—now! Hurry up!" She waved the gun at him. "Didn't think I had it in me, huh?"

Stoney released Ellona, and she moved closer to Grace. "Do you know how to work that thing?"

"I will if I have to," Grace whispered. "Just follow my lead. The police are on the grounds. Don't make any hasty moves, you two."

Ellona said, "Look who is talking now! What a fool to think you really loved me!"

Grace peeked through the keyhole to see if she could locate the guy who had manhandled her. She motioned for Azul and Stoney to get down on the floor. Grace was way too nervous to try to tie up the gangsters and hold the gun at the same time. *Where the hell is Ramos? I really need him now! Father, help me and give me the wisdom to do the right thing. This situation is in the hands of the Lord Jesus.*

They slowly backed out of the door and ran to Grace's car as the police apprehended Azul's men. She opened the door, but a hand yanked her to the ground.

Ellona climbed in on the passenger side and locked her door.

Stoney was kicking and banging on the window.

Grace raised her head, and Azul struck her across the chin with his gun. She tasted the blood flowing from her lips and rolled over.

He climbed on top of her, ready to strike again.

She spit in his face and tried to release his tight grip. Her legs were under his, and she tried to stand up.

He grabbed her waist and pulled her back to the ground.

Grace closed her eyes and prayed for strength and favor, hoping God would hear her cry. Supernatural strength bolted through her body, and it changed his grip. She jumped to her feet, and Azul pushed her against the car. Grace saw the anger in his eyes, but she also had rage boiling in her. The only time she could recall feeling that way was in the fight with Jana over Wellington.

Grace kicked him in the balls, and while he was bent over, she broke free of his grip, opened the door, jumped in, and sped off. She was trembling like a leaf. When she put the car in gear, Stoney fell to the ground.

Ellona looked back and screamed, "They are getting in their car and following us. We are going to die!"

"Stay calm, Ellona. Detective Ramos is following us too."

"How do you know?"

"Because I talked to him."

Azul chased them for several blocks, and he banged into the back of her car.

Grace swerved, increased her speed, and almost lost control. She turned the corner on two wheels and headed toward Wellington's Art Academy.

Azul pulled up beside her and shot at the car, hitting Grace in the arm. She made a quick right turn, and Azul's car crashed into the school.

Grace looked back at the explosion and brought her car to a screeching halt.

Detective Ramos pulled up to the school, but it was too late to save them. Both men were dead on impact. It was ironic that he crashed into the school's Wall of Dignity.

Ellona and Grace hugged. The sweet taste of victory and thoughts of Wellington were more than enough of a painkiller.

Detective Ramos dialed 911, and Ellona screamed, "Girl, if it had not been for God on our side, what would we do? That's what the Word says, right?"

They both smiled.

Grace said, "God is our refuge and strength and ever-present help in times of trouble."

CHAPTER

98

Jubilation in Switzerland

Dr. Wolf stopped dead in her tracks in the living room, stunned at the news report. It was surreal. "Oh my God," she screamed. "It's over!" She fell to her knees.

Wellington ran into the room. "What's over?"

"Azul is dead!" She jumped up and hugged Wellington.

"How do you know he's dead?"

"He died in a car crash. This means your hiding days are over. You are free! I know I will have to answer for my actions and face any consequences, but I'm prepared to do that. You can return to your life with Grace. Man, I'm whipped." She smiled. "It's been rough concealing you for this length of time. I never imagined we would go through all of this, but it was worth it. If you want to know the truth, I was looking for some revenge."

"Revenge?" Wellington said.

"I couldn't, but it was in my heart. I knew Azul had something to do with your plane going down. It's a pattern. He signs up the artist, makes all the money, and finds a way to get rid of them when he's finished, or something goes wrong. I tried to warn Daniel about him, but he didn't listen. He was so caught up with the attention, money, and fame. It still hurts to think about it. At one point, bitterness consumed me, but I prayed about it and let it go. God healed me from my loss, but that didn't stop me from keeping up with what was going on in the art world. I began collecting articles about Azul's dealings. When I heard about your plane crash, I felt a chilling uneasiness in my gut. It coursed through every cell in my body just pulled me to that site. It was God's will. I am thankful that I obeyed, and my service was needed."

"I'm so thankful you did too. It has been hard being away from Grace. Azul started getting a little shady when I asked about the deals we were doing. I didn't know how God was going to correct the senseless stuff he's done, but I know evil never wins. I have been praying and waiting for this day."

"I have been praying too, and it all seems to be happening so fast. There is just so much to do. I don't know where to start. There's more news."

"More? I'm in shock right now. I don't know if I can take any more," Wellington said.

"It's good news. You'll want to hear it. I had to hold it from you until the right time—so don't be mad at me. You are going to be a daddy. Grace is pregnant again!"

"You are kidding me? Oh God, how inspiring is this? I can't believe you withheld this information."

"I had to. You would have gone crazy and would be anxious to get home. Grace just told me. You can't imagine how hard it has been for her to hold in this news. Apparently, something divine happened that day you two spent together."

"Wow, that's amazing. It makes up for so much that we have been through."

"We had to wait until the right moment to tell you, and it seems fitting right now. I'm sorry I didn't tell you right away."

"With all we've been through, I can understand the dilemmas you have faced. I'm not really disturbed. I'm just a little surprised. I appreciate all you have done for me and my family. I really do." He smiled.

"That's what friends are for. I was looking out for your best interests the entire time. I must call Grace. Consideration must be given to how we report everything. I will speak with Detective Ramos and find out what our next move should be. God knew how this would end. We will have to trust him to work out the details. At any rate, you are free, and the anxiety is over for you and your family."

"No, *we* are free—and you are part of my family now." He smiled. "We will see the entire situation through together to the end."

The Aftershock

"**A**re you okay?" Detective Ramos touched Grace's hand. "Do you need medical attention? Someone has already called for an ambulance, and they should be here shortly,"

Grace exhaled loudly. "I'm okay—just a little shaken up. We could have died, or the bullet could have hit my stomach and killed my baby. I'm thankful to God it didn't. The enemy tried to take this baby from me, but he didn't succeed. There must be something significant about this child."

"Yes, he or she has been through a lot," Ellona said.

Detective Ramos said, "The police and television cameras are searching for clues. Just remember to remain calm and direct all questions from the press or officers to me. I will call your attorney. You are going to need him."

"We were going so fast. I couldn't see clearly, and we almost crashed too. I didn't know what to do. It was a close call! I'm sure the only thing that saved us was that an angel took over the steering wheel."

"I know. I was scared too," Ellona said. "Grace, I'm so sorry for not listening to you. Things may have turned out differently if I had not fallen for that wicked man and let jealousy sink in."

"No worries, my friend. You also are one of the angels in disguise who helped save us from Azul's clutches." Grace hugged Ellona and winced. "After all, I'm the one who got you mixed up in this madness. Things don't always turn out the way we expect, but it did turn in our favor, didn't it?"

They both laughed.

"Here come the cameras," Detective Ramos said. "I'll make sure they only talk to you for a few minutes before getting you to the hospital. Also, the officers at the warehouse confirmed that there were stolen goods. They collected the evidence, and we were able to get the entire conversation on tape. Don't worry about a thing. This will help clear your name, Grace."

"Thank you, Detective. We could not have done this without your help," Grace said.

"It's as much a pleasure for me," Detective Ramos said. "When the cameras start flashing in your face, let me do the heavy talking. Trust me. We'll get through this."

CHAPTER

100

Redeemed

After being released from the hospital, Grace and Ellona went to Grace's house. The yard was filled with TV cameras and newspaper reporters. To avoid them, Grace pulled straight into the garage.

In the house, Grace called her Mom to let her know that she was okay.

Ruth said she would be on the first plane in the morning.

Malcolm called and said, "Grace, what is going on? Are you okay? You are all over the news."

"Yes, I'm fine now, but what we went through was really scary."

"All the newspaper reporters are camped on your yard, and I'm here too."

"You're outside?" Grace asked.

"Yes, I had to come check on you, but I don't know how I can get through this crowd. Can you let me in?"

"Come around to the back door. I'll open it, but you better hurry because the cameras will be flashing."

"Okay, look for me," Malcolm replied.

Grace opened the back door, and Malcolm ran inside. "It's a madhouse out there!"

"Yes, and all of the reporters want to interview me," Grace said.

Malcolm smiled at Ellona and said, "Who's your friend?"

"This is Ellona. She was with me in the car chase," Grace said. "We are both still delirious. It was straight out of a movie,"

He cleared his throat and said, "I'm Malcolm."

"I'm Ellona," she replied shyly.

"Malcolm and I went to the same high school in California and were in Wellington's class together. Malcolm is a great artist."

"I see," Ellona said. "I am her personal masseuse and helped her relax as much as possible throughout this mess."

"Come on in, Mal, and have a seat," Grace said.

"I really can't stay. I just wanted to make sure you were okay." He smiled at Ellona and then turned his attention back to Grace. "I should have known something was up from the way you were acting at lunch. Why didn't you share this situation with me? It sounds so different from the Grace I know."

"You mean the quiet, simple girl you knew in California?" Grace laughed.

"Yeah. Now suddenly you are full of intrigue and a superwoman!"

"Oh, stop! I'm far from that." Grace blushed.

"Based on the reports, I'm not far off base."

"Mal, this situation was way too dangerous to tell anybody about except the people involved. Besides, once I got married, our lives went in different directions."

"You have a valid point there."

"One thing just led to another and as an artist's wife, I found myself in unknown territory. Those nefarious people ruined the beauty and glamour of the true fine art world. It was really scary and risky. Things just kind of spun out of control."

"No kidding," he said. "But you are good now, right?"

"I am definitely out of danger, and the enemy—no, let me say the devil—is dead!" Grace said. "Although this has been a painful experience, pain is a great teacher. God can use the pain we have in life."

"What do you mean by that?" he asked.

"Pain can be an undeniable game changer. I've gotten some well-earned perspective on my losses: my child, my husband temporarily, and my challenges with my faith. I withstood the turbulence of external forces that were trying to dominate my life, and through it all, I saw how God worked things out for me. My mom has always been a positive reinforcement in my life, and she always told me to let go and let God help me. Once I did, it changed my life. I really learned to appreciate the little things that I have in my life ... especially you and Ellona."

Ellona hugged Grace.

"Do you know we almost got killed!" Grace laughed nervously. "Ellona put her life on the line and was instrumental in helping bring down that murderer. She's quite the warrior."

"No, it was truly an act of bravery on Grace's part," Ellona said. "That's what nailed him."

Malcolm smiled. "It appears both of you were warriors in this battle."

Grace sighed. "I will have to tell you the whole story one day, but we are exhausted and need to relax a little and just breathe."

"Do you ladies need anything to eat—or is there anything else I can do for you?"

"No, we are good. We are going to get some rest and get ready for tomorrow. It's going to be a big day facing the media and answering questions. Also, Wellington is coming home in a few days."

"I guess that cuts short my opportunity to pursue you."

Grace smiled. "Mal, come on. You know we are just friends, and that probably wouldn't have happened."

"Yes, but I'm not going to lie and say I wouldn't have stopped trying." He laughed and looked at Ellona. "Maybe I'll have to change the lens on my camera and focus on another available canvas."

"Thanks for coming by, Mal. I appreciate you checking on me. I'll get back with you after things settle down." Grace moved to the door.

"I'll check back with you soon," Malcolm said before closing the door.

"I will be waiting," Ellona added after he was out of hearing distance. "Girl, you've been keeping back the goodies!"

"Child, please! Malcolm is just a good friend. I think he had a crush on me during college, but that changed once I got married. We never had anything going, but he sure couldn't keep his eyes off you. Looks like you may have just gained a new friend." Grace laughed.

"Yes, girl. I could use one. He appears to be a good catch. How come you didn't introduce him to me instead of Azul? It would have cut down on the drama." Ellona laughed.

"Girl, you are so crazy—but I love you," Grace said. "Wouldn't it be just like God to bless you with a great guy after all you've been through."

They exchanged high fives.

Ellona smiled. "I wouldn't be mad at him if he did."

High-Strung Gallery

"**H**igh-Strung Gallery, this is Niklas."

"Hi. It's Monica. I'm sure you heard the news about Wellington."

"Yes, we did. We are in shock—but very happy he is alive and well. We admire your bravery and incredible management of Wellington's recovery. Our telephone has not stopped ringing since the news reported this epic story. It seems like the content for a great movie. Everybody is shocked and inquiring about him. How is he—and how is Grace?"

"Wellington is doing great and is so happy that he can go home. Grace is recovering. We are headed back to New York, but I wanted to touch base with you first."

"Let us know how we can help. We are here for you. The demand for Wellington's work is really heating up. Perhaps we can still pull off that fund-raiser someday."

"He will be delighted to hear that. We are grateful to God for restoring Wellington's memory and healing his body—and his artistic gifts expanded exponentially. He is painting some wonderful things. He is so excited to reunite with Grace and return to his school. Grace calls his recovery the 'wings of mercy.'"

"Wow, I like the ring of that," Niklas said. "That sounds like a good title for an event. I'm sure there is a lot on your plate right now. We can talk about that later. When everything settles down, please call us. We would love to hear the entire story. Please give Wellington and Grace our best wishes."

"Thank you—and pray for us," Monica said before hanging up her new cell phone.

CHAPTER

102

Home Sweet Home

At the insistence of Monica, Ty accompanied them to New York. At Kennedy Airport, they were met by a massive crowd of reporters and television cameras.

"Wellington, tell us how it feels coming back home after your rumored death and months of reclusion?"

Ty stepped in front of Wellington and shielded him. "Can you back up and respect his privacy?"

"How about you, Dr. Wolf. Does it concern you that you may face jail time for not going to the authorities immediately after you found Wellington?"

"I was trying to help my friend who was suffering from memory loss and in great danger. I thought that was moral and right," Monica said. "Azul created fear within our community. Something came over me and drove me to save Wellington's life. I'm prepared to face whatever lies ahead for doing what was right." She pushed her way through the crowd and toward the waiting car.

In the car, they all took a deep breath.

Monica said, "The next few days will be challenging. The media will be clawing for answers. It's crucial that we think before we speak and stay on one accord with our replies."

Wellington said, "Ty, we can't thank you enough for what you are doing, man. You don't have to get mixed up in all of this. We don't want your name smeared in any way."

Ty said, "Man, if I didn't want to be here, I wouldn't be. I'm here to support the family. I'm thankful that you are well and that you can return to the love of your life. It doesn't get any better than that." He winked at Monica.

chapter 103

The Wait

Grace paced the floor nervously and said, "Mom, I'm so nervous I can't sit down. The baby keeps moving around as if she understands the excitement too."

"Babies are dialed into your emotions," Ruth said. "You have to stay calm. Monica called and said the plane arrived on time. They should be here any moment."

"Do I look okay? I feel so fat."

"You look marvelous, and I'm sure Wellington will agree."

"It's been such a long time since we've been together. I don't know how to act or what to say."

"He fell in love with you and loves you just as you are. You don't need to change a thing. Because you put your trust in God, the storm that seemed so overwhelming was not severe enough to overtake you.

Just relax and say to yourself, 'Peace, be still!' I think I hear a car in the driveway. Yes, it's them."

"Look at him. He looks so healthy and young—even more handsome than I remember." Grace smiled and grabbed her mom's hands. "Walk with me to the door in case I faint." She grinned.

Anderson Cooper Interview

Dr. Wolf: Yes, it's true that I kept Wellington's rescue a secret. I had to care for his health and save his life and protect him from Azul. It also helped me disconnect from the pain I felt when I lost my husband.

Anderson: Can you explain what you mean by that?

Dr. Wolf: I felt that Ricardo Azul was responsible for my husband's death. However, it was all intuition. I had no concrete proof. If I could save another individual from him, then I was going to put all I had into it—even if it meant my life. I felt that my actions could and would heal me and perhaps save Wellington, and they did.

Anderson:	You told officials Wellington had amnesia when you found him.
Dr. Wolf:	That is true. He was pretty badly injured, which included amnesia. He slowly began to recover and regain his sensibilities.
Anderson:	So you alone were instrumental in his recovery?
Dr. Wolf:	I worked with some doctors who were willing to help. It took a lot of surgeries and months of therapy. Wellington, once he was able to speak and move around, began to recover, and we built a bond of trust and a deeper friendship. I can't take credit for what God did. It's truly a miracle! I feel that I was divinely led through the steps of what to do.
Anderson:	So it sounds like the saying: "It takes a village to raise a child," but in this case, "It takes a village to restore a person's good health."
Dr. Wolf:	I would agree with that saying. Without the expertise of several doctors, he would have died. I'm thankful for their help and to God, the true Healer, who worked through them.
Anderson:	Is it true you were in touch with Wellington's wife, Grace, during this time?
Dr. Wolf:	Yes, but I did not tell her everything about Wellington or that he was still alive right away. After he got to a certain point in his recovery, the team of doctors agreed it was time to contact her. We spoke a few times, and I disclosed information as needed until he was fully recovered. As the healing process progressed, she became more instrumental in his recovery.
Anderson:	Wow! This sounds like a movie. I'm sure somebody is going to be approaching you for the rights to this story.

Dr. Wolf: At first, it was more like a never-ending nightmare. Now that it is over, the stress and pain of it doesn't seem so bad. It was worth it because we got the results we were hoping for. We are truly grateful Wellington is alive, at home, and that he can return to his normal activities with his wife and his school and continue to create his artwork.

Anderson: What are your feelings on the charges and punishment you could face with the Swiss courts for not reporting your discovery of Wellington right away?

Dr. Wolf: I acted in faith and with courage to save a friend from a terrible man who attempted to take his life. I didn't want Ricardo Azul to have another chance to ruin another family. In fact, it was a true spiritual battle between good and evil. After all, Azul was making a deliberate attempt to undermine Wellington's legacy. I never had any intention of breaking the law, but in this case, I don't know if I would change a thing.

Anderson: Is there anything else you would like to add before we end this interview?

Dr. Wolf: Yes. I want to thank the team of physicians and Grace. I also want to send a shout-out to a special friend who was by my side during this ordeal. He knows who he is without my mentioning his name. I love you.

Anderson: Thank you, Dr. Wolf, for sharing that story with us. We wish the best of health to Wellington and for his continued success. Now we turn to the latest update news of the White House and the Tax Reform Bill SB 383.

A Surprise Award

The standing ovation brought tears to Monica Wolf's eyes.

Grace said, "Monica deserves all that is awarded to her today. I will be forever grateful for her commitment to saving my husband's life—and for the diligent care of Wellington that she and her doctors took during his recovery." She hugged Monica and moved to the side of the stage.

"Ladies and friends, thank you for your generous accolades. I'm profoundly humbled to receive this award. It is truly a unique privilege to be a part of this organization. It's an honor to receive this award, but the true recipient and tribute belongs to Grace." Monica smiled, turned to Grace, and gestured for her to stand next to her at the podium.

Grace blushed, and everyone began clapping and cheering.

Wellington joined them on stage.

Monica said, "Grace, you have displayed unwavering bravery, courage, and strength that exemplifies the core values and virtues of the this organization. Thank you for keeping Wellington's vision alive despite the unnerving trials you both have endured. We salute you." She hugged Grace.

"Thank you. Thank you." Grace waved to the audience as the cheers continued. Tears streamed down her face. Her heart was full, and she slowly walked to the microphone. "I humbly accept this honor, and, ladies, I look forward to our future projects."

Monica's face was radiant as Ty helped her down the stairs.

Grace smiled because she had found love again. The reunion with Wellington was a beautiful reminder of what can happen when you trust and open your heart—even after it has been terribly damaged.

Monica stopped Grace at the bottom of the stairs. "Girl, you are something else. You remember how the girls used to talk, laugh, and share stories of being an artist's wife? That used to be so much fun. I really miss the fellowship and can't wait to get back."

"I think you broke the code and set a new standard for the artists' wives. It's one thing to be an artist, but it's another to be married to one and succeed at being the artist wife. You are a go-getter, a believer, and an achiever. Congratulations on your accomplishments!"

Grace blushed and said. "Thank you, Monica,"

The Artist's Wife Organization raised a million dollars for Wellington's Art Academy and another million dollars for Monica's charity. The Angel Baby Foundation's mission was to support children like Javier and research a cure for rare and deadly diseases passed from mothers to their children.

In the weeks and months following Ricardo Azul's death, millions of dollars from the stolen art were recovered—and several criminals were prosecuted. Based on Azul's extortion and Detective Ramos' tapes, Grace was completely exonerated.

Monica was looking at facing one to five years in prison for concealing Wellington. Ty hired the best defense lawyer in

Switzerland to handle her case. The Swiss courts considered her motive and were sympathetic since she did not have a criminal record and fully cooperated.

Grace needed to clear up her relationship with the Johanssons and Ty. They were due apologies because of Grace's deception. They genuinely accepted Grace's urgent plea for forgiveness, and they all agreed to work together on future projects, including a fund-raiser to feature *Amnesty* and *Angel in Disguise*.

Grace called Ellona and said, "Girl, God is so good! They all forgave me!"

"That is awesome!" Ellona said. "I knew God would work it all out."

"There is one more thing," Grace said. "I appreciate all the help and support you gave me, my friend. I have a very special gift for you, and you better not say a thing."

Ellona laughed and said, "Okay, I won't."

"I paid the registration fee for you to attend an acupuncture school."

"You didn't?" Ellona screamed. "I always wanted to do that."

"I heard you mention it in one of our sessions. You thought I was asleep, and I guess you were talking to yourself about your dream job. I realized how much you want to further your career, and I just want to bless you after all you've done for me. Is that okay?"

"Girl, I don't know what I'm going to do with you, but I surely can't do without you."

They both laughed.

Ellona said, "God's grace just keeps getting better by the moment."

"I know. That's why I always say, 'It is well with you, my sista,'" Grace said with a big smile.

106

A Time to Heal

Time is a great healer of brokenness. Forgiveness is essential for life, and faith and a sincere willingness to change can elevate one's life enough to provide a fresh start. We all know that life is not without wrinkles or detours. How one perseveres and adapts to change, when one changes their attitudes and elevates their faith, there are many new things to discover.

"Grace, I apologize for not telling you about Sonya and Javier," Wellington said. "It should have been an easy thing to do, but I kept waiting and hoping I could find the right words. Time just kept passing me by, and I kept putting it off. I was afraid I might lose you. I knew it was going to be difficult for you to understand. That's why I wrote it down. I kept practicing what to say. I know that sounds crazy."

"Yes, that's ridiculous. How could you be so careless? You should have trusted me and taken the chance of me believing you. I thought I knew you until I found that letter. My heart bled incessantly after I read it. It really hurt that I did not hear it from your own lips. It also made me question whether more relationships would pop up. It was extremely hard to accept."

"I am so sorry I hurt you. I'm also disappointed in myself for not talking to you. I promise you that was one night I regret. Please believe me when I tell you I'm not hiding anything else from you."

Grace rolled her eyes and shot him a look that could kill.

He said, "But you will never know how betrayed I felt when you went behind my back and sent your own artwork. You knew how much that commission meant to me. On top of that, you waited until we got all the way to Switzerland to tell me the painting was yours. I couldn't understand how you could do that to me. It was as if you were trying to get back at me. But for what? That's why I blew up in the hotel room and lost my cool."

"It wasn't my intention to hurt you. I just didn't know how to fix my mistake. It just grew and got out of control. After your accident, the weight of this matter rested very heavily on my heart, producing a lot of sleepless nights. I blamed myself for your death. All that stress on my mind and body was the cause of me losing the baby. I made a huge mistake, but I paid for it dearly. I'm sorry for sending that painting. It was not my place to send anything to the gallery without your permission, especially not my artwork." Grace wiped the tears from her eyes.

"You definitely are not to blame for all that has happened. I could have prevented all of this." Wellington pulled her close. "I realize how irresponsible it was to leave you alone in that hotel room that night. I hope you will forgive me, and I hope we can start over."

"I forgive you and hope you forgive me too. I never want to experience anything like that again. It took a long time to get that officer's voice out of my mind after he gave me the distressing news about your plane crash. My heart didn't settle down until I met with

Monica and heard the great news about you being alive. That's when I started living again. It confirmed that there is a God who cares." Grace squeezed Wellington's hand.

"I can attest that God is good to us. He healed me and restored my memory. Those days of recovery were tough, and it took a lot of strength and courage to fight through it. There were days when I just wanted to die. I appreciate life more than ever and will never take it for granted. We have many bright days ahead. I believe the goal is for us to complement each other and not compete. Don't you agree?"

"I do." Grace smiled.

"With all that has happened, I want you to know how proud I am of you. You have been tenacious in undertaking my business, embracing my son, and fighting that devious Azul. I don't know how you did it. You were right about Azul." He laughed. "I heard you fought him like a superwoman—but with a gun? What's that all about?"

"That was the detective's suggestion. I was scared for my life. My hands were shaking the entire time. I was relieved when it was all over." Grace sighed.

"He bragged about your resolve throughout this entire ordeal. I need to apologize to you for something else," Wellington said.

"What?"

"I have to admit I had little faith in your talents at first, and I didn't give you enough encouragement in class. In fact, I was downright hard on you because I wanted to push you to be the best. I guess I'm always the teacher, huh?"

"Yeah, I know," Grace laughed. "You were very tough on me. That's one of the reasons why I switched classes."

"Is that the only reason?" he asked.

"I think I needed some separation to work through my unrealistic expectations." Grace smiled.

"Well, you proved me wrong again. I admire your courage to fight for your passion in art and to keep learning and fight for me. Now look at you. I think you hit the ground running with that awesome abstract you created. And you created that for my birthday?"

"Yes, it was meant for you. I worked extra hard on that piece to please you—and look at the trouble it caused. Do you like it?"

"I do. It's a winner. But more importantly, you got the attention of well-known art collectors. I believe I'm going to have to scoot over for the new emerging artist of the family." Wellington flashed his contagious smile.

CHAPTER

107

Radiance's Introduction

Six months later, Grace delivered a healthy baby girl named Radiance. When Grace met Wellington, he said, "There is something radiant about her." That how their precious little girl got her name.

Radiance was a true miracle from God, and she certainly helped mend their broken hearts after losing their first child. As soon as Radiance could hold a spoon, they put a paintbrush into her tiny hand. At age three, she began showing real signs of artistic ability.

One morning, the three of them were painting in the studio, and Radiance was running around with a paintbrush in her left hand.

"Mommy, look at the man." She accidentally kicked over a paint can and spilled paint all over her canvas.

Wellington and Grace stopped in their tracks and stared at the angelic image. They were witnessing a special artistic gift flowing through their child. To their amazement, the colors were shaped like an angel. It supernaturally formed right before their eyes. Angels break barriers and the chains of evil. They knew God was showing more of their blessings in their little angel and her miracles, but that was an angel with no disguise.

Printed and bound by PG in the USA